# TERMINAL SILENCE

*The Cause* Book III

By DAN KLASING

Publisher, Copyright, and Additional Information

*Terminal Silence* – The Cause Book III

Copyright © 2025 by Dan Klasing


All rights reserved. No part of this book may be reproduced or transmitted in any form or by any means, electronic or mechanical, including photocopying, recording, or by any information storage or retrieval system without the written permission of the author.

For permissions contact: danklasing@gmail.com.

This is a work of fiction. The characters, events, and technology portrayed herein are fictitious. Any similarity or resemblance to actual events, locales, or real persons, living or dead, is coincidental and not intended by the author.

All rights reserved.


ISBNs:
979-8-9881498-4-2 (paperback)
979-8-9881498-5-9 (ebook)

Cover design and interior design by Rafael Andres

# CHAPTER ONE

Central Chile
Maule Region
150 miles south of Santiago

A cold wind washed across the broad grasslands at the foot of the Andes Mountains, painting the rural farms and sweeping ranches of Chile's central valley in a silver-gray early morning frost.

Inside her cozy but weathered one-bedroom house, Tella Hernandez set down her steaming cup of coffee, threw another log into the fireplace, and pulled on the faded green coat she had worn for so many years she couldn't remember where or when she bought it. Now over seventy, the coat hung loosely from her shoulders, and the sleeves nearly covered her bony hands. Before leaving the house, Tella slid her feet into a pair of muddy rubber boots and pulled on a thick wool multi-colored toboggan.

Like every day of her life, Tella stepped into the dark morning to make the fresh cheese, or *queso fresco,* she sold to several high-end restaurants in Santiago. In a few hours, a driver would show up at her house to pick up the cheese and hand her 20,000 pesos, or about 25 dollars. Tella's cheese was some of the best in the country, but it would never make her rich. And she didn't care. She had never

3

married, choosing to remain on the tiny farm her family had settled decades before. Tella lived simply and happily, unable to understand why her younger brother chose to live in Talca, a city of 200,000, thirty miles to the west.

A biting gust of wind took Tella's breath away as she closed the door behind her. Ignoring the cold, she opened a flimsy gate and stepped into her ancient pole barn. After grabbing the long walking stick she always left leaning against the wall, she flipped up the power switch on her brand-new milking machine. Until just a few months before, Tella milked her cows by hand. It had taken several lessons from her nephew to learn how to use the amazing device correctly, but once she got the hang of it, her arthritic hands didn't hurt quite so much at night. She loved her new machine and lovingly polished its stainless-steel tank and fittings every morning. To her, it was nothing less than a miracle from God.

Leaving the barn, Tella tramped across her muddy pasture using the walking stick to keep her balance. With the first morning light seeping through the mountain passes, she could just make out her three precious milk cows standing together near the fence at the far end of the half-acre enclosure.

"What are you silly girls looking at? Come in! Come in out of the cold!" she shouted in Spanish.

At the sound of her voice, the cows turned and started ambling in her direction. While they slowly made their way toward the barn, Tella looked to the east. About this time of day, the rising sun backlit the snow-covered peaks of the Andes, creating majestic patterns in the morning sky. She never tired of the daily light show and looked forward to its calming certainty every morning.

But today, something wasn't right. Instead of dawn creeping over the high summits, something else caught her eye. A bright orange glow appeared between two of the mountains. A moment later, the strange light started to lift into the air and grew quickly, transforming into a long white flame that rose higher and higher into the sky. Ten seconds later, Tella felt more than heard a low rumble wash across the valley.

The short Chilean cheesemaker couldn't pull her eyes away from the incredible scene. She had never seen a light so intense. It blotted out the stars just before what looked like ethereal blue and green wings flared outward from its center. If she hadn't known better, she would have concluded some mighty angel had emerged from the mountains to fly back to heaven. Forgetting the cows, she stood motionless, watching the brilliant light become smaller and smaller until it finally disappeared into the east.

Tella didn't have much education, but the simple Chilean chee-semaker who lived deep in the country, or *campo,* knew she had just witnessed a rocket launch. She remembered news reports about the Americans landing on the moon and space airplanes that glided back to Earth. But nothing could have prepared her to witness such a thing in person, and she had no idea what it meant. Tella had not been to mass in many years, but just to be on the safe side, she dropped painfully to her knees and prayed for protection and peace.

As the morning returned to normal, she pulled herself slowly back onto her feet, took one last look at where the rocket first appeared, shrugged, and followed the cows inside.

Later, she would call her brother and ask him about what she witnessed. But first, her girls needed milking, and then she had cheese to make, rocket or no rocket.

## North American Air Defense Command
## Cheyenne Mountain, Colorado
## Central Operations Command

Technical Sergeant Eugene Bailey picked up his coffee and took a sip. A scowl crossed his face as he forced himself to swallow the cold, bitter liquid left at the bottom of his mug. After nearly six straight hours staring at three computer screens, he hoped someone had made a fresh pot of the wickedly strong brew he needed to stay alert until the end of his shift. Bailey stood and stretched a moment. Manning the deep underground command center and monitoring the immense amount of information gathered by NORAD's early warning satellites could be mind-numbingly dull. But the men and women of the United States Air Force and Royal Canadian Air Force tucked away deep under Cheyenne Mountain in Colorado had to be on their toes just in case the Russians, Chinese, or North Koreans went insane and started lobbing missiles over the Arctic.

Just as he turned to go in search of a hot refill, his eye caught a bright red light blinking furiously on one of his three monitors.

The coffee forgotten, Bailey jumped back into his chair and expertly typed a set of commands into the computer. The screen immediately changed to display an outline map of South America. On what looked like the border between Chile and Argentina, a dotted line appeared and began crawling across the screen to the northeast.

The technical sergeant's eyes grew wide. NORAD's launch detection satellites had never picked up a potential threat originating from this part of the world.

Without hesitation, Bailey flipped up a clear plastic cover and pressed a red button marked 'Launch Warning.'

As several red lights mounted to the ceiling began flashing, the entire control center came to life. An unannounced ballistic missile launch could mean many things, from an unexpected test of a new spacecraft – to the start of a nuclear war. The thirty highly trained men and women staffing the control room donned headsets and furiously typed away at their stations, beginning a series of well-rehearsed protocols. They moved quickly but professionally, working to decide whether or not the launch represented a threat to the United States or Canada.

Sergeant Bailey began the process of authenticating the launch by initiating a diagnostic check on the Space-Based Infrared Satellite that transmitted the early warning message. The satellite responded perfectly, confirming its assessment that a ballistic missile had just lifted off from the mountains of Chile.

Still not satisfied, Bailey tasked the military's newest WFOV or Wide Field of View surveillance platform with verifying the suspected launch. While the WFOV spacecraft's primary responsibility covered North America, its wide-angle vision allowed it to 'see' most of the Western Hemisphere. The suspected launch occurred at the extreme limit of the WFOV's capability, but the data from both satellites matched.

"Well, I'll be damned," Bailey said under his breath as he snatched an old-fashioned telephone receiver from its cradle.

"Sir, launch from central Chile is confirmed," Bailey stated without emotion when his supervising captain answered the call.

The captain's almost bland response matched Bailey's. "Acknowledged. Begin a track, mark position of origin, and run full telemetry."

"Yes, sir," Bailey acknowledged, his intensive training ensuring he responded properly to the situation despite the fact this was the first time he had encountered an unanticipated launch scenario.

With a few commands, the gigantic screen covering the operation center's far wall changed to depict the entire continent of South America. A long arching red line originating in the Andes Mountains slowly ticked across Argentina. Displays next to the rocket's current position indicated the object's altitude and speed. A white line extending ahead of whatever now flew high over the Atlantic Ocean anticipated its expected trajectory.

"What have we got, Sergeant?" a voice asked from over Bailey's shoulder.

Bailey hadn't noticed General Nathan Selkirk, the current NORAD commander, standing over his shoulder.

"Sir, we have a confirmed launch. Position of origin 35°22'2.43" south latitude, 70°39'46.31" west longitude."

"Chile?"

"Yes, sir. Right in the middle of the Andes," Bailey responded, using his cursor to point at an obviously uninhabited and inhospitable point deep in the massive mountain range.

"Tracking?"

"Yes, sir. The vehicle is now over the Atlantic and still climbing. Analysis reports the launch poses no threat to CONUS."

"Okay. No threat to the continental United States. Then where the hell is that thing going?" the general asked.

"Speed, altitude, and angle of climb are consistent with an attempt to achieve orbit, sir," Bailey reported. "Wait. We may have staging."

On the giant display, the red line flared and then continued on its original path.

Bailey checked his readings. "Staging confirmed. No doubt about it now, sir. It's headed into space."

"Any data available on the type of launch vehicle? Can it be identified as Russian, Chinese, North Korean, or maybe Indian?" the general asked.

"No, sir. We barely caught the launch at all. No further identification was possible at that extreme range."

"Chile?" Selkirk repeated with disbelief. "I'll be damned."

"Yes, sir. That's just what I said."

"Chile has no space program anyone has ever heard about. And I seem to recall they have massive internal political problems. This doesn't make any sense."

"No, sir. It sure doesn't," Bailey agreed.

"It may not be an immediate threat, but whoever pulled off this little surprise must be up to something. And I doubt it's good."

# CHAPTER TWO

Later the same day
FBI Laboratory
Quantico, Virginia

Special Agent Frank Deal leaned back in his chair, placed both hands behind his head, and swiveled around to face the windows of his third-floor office. The heat of summer had not yet taken hold of the Virginia countryside, and the dense tree line that obscured the general public's view of the FBI's modern laboratory building glowed in the late afternoon sun.

Deal's job as Special Agent in Charge of the FBI's elite Fast Response Team usually kept the fifty-year-old ex-JAG officer on the move around the globe. But for the past several months, the terrorists, warlords, dictators, and other assorted bad guys seemed to be taking a break. Not that Deal and his team ever truly relaxed. They had taken advantage of the lull in the pace of real-world crises involving weapons of mass destruction to train, regroup, and prepare for their next assignment.

The sudden buzz of the intercom jolted Deal back to the present. "Sir, the Director is on his way over," his assistant announced. Deal took a moment to answer.

"Okay. Let me know as soon as he's in the building," Deal said, trying not to sound irritated while rubbing both hands across his head of short, gray, wiry hair.

With a silent sigh of resignation, Deal stood and fastened the top button of his white shirt, straightened his plain dark blue tie, and pulled on his suit coat.

*Looks like it's time to get back to work.*

"Also, Mr. Adcock is in the office. He says he had a message to meet with you and the Director."

"Okay. Send Bubba on in," Deal responded.

A few seconds later, Lawrence "Bubba" Adcock strode through the door wearing a white lab coat over a t-shirt advertising some NASCAR racing team and a pair of khaki shorts. The lab coat barely hid Bubba's impressive beer belly and did nothing to disguise his obvious southern good-old-boy demeanor.

"Afternoon, Frank!" Bubba exclaimed with a wide grin. "You look like you missed out on the last piece of mamma's apple pie."

Deal just shook his head. Over the last few years, he learned that he couldn't suppress Bubba's sometimes overly effusive personality.

"Bubba, can you at least call me Agent Deal when the Director gets here?" Deal asked.

"Okay, boss. I'll try. So, the big cheese is coming here himself. Something must be up," Bubba commented as he walked over to the windows. "Nice view. No windows down in the labs where I work."

"Yeah. It's terrific," Deal replied absently.

"I'm meeting up with Michael and Sarah later for a beer. They have a couple of days off from the Academy. We might even drive up to Georgetown and try to get Zack's nose out of the books for a night. Want to come?" Bubba asked, mostly to pick at Deal, knowing the FBI Special Agent would decline.

"No. Thank you."

"Okay, but the kids miss the boss being around," Bubba continued.

"Bubba. Cool it. The Director will be here any minute," Deal said, holding out one hand like a stop sign.

"Alright. I'll behave for a while," Bubba replied, feigning contriteness.

The buzz of the intercom announcing that the FBI Director was on his way up saved Deal from more of Bubba's antics.

A minute later, FBI Director William Glover walked into Deal's office, closed the door, and had Deal and Bubba take a seat.

"Frank, we have a situation," Glover said, skipping any friendly chit-chat. "I've asked Mr. Adcock to join us as this falls within his area of expertise."

While Bubba often acted like a country boy from rural Alabama, where he grew up, he was actually an acknowledged genius in aerospace technology, chemistry, and physics. To add to his impressive accomplishments, he had just become the youngest person to receive a master's degree in orbital dynamics and would receive a doctorate in physics in less than three months.

"Yes, sir. What have you got for us?" Deal asked, already dreading the answer.

The lines on Glover's mahogany face darkened.

"Less than twelve hours ago, NORAD detected an unscheduled and unannounced missile launch," Glover began.

"North Korea?" Bubba asked.

Glover shook his head. "No. And not Iran, Pakistan, China, Russia, or any of the usual suspects. Just after 05:30 a.m. local time, 06:30 a.m. here, a vehicle with at least two stages lifted off from a location in the Andes Mountains inside the border of Chile. Whatever that rocket delivered is now in low Earth orbit."

Deal and Bubba sat a moment in stunned silence.

"Chile?" Deal asked. "I've never heard they had anything like that. Or any country in South America, for that matter."

"They don't. Or at least we didn't think so. I checked with the CIA on this as soon as I heard. They don't have many assets down there, and this launch caught them by surprise," Glover responded.

"Wow," Bubba exclaimed. "Did NORAD send over its data? I'd love to take a look at its orbit. A launch from Chile would most likely take the vehicle over Argentina. Unless, of course, they were going for a polar shot."

"You're living up to your reputation, Mr. Adcock. Our current information shows whatever they launched is not in a polar orbit. But that's preliminary."

"Wait," Deal interrupted. "In plain English, please, Bubba."

"Sure," Bubba said, looking around and picking up a round snow globe depicting a quaint scene of Oxford, England, that Deal kept on his desk. "The Earth spins on its axis. If you shoot a rocket up and to the east from the equator, the Earth's rotation helps throw the rocket into space. That effect decreases as you move the launch point further north or south. If you want the vehicle to go around the planet at an angle to the equator, you point the rocket north or south. You still get some help from the Earth's rotation, but not as much."

Bubba moved his finger around the snow globe to demonstrate.

"Now," Bubba continued, "if you want the orbit to go over the north and south poles, or a polar orbit, the Earth's rotation provides no help at all. You need bigger engines, more fuel, and such. I'm not saying that can't be done by Chile or whoever, but it's considerably more difficult."

"The State Department already sent our ambassador to speak with the Chilean Foreign Minister. They flatly denied any knowledge of the launch," Glover explained.

Deal grunted in disbelief. "They're hiding something."

"You said the launch originated in the Andes Mountains. That's really weird. Do you have the exact coordinates?" Bubba asked. "Can we take a look at the origination point on a map?"

Glover reached into his pocket and retrieved his phone while Deal turned on the 65-inch high-definition monitor on the wall across from his desk. Glover tapped a few buttons and cast a map of south-central Chile onto the screen. A red pin appeared deep inside the mountain range.

"Zoom in and take a look at the satellite view," Glover said, handing his phone to Bubba. "You can do that faster than me."

Bubba took the phone, switched the view to an image taken just a couple of months before by one of NASA's satellites, and zoomed down to the exact launch site.

"That doesn't make any sense," Deal pronounced. "There's nothing there."

Deal was right. The area appeared to be a shallow valley set between several steep ridges. Just to the east, a narrow ribbon of water cut through a deep river gorge.

"No man-made structures, launch towers, support buildings, or even roads to that location," Bubba observed.

"Yeah. It doesn't look like anyone has ever stepped foot on that place. It reminds me of pictures from Mars," Deal added. "Is the Air Force sure this is the correct point of origin?"

"NORAD confirmed the position with two of our newest early-warning satellite systems," Glover responded. "But I see what you mean."

Bubba walked closer to the monitor with his head tilted slightly to one side. For the next couple of minutes, he studied the picture on the screen carefully, scratching his head of unruly light brown hair as he zoomed in and out and changed the view angle.

"What do you see, Bubba?" Deal finally asked, noticing Bubba's concentration on the low hills surrounding the valley. The FBI agent had learned to trust the eccentric young genius's intellect and judgment during two previous operations. If Bubba saw something out of place, Deal wanted to know about it.

"Maybe nothing. I'm no geologist. I took a few courses as an undergrad. Mostly because they were an easy A, but this anticline doesn't look natural."

"A what?" Glover asked.

"An anticline is an upward fold in the rock. You can see the folded layers right here," Bubba explained, pointing to an area along one side of the plateau where bands of rock looked like a bell curve or wave. "I can't be sure from this view, but below the folds, it looks like the supporting rock has been removed, dug out, and replaced with, well, something else."

Deal and Glover both walked closer and peered at where Bubba was pointing.

"I don't see anything," Deal said, squinting at the spot Bubba identified. "What do you think it means?"

"You're thinking that might be a camouflaged entrance to a tunnel?" Glover asked.

"Maybe. It's difficult to be sure by the high angle of this shot. If it is, it's certainly big enough to accommodate a mobile launch vehicle. If I'm right, and I think I am, whoever launched a rocket capable of achieving orbit from this place is clever as hell and did a great job covering their tracks."

"Let's assume your theory is correct. Where would a tunnel go from there? And where would it begin?" Glover asked.

Bubba walked back to the map.

"Assuming this is a hidden door, it sits on the east-facing wall next to the plateau," Bubba began. "If we draw a line from that point to the west..."

Glover and Deal watched as a red line extended to the west from the launch point.

"... you find the city of Talca."

"But that's what? Fifty miles away?" Deal asked.

"Fifty-two," Bubba corrected. "I'd bet my daddy's pickup truck that our theoretical tunnel would connect the launch site to another entrance somewhere near Talca."

"Explain your thinking, Bubba," Deal said.

"Okay, boss. No problem. First, the tunnel entrance leads into the ground facing west into Chile. To the east is Argentina. That's in the wrong direction. A tunnel would have to make a big loop to go back that way. And it's really difficult to dig a tunnel with a lot of turns in it. To the north and south are just a thousand miles of massive mountains. The most likely and most logical direction for some traversable underground transportation system is west. Toward Talca."

"But why Talca? Why not one of these other little cities?" Deal asked, challenging Bubba's conclusion. "A couple of them are closer and not far from the line between the launch site and Talca."

Bubba gave Deal a self-satisfied grin.

"The answer is rivers. As you can see on the map, several rivers run out of the Andes, cutting across Chile and flowing toward the Pacific Ocean. Talca sits directly west of the launch site and between the Maule and Lontue' River systems. Of course, a tunnel can be built under a river, but you need extensive supports and other structures to keep water out. Plus, at first glance, these appear to be seasonal rivers that flood in the spring. Vast areas around these systems will be boggy most of the year. Digging a tunnel through soft ground is next to impossible."

Deal looked at Glover. The FBI director stood rubbing his chin and scowling at the screen.

"Director, I don't suppose you drove down here just to spitball a few theories, did you?" Deal asked.

"I did not," Glover responded. "Bubba's analysis is compelling, but we need real answers. Get your team on the ground down there as soon as possible. We have no idea what the Chileans just put into orbit. It could be completely harmless. A research satellite or something. But they are being way too evasive for this to be something that mundane."

"Will the Chileans cooperate?" Deal asked. "Or do we go in quietly to snoop around?"

"The Chilean government is, as usual, squirrely. Sometimes they like us, sometimes they don't. Right now, they don't because we've been leaning on the current president down there to clean up his act. So, do this quietly. Very quietly. Leave your tactical people staged at one of our abandoned bases in Panama in case you need them for muscle. You and a small team get down to Talca, or whatever it's called. Go undercover. Tourists or something."

"I'm not sure the locals will believe we're tourists. Americans showing up in a small, out-of-the-way city in central Chile, in winter, mind you, might raise some eyebrows. Especially after a surprise missile just flew out of the mountains," Deal replied, more thinking out loud than objecting to Glover's suggestion.

Glover patted Deal on the shoulder as he turned toward the door.

"You'll think of something, Frank. You always do."

After the Director left, Deal ambled back to the windows. Summer was just around the corner. But it would be winter where they were going.

"Boss, I may have an idea," Bubba offered. "Let me work on it, and I'll get back to you first thing in the morning."

# CHAPTER THREE

The Pacifico Hotel
Santiago, Chile
The next day

The windows of the ultra-luxurious Pacifico Hotel overlooked the sprawling city of Santiago from its hilltop perch outside the central downtown area. The hotel catered to only the wealthiest travelers, visiting officials from other countries, and celebrities. But the entire top floor had been permanently reserved for the hotel's shadowy owners. Just a few of the longest-serving and most trusted staff had access to the twelve suites, gourmet kitchen, meeting rooms, and spa that took up the entire floor. The twelve current owners always arrived at the hotel by helicopter and rarely ventured into other parts of the building.

And nobody knew their true identities, including the executive manager.

The top floor had remained vacant for nearly a year. But after the executive manager received a call that two of the owners would arrive with VIP guests in just a few hours, followed later in the day by the other ten, the hotel's personnel exploded into a flurry of hurried preparations. Staff placed fresh flowers in every room, bartenders meticulously stocked the private bars with each owner's favorite liquors and wines, and the hotel's five-star chef gathered fresh ingredients and supplies for the private kitchen.

Just as the executive manager finished personally inspecting every inch of the top floor, he received a message that the first helicopter was only minutes away from the rooftop helipad.

Dressed in an impeccably tailored Armani suit, he sprinted up a set of stairs, unlocked the private elevator, and rolled out a sumptuously thick dark blue wool carpet across the rough asphalt roof to the edge of the helipad.

Then he waited.

Within minutes, a gleaming black Airbus Dauphin 2 appeared from the west and settled onto the roof. As the manager watched from his post near the highly polished elevator doors, the side of the aircraft opened, and a set of stairs automatically reached toward the ground. A moment later, three men and one woman descended the stairs and walked briskly across the carpet.

The manager had to stifle a gasp of surprise when he recognized one of the men as the president of Chile, Juan Mateo Cayo.

The four passengers chatted amiably as they made the short walk from the helicopter. As they approached, the manager opened the doors to the elevator and gave a slight bow as the group passed by and stepped inside. None of the new arrivals even looked at him, much less offered so much as a perfunctory greeting or insincere 'thank you.'

The group of four rode the elevator down one floor and stepped into the twelfth floor's wide, brightly lit main corridor. The décor could easily be mistaken for a French king's chateau. Crystal chandeliers hung above antique Persian rugs. An eclectic collection of paintings, including an original Monet and two Picassos, adorned the walls bathed in museum-quality lighting.

"An impressive collection," President Cayo commented as they passed by twelve closed doors, each bearing a single gold number. "I had no idea such artwork existed here in Chile."

"Thank you, Mr. President. Some of our colleagues enjoy collecting such things. They keep the most valuable pieces at their homes, of course. I'm more partial to horses than paintings," Alexander Monroe, one of the hotel's owners, replied, walking next to the president.

"I, too, love to ride. Perhaps you can join me at my estancia in the future."

"Estancia?" Monroe asked.

"You would call it a 'ranch,' I believe," Cayo explained. "It is quite beautiful. As you know, I have no wife or family to share it with. So, I very much enjoy bringing friends there whenever possible."

"Thank you, Mr. President. I'd be honored," Monroe answered.

At the end of the hall, Monroe opened the door to a conference area. The ultra-modern furnishings within clashed with the opulent hallway but offered a comfortable and secure environment well suited to high-level discussions and decision-making. Floor-to-ceiling windows across the entire space offered a breathtaking view of Santiago and the mountains beyond.

Bypassing a massive round conference table, Monroe showed the president to one of two soft black leather club chairs next to a marble fireplace. A matching couch filled out the seating area.

"May I offer you a drink?" the only female in the room, who Monroe had introduced as 'Miss Kent,' asked when the president had settled his 5' 10" muscular frame into one of the chairs.

"Yes. Dark rum. El Dorado. Neat."

The president watched approvingly as Amina Kent glided across the room to the chrome and glass bar and poured two fingers of the rare black rum into each of two matching crystal tumblers. Like most men, Cayo had a difficult time pulling his eyes away from Amina's slim figure and silky black hair that seemed to flow from her head and dance lightly off her shoulders. Her form-fitting dress matched her perfectly applied red lipstick, which, in turn, set off her wide-set black eyes. He couldn't quite place her nation of origin. She spoke with a light British accent but looked too exotic to be from England or Northern Europe.

"Would your security man like something to drink, Mr. President?" Monroe asked, gesturing toward the only other person in the room.

"Eduardo will be fine. He has been at my side many years and would refuse even water while he stands in protection of me," Cayo replied.

"Of course. Such loyalty is a rare gift."

Amina placed the tumbler into the president's hand, allowing her fingertips to just brush his as she did so.

"Thank you, Miss Kent," Cayo said before turning back to Monroe. "Alexander, you have been a major supporter of mine for several years. Your donations to my campaign and others from my party have been extraordinarily generous. So, I was happy to grant your request for a private meeting away from the Presidential Palace. Yet, my country has many issues to address, and my time is limited. Please, how may I be of service?"

"I understand completely, Mr. President. Let me get right to the point. My companies have invested heavily in Chile. Mining, agriculture, manufacturing, and shipping, to name a few. And I know you will understand our need to keep those businesses secure. With backing from your government and the favorable business environment you have created, they have been profitable for us – and I believe for you as well."

Cayo answered Monroe by lifting his drink in the air. He knew better than to verbally acknowledge the allusion to the money he received from Monroe's companies that went far beyond campaign contributions.

Monroe continued. "So, when we heard about the rocket launched from the Andes within Chile's territory, we became concerned. Chile is a peaceful country with excellent relationships around the globe."

"And you wish to know if my country has decided to spend vast sums enhancing our military with ballistic missiles?" Cayo asked.

"Or undertaking some kind of secret space program. Yes," Monroe answered. "Either could be destabilizing, which is not good for business."

Cayo ran his fingers across his trademark black and gray goatee while he studied Monroe before answering. News of the incredible missile launch had not yet broken in the media, but it would. A few grainy pictures had already appeared on the internet, and he suspected Monroe knew more about the launch than he did.

"Alexander, we were as surprised as the rest of the world. I do not know who has done this thing in my country and without my permission. But I will find out. I have ordered my federal security service, the ANI, to investigate and I have assured the Americans, Chinese, Russians, and Argentinians that we would share our findings. I will be happy to keep you apprised as well," Cayo explained.

"I'm sure the Americans offered to assist?" Monroe asked.

"Oh, yes. They contacted my government within hours. Our military and aviation radars barely detected the missile. The American satellites not only picked up the launch immediately but pinpointed the exact location and path of the vehicle into space. After we denied any knowledge of the event, the Americans offered to send resources through their NASA agency."

Monroe had guessed as much.

"And you refused?" Monroe asked.

"Of course. The Norte Americanos use the smooth language of diplomacy to offer their help. But I know better. They will use this as a pretext to insert CIA agents into my country and try to undermine my administration. I will not allow foreign spies into Chile. It is no secret that America has meddled in Chile's affairs before. Given the opportunity, they will certainly do so again. This is an internal matter and the business of no other country. We have made that perfectly clear. How I run *my* country is *my* business."

Monroe offered an approving nod before throwing back the remainder of his drink. He barely managed to keep from laughing at Cayo's bluster. The president of Chile was nothing more than a tinpot dictator chosen and placed in office by The Cause, as Monroe and his associates called themselves, to do their bidding.

*My country. My business. Hilarious.*

"Excellent. I appreciate your time, Mr. President. I can reassure my people that the matter is being handled with wisdom and care," Monroe said as earnestly as possible. "Now, if you can indulge me with just another moment of your time, I would like to introduce you to someone who will take your presidency to the next level."

Cayo cocked his head to one side.

"I don't understand," the president said, maintaining his phony politician's smile.

Monroe raised one finger and pressed a button on an intercom panel next to his chair.

"Dr. Knox, will you please join us?"

Cayo's brows knitted together, but he remained seated.

Next to the fireplace, one panel of the wall slid open, and a man stepped out.

Cayo looked at the newcomer for a moment before recognizing who now stood behind Monroe.

It was him.

Cayo's eyes popped open, and his jaw dropped.

"What...what is the meaning of this? Is this some sort of joke? Who is this...this imposter?" Cayo demanded.

"What a ridiculous question!" Amina replied, standing. "You don't recognize Juan Mateo Cayo, president of Chile?"

*"I am the president,"* Cayo blurted.

Amina took a few steps, sat on one arm of Cayo's chair, and snaked her right arm around his shoulders. Leaning down, she whispered in his ear: "Not anymore."

In one lightning-fast move, she drew a thin piano wire around Cayo's neck and pulled it tight.

Cayo's eyes bulged from their sockets, and he tried to stand, uselessly attempting to wedge his fingers between the garrot and his neck. The president's body tensed, and his back arched upward from the chair, but nothing could loosen Amina's grip. As his vision began to blur from lack of oxygen, Cayo's eyes locked on his bodyguard, Eduardo. His last thought was a question – *why?*

"Thank you, Miss Kent. I appreciate you not making a mess on the carpet," Monroe said.

"My pleasure, as always," Amina replied. "I'm sure my bank account reflects the usual payment?"

"Of course," Monroe answered. "We would not like to upset you."

"No, you would not," Amina said without emotion.

Monroe and Dave Knox watched the assassin casually walk away as if she were leaving a favorite restaurant.

"Mr. President, are you ready to leave?" Eduardo asked Dr. Dave Knox after Amina disappeared.

"Yes, Eduardo. Just a moment," Dave said, tossing down Cayo's untouched drink.

Monroe looked at Knox one more time. The transformation was absolutely perfect. Knox looked, sounded, and walked just like Cayo. He had even perfected Cayo's habit of stroking his goatee.

"Good luck, my friend," Monroe said. "You look great."

"You look great, *Mr. President,*" Dave corrected.

Less than a minute later, Eduardo and Knox emerged from the elevator onto the roof. The hotel's manager still stood near the doors.

Knox nodded as the pair headed to the waiting helicopter.

The manager bowed slightly. "Mr. President."

# CHAPTER FOUR

Washington, D.C.

"What's the rush, big guy?" Michael King asked from the passenger seat of Bubba's brand-new pickup truck. "You're driving like you're on a mission from God."

"Don't listen to him, Bubba. This is fun," Michael's long-time girlfriend, Sarah Marshall, said from the back seat. "Like the evasive driving class at the academy."

Michael just rolled his eyes. After they had joined the FBI on Agent Deal's strong recommendation and started their training at Quantico, Sarah had uncharacteristically become an adrenalin junkie.

"You got it, little lady!" Bubba said, goosing the accelerator.

The big truck shot ahead, causing Michael to grab the door handle.

"Bubba!"

Bubba and Sarah both laughed.

"I thought you liked fast cars," Bubba said, lifting his right foot and slowing back to the posted speed limit on the Francis Scott Key Bridge that connected Virginia with Washington, D.C.

"I do. When *I'm* driving," Michael responded.

"I know. Don't worry. You're still the designated wheelman of our little group," Bubba said. "How's the academy? You guys know all about being secret agents or whatever yet?"

"It's been awesome. But we're almost done. Academy training takes 20 weeks. It will be another few years before we can be full-fledge agents," Sarah explained. "Your boy Michael here is on track to graduate at the top of the class."

"Sarah isn't far behind. She's giving me a real challenge for the top spot," Michael said with pride.

"Uck. Stop," Bubba said, laughing from behind the wheel. "You two are making me sick. Not to make you more irritating, but the boss sometimes drops his 'tough guy' act and lets it slip how well you're both doing."

Deal had encouraged Michael and Sarah to join the FBI and work toward becoming agents after they both finished college the year before. He had also hired Bubba on the spot to work directly with his Fast Response Team at the FBI Laboratory. The fourth member of their group, Zach Self, now attended the School of Foreign Service at Georgetown University. His magnetic personality and ability to make friends with anyone made a career in the Diplomatic Corps or politics a natural fit.

"Where are we meeting him?" Michael asked. "The sooner I get out of this monster truck, the better."

"Right here," Bubba announced as he pulled up to the curb outside The Tombs, one of Georgetown students' favorite hangouts.

The two-story yellow building with turquoise trim and dark red metal roof looked like an inn from the 1800s – exactly what it used to be.

Bubba and Michael followed Sarah through the double doors. Inside, long tables lined with wooden chairs filled the space between the old-fashioned oak bar and a row of cozy red leather booths set against the wall. The air smelled of fried food and beer, perfectly matching the cool, dark, casual atmosphere.

Sarah squealed with delight when she saw Zach stand up from one of the booths and wave. She ran to her old friend, threw her arms around his neck, and kissed him on the cheek.

"Well, well. Have I got something to worry about here?" Michael chided.

"You certainly don't deserve this girl, buddy," Zach kidded back, hugging Sarah tightly.

Zach and Michael had been best friends since meeting in elementary school. They had been inseparable ever since.

"How are they hanging, giant genius?" Zach asked Bubba.

Bubba laughed. "Is that the kind of language they're teaching you in that fancy diplomat school? And, to answer your question, they are hanging just fine. Now, how about we do what we came here to do? I got a powerful thirst and a need for a dozen or two onion rings."

"First round is on the way," Zach said as they slid into the booth. A moment later, four frosty mugs of beer appeared on the table.

During two previous high-stakes operations with the FBI and Agent Deal, the four friends had endured multiple life-and-death situations together – bringing them closer than most families. Now, they didn't see each other as often as they had in college and spent the next half-hour catching up.

"Man, it's great to see you guys!" Zach declared. "I'm loving school, but most of my classmates are way, way too serious. I like a little more, you know, excitement."

"Sure you do, buddy," Michael joshed. "Just what in the heck do you study at foreign service school anyway? Not to bust your chops, but it sounds kinda boring."

Zach nodded his head.

"Compared to the FBI Academy, I suppose it must seem that way. It's actually really exciting. Diplomacy is the art and science of maintaining peaceful relationships around the world. But it's not all shaking hands and kissing butts. In a lot of ways, practicing foreign relations is like high-stakes poker. You have to know who's sitting across the table, be able to figure out what hand they are holding, and try to predict their next move."

After his second beer and first plate of hot, crispy onion rings, Bubba rubbed his expansive belly and leaned back into the soft cushions. He didn't want to ruin the tranquil mood but knew he was about to do just that.

"Hey, guys," Bubba began. "I need to talk about something that's going on. You up for some shop talk?"

Zach's dark eyebrows raised.

"Something serious?" he asked, noticing Bubba had dropped his country-boy persona.

"Yeah. I'm afraid so."

Michael put his beer down, and Sarah, sensing the change in mood at the table, slid a bit closer to her boyfriend.

"Okay, big guy, shoot. We're listening," Michael answered.

Bubba took a breath before getting into his idea about how to help Deal. But he suddenly hesitated to suggest a plan that might put his friends in danger yet again.

"You look like you might not want to talk about this," Sarah said, reaching over and touching Bubba's hand.

"Just spit it out," Michael prompted, not catching Bubba's sudden reluctance to involve his friends.

Sarah shot Michael a disapproving look.

"It's okay," Bubba said. "Michael's right. Okay, here goes. Have you heard about the rocket launch in Chile that happened yesterday morning?"

Three blank faces looked back at the genius physicist.

Bubba continued. "That's not too surprising. I've seen a few posts on the internet, but it hasn't made the national news yet and might not ever. But it's a big deal."

Zach cocked his head to one side. "Why? If Chile wants to shoot a rocket or something into space, they certainly have the right to do it. There's no international treaty or even agreement limiting what a country can send into orbit."

Bubba nodded in agreement.

"I know. But here's the thing – and it's classified."

Michael, Sarah, and Zach now sat up and leaned in toward Bubba.

"The rocket took off from deep inside the Andes Mountains. We looked at satellite photos of the precise spot, and there's nothing there. I mean nothing at all. No buildings, launch towers, vehicles, people – nothing. And there's more. Right after NORAD detected the missile, the State Department contacted Chile's Foreign Minister. Get this. The Chilean government denies knowing anything about it. They claim they were as surprised as we were."

"What?" Zach exclaimed. "That's sketchy as hell. Either they did it and have something to hide or..."

"Or they don't have control over their own territory, and there's some rogue actor out there shooting billion-dollar rockets into space," Michael said, finishing Zach's thought.

"Not to throw cold water on a hot story, but what does that have to do with us? I mean, the United States?" Sarah asked.

Bubba understood Sarah's question.

"Usually, we wouldn't care. But then, this isn't a usual situation. Most countries announce their space programs to show off their technical prowess, like India landing a rover on the moon recently. Heck, even North Korea makes a big deal every time they launch a new ballistic missile. But not this time. We don't know what it is or what it will be used for," Bubba explained.

"Could it be a weapon of some kind?" Michael asked. "Could they have put like a bomb or something in orbit and threaten to drop it on..."

"The United States?" Bubba said. "Yes."

All four sat silently for a minute, pondering the implications of Bubba's news. Someone just demonstrated the ability to launch a ballistic missile capable of threatening, essentially, every person on Earth. Whether the Chilean government told the truth about its lack of knowledge made no difference. The United States needed to know what really happened.

"Alright. So, where do we come in?" Michael asked, cutting to the chase.

Before answering, Bubba took a long pull on his beer.

"Just a couple of hours ago, I met with Deal and Director Glover. Glover assigned Deal and his team to go down to Chile and investigate this thing. The rub is that Chile has refused any outside help, even threatening to arrest foreigners caught meddling in Chile's business. On top of that, the launch site is up in the Andes, and the nearest town of any size, a place called Talca, isn't exactly a tourist destination."

"And a bunch of burly FBI agents appearing in the area would draw unwanted attention and cause an international incident if they got caught," Sarah concluded.

Bubba raised his mug. "Yeah. Exactly."

Zach could see what was coming. "But four college-age gringos might not raise so many eyebrows."

Bubba nodded. "We would still need a good cover story."

"I have an idea," Sarah volunteered. "I have several friends who went to South America to teach English. They stayed with families in the cities and towns where they taught. I bet we could do something like that."

The idea made sense. They would have a perfectly good reason for being in the area that wouldn't arouse the attention of the Chilean government.

Only two things stood in the way. First, they had to convince Deal. Second, only Sarah spoke more than a few words of Spanish.

FBI Laboratory
The next morning

Deal sat stoically behind his desk with his arms crossed over his chest while Bubba described his discussion with Michael, Sarah, and Zach the night before. But Bubba wasn't deterred by Deal's gruff demeanor. He knew the scowl on the FBI agent's face meant he was seriously considering their idea.

When Bubba finished, Deal sat forward and looked Bubba in the eye.

"You didn't tell them anything classified, did you?" Deal asked.

"Well, not much. Just what they needed to know," Bubba responded a bit sheepishly. "Nothing too sensitive anyway."

Deal just nodded. The question was academic. He had worked with Bubba and his friends long enough to know they wouldn't take classified information lightly.

"And *all* you guys speak Spanish?" Deal asked skeptically.

"No. But that doesn't matter. Sarah and I researched organizations that provide English teachers in various South and Central American countries. They don't require any real language or teaching skills. They need warm bodies who can help students with their English, mostly in high school. And we found two different companies looking for teachers in the Maule Region, or what they also call the 7th District. Talca is in that District, as is our launch site," Bubba said proudly.

"Did you contact these companies?" Deal asked. "Do they need teachers now?"

Bubba grinned widely.

"A new term starts in a week. They jumped at the chance to get four new college graduates down there."

Deal sat back again and looked out the windows. In the 18 hours since the director stood in his office, he had considered numerous ideas about how to quietly get his people into Talca but had discarded each in turn. He didn't like the idea of pulling Michael and Sarah out of the academy, even if only for a short time. But he could smooth that over. Zach could make up his work at Georgetown, especially after the Dean of the School of Foreign Service got a call from the FBI Director. And Bubba already worked directly for him.

"Have Michael, Sarah, and Zach agreed to go? You guys will be on your own down there until I can figure a good cover for me and Agent Sims."

"I think you know they jumped at the chance. Once we get down there, I'll look around for a good cover story for you guys. And is Agent Sims back? Last we heard, she was hot and heavy with good old Sheik Ali," Bubba said.

"I think Ali would have married her. But the other sheiks objected. Anyway, yeah, she's back. I have her setting up our tactical operators in Panama right now. Then she'll head back here," Deal explained.

"So, boss, are we a 'go' for this thing? We can be on a plane to Santiago in three days and be in Talca by Monday morning."

Deal didn't hesitate. "Yes. Approved. Get secure cell phones set up and whatever else you need from the equipment department. I'll call the academy and get Michael and Sarah released from their classes. Keep me informed. Check in every six hours once you're on the ground. Red and Blue teams will be 8 hours away if you get in real trouble. So be careful. Chile is like the Wild West in a lot of ways. Crime is rampant, especially in Santiago."

"You got it, boss!" Bubba exclaimed as he nearly sprinted out of Deal's office.

Deal didn't share Bubba's enthusiasm. His gut churned imagining the wide range of threats that might already be hanging over their heads.

# CHAPTER FIVE

The Cause's Underground Complex
Near Talca, Chile
One day later


"Separation of sub-satellites from the main body is ready to commence, sir," a technician wearing a dark blue jumpsuit said from his seat at one of the massive operation center's six monitoring stations.

Alexander Monroe stood behind the technician, a glowing cigar jutting from his overly white teeth.

"Proceed."

"Separation in five, four, three, two, one – mark."

Monroe looked up at the giant screen that overlooked the laboratory, where a depiction of the globe rotated slowly on its axis. Monroe could identify the outline of the Iberian Peninsula and the edge of the British Isles coming into view. A bright yellow line advanced across the Atlantic toward Europe, indicating the current position of the satellite The Cause placed in orbit just days earlier.

As he watched, the view on the screen zoomed in, showing the one-ton satellite releasing several smaller objects into space. As the main body of the satellite continued on its path, the ten smaller objects stopped, remaining in a fixed position.

It took the mother satellite less than five minutes to deploy the cargo over Western Europe before disappearing over the 'horizon' and into the vast continent of Asia.

Monroe waited patiently for the team of orbital scientists to analyze the positioning of the sub-satellites, or what Dave Knox called 'cubesats.'

"Sir, we have ten nominal-functioning devices deployed as planned over Europe. They are all holding station at the coordinates Dr. Knox provided," the technician sitting in front of Monroe reported.

"Prepare the demonstration scenario as planned, but proceed only on my order," Monroe said, patting the tech on the shoulder. "When is the next cubesat deployment scheduled?"

The tech punched a few buttons on his keyboard, and the line following the mother satellite on the screen raced ahead around the globe multiple times before stopping over the South China Sea.

"It will take a few days for the satellite's orbital path to reach the next release point that will cover China, Taiwan, North and South Korea, Eastern Russia, and Japan, sir."

"I'll call you shortly," Monroe said, turning to leave the control room.

Monroe walked down a brightly lit hall and pushed open a heavy, dark glass door.

Inside, ten stern faces already seated around an ornate conference table turned in his direction. An untouched heavy crystal tumbler sat on the table before each man filled with the finest Kentucky bourbon whiskey money could buy.

The men in the room remained silent as Monroe walked confidently to the head of the table and carefully placed his cigar in a green glass ashtray. He didn't allow himself to smile, preferring to let ten of the twelve Directors of The Cause stew in their anxiety over the success of their boldest and most expensive operation to date.

For a long moment, the tension built around the table until finally, one of the Directors wearing slim, stylish glasses on the end of his nose slapped the table loudly.

"Well, Monroe? I hope the fact that you summoned us all down here to these god-forsaken mountains means you have good news to report. We've gambled the resources of a small country on Dr. Knox's latest scheme. I think it's past time we get a look at what we've invested in."

Monroe stood.

"I agree. Gentlemen, please turn your attention to the screen."

A 120-inch monitor descended from the ceiling, showing a high-definition picture of an oil rig sitting in the middle of an ocean.

"What is this?" the same Director demanded.

"You are looking at Oil Platform 21A. The company that owns this rig shut it down two days ago with the intention of moving it to a new spot in the North Sea. This picture is from one of the remote cameras they use to keep an eye on their asset while it is unmanned. We tapped into their feed so we can watch what happens next."

"Fascinating, Monroe," the impatient Director commented. "We have all seen an oil rig before."

Monroe just smiled and pulled a small walkie-talkie out of his pocket.

"Proceed with the demonstration."

High above the Earth, a door slid open in the back of the tenth cubesat stationed over Europe. A gray 4-inch diameter sphere appeared in the door and stopped as if hesitant to step into space. A moment later, a tiny burst of blue from the back of the sphere propelled it into the black void.

After it floated a few yards away, miniature thrusters spun and twisted the sphere until its internal navigation system calculated a precise orientation and reentry trajectory. When the computer confirmed the sphere's position, one of its six exhaust ports fired, slowing the sphere until it fell behind the line of cubesats and into the clutches of the Earth's gravity. A moment later, the relatively tiny device began a suicidal plunge toward the surface at over 17,000 miles per hour.

Completely invisible to even the most sophisticated radar, the weapon sliced through the clouds, an unstoppable mass moving at extreme velocity.

"Keep your eyes on the screen. You won't want to miss this," Monroe said, stepping aside so he could watch the other Directors' reaction to what was about to occur.

A second later, the massive oil drilling platform that stood six stories over the cold North Sea disappeared behind an instantaneous cloud of steam that obscured the entire area. There was no fire. No explosion. Thirty seconds later, the wind cleared the air.

The massive steel structure no longer existed.

"What the hell was that?" another Director asked, astonished.

Monroe walked over to a long credenza placed by the windows, opened a drawer, and removed a four-inch diameter gray metal sphere, holding it up so everyone could see.

"Are you trying to tell us something like that just destroyed an entire oil rig?"

The room erupted in questions, accusations, and demands for answers. Monroe stood silently, waiting for the Directors' initial astonishment to subside.

"The answer to your questions is yes. A very special ball of titanium alloy this exact size just took out that entire platform," Monroe explained. "I'm sure Dr. Knox could enlighten us as to the physics involved. As I understand it, the immense energy released when the sphere hit the oil rig was not from any explosive, nuclear or conventional, but simply the mass of the sphere times its incredible speed."

The still skeptical Director stood and held his arms out as if encompassing everyone sitting around the table.

"Are you saying that we spent untold billions for some kind of crazy Star Trek space weapon? Other than the obvious chance to blackmail people who don't want us blowing things up, or pissing off every superpower on Earth, what good is something like this? How does this make us *money*?"

Monroe just smiled. "Oh, this is just how we make sure nobody messes with our satellites once they are in orbit. Dr. Knox has assured me his satellites are capable of far more and will easily redouble our fortunes."

Monroe ignored the skeptical looks some of the Directors shot in his direction. He and Dave had agreed to withhold details about how they would utilize the satellites' full capabilities until the launch protocols were complete.

As the meeting subsided, one of the men approached Monroe and shook his hand. "Quite the demonstration, Alexander. Congratulations are certainly in order. But where is Dr. Knox? The Directors are, at the core, investors. And, as you are well aware, investors covet information. While Knox's reputation buys him considerable leeway, they will only withhold their demands for a full accounting and plan of action for so long. I suppose he is occupied managing this technical marvel of his?" the man asked in a nasally British accent.

"I'm sure he is," Monroe replied. "He told me to pass on his gratitude to all the Directors of The Cause for their faith in his leadership and willingness to stand behind his newest endeavor."

"How could we not? He has proved superbly effective, and his projects have all paid off handsomely. But past success only goes so far. Can we expect to have him with us for the next meeting?"

"We'll see. But I'll pass along the Duke of Albans' congratulations and well wishes," Monroe said, placing one hand on the duke's tailored gray suit.

The duke ignored Monroe's lack of deference to his title. *Americans.*

"We shall all be interested to talk to him about how he will use our new, uh, toys. I am given to understand it will require three further launches to complete the dispersal of all the satellites required to fulfill his vision?"

"Correct," Monroe responded. "If all goes well, perhaps you'll invite us to Buckingham Palace one day. Maybe you can talk me into bowing and calling you 'Your Highness' then," Monroe said with a wry grin.

Monroe knew everyone in the room had lofty ambitions. And the Duke of Albans', while immense, didn't eclipse anyone else's.

The duke chuckled. "You may be assured I'll do just that. But with the United States, Great Britain, and others rather intensely curious about our first successful deployment, do you and Dr. Knox believe security can be maintained?"

Monroe had anticipated some handwringing. "Oh, yes. We have the complete cooperation of the entire government of Chile."

The duke's eyes betrayed his doubt. "I must say, old man, that would be quite the feat."

"Yes. Quite," Monroe agreed. "Even as we speak, Dr. Knox is making the final, shall we say, arrangements."

# CHAPTER SIX

The Presidential Palace (Palacio La Moneda)
Santiago, Chile
The same day

The president of Chile, Juan Mateo Cayo, aka Dr. Dave Knox, stood behind the table that served as his desk, eyeing a group of twenty high-ranking military officers and cabinet ministers. This meeting would be the first real test of his new identity. Cayo had known some of these people for many years, so Dave's appearance, voice, mannerisms, and dress had to be perfect. Any lapses on his part would bring immediate, fatal consequences.

But while recognizing the danger, Dave had no doubt that his immense intellect, complete mastery of Spanish in the correct dialect, and months of studying every minute detail of Cayo's life would easily fool everyone in the room. Today, he was no longer genius physicist Dr. Dave Knox.

He was Juan Mateo Cayo.

The presidential office could only be described as immense, dwarfing the Oval Office in sheer size. Ornate Spanish-style furniture filled the gilded space from end to end, and paintings by famous artists, primarily European, covered every wall. Heavy blue drapes framed massive windows that overlooked the interior courtyard, allowing the afternoon sun to glint off the polished parquet floor. Adding to these trappings of power, Dave wore the red, white, and blue sash over his right shoulder reserved for Chile's president.

The military officers and ministers stood in a rough semi-circle around the desk, wondering why their president chose to call a meeting that included military and civilian authority. While not entirely unprecedented, such gatherings were usually reserved for crisis situations – most recently, an earthquake that devastated several towns in the northern districts. They all suspected this meeting would address the missile launch in the Andes Mountains. Indeed, the president's formal attire and solemn demeanor hinted at an important announcement of some kind.

Dave allowed his somewhat grim expression to soften. Throughout his life, he had honed his skill at manipulating people to get whatever he wanted. And he was about to need every bit of that experience.

"My friends," Dave began, using the usual opening greeting of the real, and now late, President Cayo. "I appreciate your prompt response to my call for this important gathering. And I further thank you for your discretion in arriving at the palace this afternoon so as not to cause the media any concern or draw its attention.

As you may suspect, I have exciting news to pass along to my trusted generals, admirals, and ministers. Please consider everything I am about to tell you today to be top secret as it affects the national security of our great nation."

Dave already knew that almost everyone in the room owed their position to Cayo, either because Cayo had appointed them to their current ministerial offices or promoted them to high-ranking military assignments.

Dave paused for effect, allowing the gravity of the meeting to settle on the gathering.

"You have all heard by now about the space launch that took place within our borders several days ago. To date, I have deflected questions about that event, choosing to deny that the government of Chile had anything to do with it. In fact, I have outright denied that Chile had any hand in the launch. I can tell you now that this is both true and untrue."

A sea of scowls and quizzical looks appeared before him.

Dave held up a hand, a quiet request for patience.

"I know that statement is confusing. So, allow me to explain. Approximately one year ago, a consortium of wealthy investors approached me with a proposition I could not turn down. These are all immensely powerful people from several different countries around the world. Their identities are not important for our discussion today. Still, I can assure you the resources they bring will help Chile become not only relevant on the world stage but a nation of the first order, on the same economic and military level as any European country and the leading power on the continent of South America."

As Dave let this sink in, the men and women in the room grew restless, each obviously holding their tongues with increasing difficulty. Dave held up his hand once again.

"Please bear with me a few more moments. This group of investors offered to finance my campaign to become president of Chile. In exchange, they asked only for an open-ended lease of land I have owned for many years in the 7th District. Many of you have visited my ranch. It encompasses a broad swath of grassland outside Talca and runs into the foothills of the Andes. After a short negotiation, I agreed. As you know, our party's campaign budget became all but unlimited, sweeping me, and consequently, all of you, into office."

The Minister of the Interior, Sergio Aybar, could no longer remain silent. "Mr. President, I have heard nothing of a major industrial or agricultural undertaking in the 7th District. This is unusual at best and could border on illegal interference in Chile's internal affairs."

Dave took Aybar's comment in stride.

"Sergio," Dave said, using the minister's first name. "You are correct. In fact, should this come to the attention of the Judicial Branch, I'm sure they would find the deal I made quite illegal. No doubt I would be indicted on many counts of election finance violations, accepting bribes, and probably a host of other charges from fraud to crimes against the environment – perhaps even treason. But that is not all."

Dave ignored the many gasps of surprise and quickly moved toward the climax of his presentation. "Shortly after acquiring the lease, this group began constructing an underground complex and tunnel system stretching from the countryside twenty kilometers outside Talca into the Andes. Inside that complex, they assembled the launch vehicle, transported it high into the mountains, and, as you already know, sent it into space."

Stunned silence turned quickly into shouted questions. Dave's cavalier admission of multiple crimes couldn't have been more jarring. Nobody in the room expected the president to boldly reveal he had colluded with some unnamed cabal of foreigners with a completely unknown agenda to use their country as a launch site for flying missiles into space.

"This is unacceptable!" the Attorney General, the country's top law enforcement officer, shouted, pointing at Dave. "I will begin an investigation of this immediately!"

"You have poisoned this entire government. You should resign!" an Army general bellowed. "You may have forced the military into taking control of the government and imposing martial law."

Almost everyone in the room threw some accusation or threat at Dave at once. The Foreign Minister challenged Dave to explain how he could ever repair diplomatic relationships with the countries he had lied to by assuring them Chile had nothing to do with the launch. Argentina had made particularly boisterous objections to the surprise overflight of their territory, and the United States expressed concerns about Chile developing a ballistic missile that could carry military warheads, potentially shifting the balance of power in the entire Western Hemisphere.

Dave let the explosive response burn itself out. For the next few minutes, he didn't try to argue or explain anything. Instead, he stood confidently, absorbing the shots fired at him from all directions. When the pandemonium subsided, Dave remained standing with his feet slightly parted and his hands on his hips.

"That's enough. Everyone calm down and take a seat. You will now listen to me."

The assembled government officials, still grumbling and whispering among themselves, reluctantly moved to a large seating area, obeying their president's order. But the mood in the room remained poisonous.

Though still seething, Sergio Aybar managed to ask a question in a practiced diplomatic tone.

"Mr. President, what is your plan for when this news breaks in the press?"

"That will not happen," Dave said confidently.

"And how, may I ask, can you be certain of that, sir?"

Dave nodded, indicating he had an answer at hand.

"First, nobody except the people in this room knows the truth. And I am certain none of you will divulge what I have told you."

A sea of doubtful faces looked back at him, but everyone held their tongues – at least for the moment.

"Please allow me to show you why I am so confident. Everyone, please take out your cell phones and check the balance of your personal bank accounts."

One by one, cell phones appeared in everyone's hands, and passwords were quickly entered. Just ten seconds later, an admiral gasped. As each person looked at their balance, exclamations of surprise flew around the gathering like a whirlwind.

The Attorney General was the first to speak the obvious question out loud.

"What is this?"

Dave gave the group a wide smile.

"As you can now see, the equivalent of twenty million U.S. dollars has been deposited into your accounts."

"More bribery, Mr. President?" the Attorney General asked.

"No, Mr. Attorney General. Those deposits have been freely given and faithfully recorded by each of your banks. They cannot be erased. That is now your money to keep, invest, or spend at your discretion. The only caveat is that you cooperate with a plan that is already in motion and cannot be stopped."

"And if we choose not to cooperate?" the Attorney General asked.

"Then you will be implicated by those deposits and will be imprisoned. And to further ensure your cooperation, the money can be easily traced, if necessary, to Columbian drug cartels."

# CHAPTER SEVEN

FBI Laboratories
Quantico, Virginia
The next morning

Bubba stood alone in Agent Deal's office with his hands buried deep in the pockets of his white lab coat. The light from the massive monitor on the wall illuminated a rare scowl on the genius physicist's face as he tried to make sense of ten yellow dots that traced a line across a map of Europe from the coast of Portugal across Spain, France, and over the English Channel, ending at a point over the Scandinavian Peninsula.

Without taking his eyes off the screen, Bubba pulled one hand out of its pocket and scratched at his chestnut hair.

"Well?" Deal asked from behind his desk. "Any idea what those could be?"

Bubba didn't respond to Deal's question and ignored the rhythmic tapping of the FBI agent's foot against the side of his desk. Instead, he grabbed a now wrinkled computer printout off the conference table behind him and studied the lines of numbers arranged in ten neat columns. After another minute of allowing his brain to run through myriad possibilities, Bubba slowly turned to Deal and shrugged.

"I have no idea."

Deal rose to his feet. "That's not what I wanted to hear."

"Don't know what to tell you, boss. NORAD confirmed what the British and French radars detected after the spacecraft, or whatever it is, spit those things out a few hours ago. The only thing we know for sure is there are ten microsatellites in geosynchronous orbit over Europe. They are emitting no signals whatsoever. And as far as we can tell, they aren't receiving any signals from Earth. Until they either turn themselves on or someone goes up there and snags one, we don't have any data to analyze."

"That's it?" Deal growled. "And what the hell is a mini satellite?"

"A *micro*satellite falls into a range of 10 to 100 kilograms. They might have been missed as just space junk if they were still orbiting the Earth and not just sitting over a fixed point. Other than that, I can make a few educated guesses. I expect they are probably cubesats. Square boxes," Bubba said, using hands to approximate their shape. "We don't have the technology to determine their exact size. Cubesats can be efficiently loaded onto one vehicle and ejected one at a time. Mostly, they are used as a platform for scientific investigations and testing new technology. Lately, several companies have used them for advanced missions to prove various communications concepts in constellations, swarms, and disaggregated systems. Some idiots even want to use them for massive advertisements covering the night sky. Instead of stars, all you will see is massive glowing billboards hawking beer or boner pills."

Deal had never heard of cubesats or micro satellites and could only accept Bubba's theory at face value. The surprise launch out of Chile caught everyone off guard. And the ten unidentified satellites hanging directly over Western Europe set off alarm bells in his head. They looked like a threat that nobody could touch.

"So, we don't know shit," Deal spat, using a rare expletive. "That has to change. Are you guys all set up on flights to Santiago?"

"Yep," Bubba responded. "D.C. to Atlanta and then overnight down to Santiago. We'll register with the company that supplies English teachers in Santiago and then take a bus to Talca a day later."

Deal stood looking at the display for another few seconds. His mind raced, trying to work out the implications of the mysterious satellites. They could be nothing more than communications platforms. But he didn't think so. Nothing about the launch or the dispersal of the constellation of cubesats, or whatever, made sense. He needed answers and realized the best candidate for figuring out this enigma was standing right next to him.

"Change of plans," Deal announced suddenly. "You're not going."

Bubba spun around to face his boss. "What?"

"I need you here. Michael, Sarah, and Zach can handle things on the ground in Chile."

"But..."

"No buts. You're more valuable right here using that giant brain of yours to figure out what those things are and what might happen next."

Bubba wanted to challenge Deal's decision. He and his three friends were a dynamic and effective team. But once Deal made a decision, Bubba knew nothing he said would change the steely FBI agent's mind. And if he was honest with himself, he knew Deal was right. But that didn't relieve his deep disappointment.

"I can't say I like it," Bubba responded, obviously still wanting to join his three best friends on what could be a dangerous mission. "But, okay."

"Where will they stay once they're on the ground in Talca?" Deal asked.

"Good news on that front. All four of us, well now three, will be living with a retired couple that own a bed-and-breakfast near the center of town. They'll get their specific teaching assignments and have to be in class several hours every day. But it looks like they'll have plenty of free time to poke around," Bubba explained.

"They'll have to do more than poke around. They need to get into the mountains and surrounding countryside to figure out if there's actually a tunnel. I want to know where it starts, where it goes, who dug it, and why," Deal said. "I'm still working on how to get Agent Sims and me into the country. This operation is too big for two junior agents and a budding diplomat."

"They can handle it, boss," Bubba said confidently.

"I don't want them screwing around down there. They need to get as much information as possible without blowing their cover. I bet those microsatellites or whatever aren't the last."

"Agreed. And the government in Chile seems pretty touchy about the whole thing. Sketchy as hell," Bubba commented.

"That's what the State Department said, but they said 'evasive' instead of 'sketchy,'" Deal agreed. "But their president is taking a hard line. State believes he's scared outside interference will make him look weak. But that's diplomatic baloney. I think he's hiding something. Either way, you don't want to wind up on the wrong side of a guy who wants to be the next Augusto Pinochet."

"Isn't he the general who overthrew the democratically elected government back in the 70's?" Bubba asked.

"Yeah. He grabbed power with the help of the United States in a military coup after the people elected a new president Pinochet considered too "socialist." After he took over the government, he spent the next 16 or 17 years staying in power the way dictators always do – threats, violence, persecution, torture, and murder. Not to mention one of the favorite tools of autocrats – concentration camps. This new guy, Cayo, is headed down that same path."

Deal wasn't making Bubba feel any better about talking Michael, Sarah, and Zach into volunteering for this mission.

Deal added, "The Chileans have hardened their position in the last few days. They have not only refused outside help investigating what happened but threatened to arrest anyone getting too curious and prosecute them as spies."

# CHAPTER EIGHT

The Andes Mountains
Near the suspected launch site
The same day


Lieutenant Violette Ruiz couldn't remember ever being so cold. Even dressed in gear worn by professional mountaineers, she had to concentrate on holding the high-powered binoculars steady as she scanned the desolate mountains that seemed to stretch out in all directions as far as the eye could see. Her elbows ached from digging into the hard rocky ridge where she had laid in a prone position for the last two hours.

*This must be the loneliest place on Earth.*

Another twenty minutes passed before she heard footsteps climbing the steep slope toward her observation post. The Argentinian Air Force officer chose the high ridgeline earlier that morning as the best bet to get a look at the suspected launch site and because it offered concealment behind a line of huge rocks perched precariously over the valley below.

The footsteps got closer until her partner, Bruno Miranda, flopped down on the ground at her side, resting his back against one of the cold, hard granite stones. Panting heavily in the thin mountain air,

Miranda remained motionless, his forehead resting in the crook of his right arm.

"Tough climb?" Ruiz asked, not hiding the sarcasm in her voice.

Miranda slid onto his back and sucked in several deep breaths before responding.

"Funny. Very funny, Ruiz," Miranda managed to gasp.

Ruiz didn't pull her eyes away from the binoculars as she chuckled at Miranda's discomfort.

"I climbed the same slope two hours ago and didn't look like I was going to die when I got up here," Ruiz chided.

"Yeah, well, while you've been up here sitting on your butt having a look around, I've been marching up and down these mountains looking for outposts, observation emplacements, or anything built by man. Just as you ordered, ma'am," Miranda said, throwing a mock salute while still lying on his back.

"See anything?" Ruiz asked.

"Rocks, boulders, cliffs, snow, and one big bird of some kind. No buildings. No soldiers. No people. Not even a tree."

"You're certain?" Ruiz responded. "The Chileans would be a little displeased if they found an Argentine Air Force officer and an out-of-shape aerospace engineer snooping around on their side of the border."

Miranda rolled onto his side and supported his head with one arm. Even dressed in heavy cold weather gear, he had a hard time taking his eyes off Ruiz's silky black hair that escaped from her knit cap and blew back across her shoulders. The Air Force officer's eyes seemed to glint in the late afternoon sun, even though partially hidden between the massive binoculars that seemed permanently attached to her face.

"As sure as I can be, Lieutenant," Miranda responded. "But I'm not trained for this sort of thing."

Ruiz could feel Miranda studying her. But she didn't mind. At least not anymore. When she and Miranda were thrown together as a team, the engineering professor had struck her as stiff and more than a little inept. But after a helicopter dropped them at the border, Miranda had proven himself more than capable of keeping up with her on the long, grueling hike across the mountains. She even found him attractive in a geeky, Clark Kent sort of way.

"Keep your eyes and mind on the mission, professor," Ruiz scolded. "This isn't a picnic. We're here to determine what the Chileans are doing. Argentina can't have its next-door neighbor firing missiles over its territory. You and I have been charged with figuring out how they managed to get a rocket into space from this god-forsaken place."

"You never said why they chose you to lead our little expedition. Do you want to fill me in on that?" Miranda asked.

"No."

"That can only mean I've been deceived into going on a secret mission with a spy," Miranda concluded.

"*If* I am a spy, then so are you. Congratulations. I can assure you of one thing, though, if we get caught, that's exactly how we'll be treated. So, stay alert and quit asking useless questions. With any luck, we'll be out of here before anyone even knows we stuck our noses over the border."

Another half-hour passed in relative silence as the pair continued to scan the landscape in all directions for any clue that could help them pinpoint the launch site. But they might as well have been searching a desolate alien planet.

As night approached, throwing their observation post into deep shadows, Ruiz ordered them back to the tiny base camp they set up a half mile down the ridge next to a freezing, narrow river. Miranda was packing away their cameras when the faint but unmistakable sound of helicopter blades chopping through the cold air began bouncing ominously off the mountainsides.

Ruiz pulled Miranda down onto his knees and tried to determine where the sound was coming from. But the mountains tossed the sound back and forth across the valleys, making it impossible to locate. One thing was certain, the sound was getting louder.

"Get down," Ruiz ordered. "Stay absolutely still. We're exposed up here. Don't worry. The shadows will provide cover."

Ruiz's reassurance rang hollow to Miranda. Her words sounded confident, but he could sense the tension in her voice. He tried to relax, forcing himself to take shallow breaths as he curled into a ball next to the freezing cold boulder.

Suddenly, a strong wind from above assaulted them with bits of dirt and small rocks flung into the air by the helicopter's rotors. Miranda envisioned a squad of angry Chilean Special Forces repelling out of the aircraft and taking them to prison.

But that didn't happen.

The helicopter moved over the valley and began descending, apparently unaware he and Ruiz existed.

"Quick, give me the video camera," Ruiz demanded.

With his hands shaking almost uncontrollably, Miranda unzipped his pack and handed the high-definition camera to Ruiz.

As they watched, the helicopter moved slowly over the valley floor. In the next instant, the Argentinians had to shield their eyes as several powerful floodlights suddenly bathed the entire valley in brilliant light. Despite their intense inspection during the day, Ruiz and Miranda had failed to pick out any artificial light sources. Then something even more startling happened.

On the side of a low ridgeline directly across the shallow valley and below their position, the Earth seemed to crack open. The two Argentinians could feel as well as hear a low rumble as two perfectly camouflaged doors separated, revealing a wide entrance into a darkened tunnel.

The aircraft almost delicately touched down on the valley floor. Then, as soon as it settled onto its landing gear, it began to move, as if on an invisible conveyor belt, into the opening.

The helicopter's blades were still slowly turning when it disappeared inside, and the doors closed. In the next instant, the entire valley returned to utter darkness and silence.

Miranda's eyes could barely accept what he just witnessed.

"I'll be damned," he said, astonished.

"If we don't find out what's going on in there, we all just might be. Let's get back to camp," Ruiz said, handing the video camera back to Miranda. Miranda packed the camera away, his mind still trying to come to terms with the sheer magnitude of the technology and engineering prowess it took to construct and hide an underground launch facility in the middle of the Andes.

"Go ahead," Miranda replied. "I want to get a few quick measurements of the area."

"Five minutes," Ruiz said, pulling on a set of night vision goggles with infrared capability. "No more. We have what we came for. I don't think we were spotted, but let's not press our luck. I'll start breaking down camp."

"Agreed. See you shortly," Miranda responded, rolling back onto his stomach and raising a range-finding sight to his eye. "I'll be right behind you."

Ruiz slung her pack over her shoulders and moved off down the steep, rock-covered slope. The loose, crumbly surface forced her to move downhill in a sort of controlled slide. It didn't take long for her to reach the campsite where they left their two-man tent and supplies just the night before.

As she strode up toward their tent and pulled off her pack, she felt more than heard someone step out from the darkness behind her.

Ruiz spun around, suddenly facing the barrel of a nasty-looking assault rifle pointed at her face.

"Don't move," the man dressed in combat fatigues ordered from behind a black ski mask.

Ruiz dropped the pack and slowly raised her hands. She had only seconds to act while the hulking soldier still believed he had the upper hand.

"Please don't hurt me," Ruiz pleaded pitifully just before glancing to her right and inhaling sharply.

The man behind the gun made the mistake of following Ruiz's eyes in the same direction.

In an instant, Ruiz's right hand shot out, knocking the barrel of the rifle away. At the same time, she spun to her left and landed a vicious blow to the gunman's face from her left elbow. As the stunned attacker sank to his knees, Ruiz yanked the assault rifle from his hand and smashed the butt of the weapon into the side of his head. With a quiet grunt, the much larger man fell face-first onto the hard rocky ground.

Ruiz wasted no time. She snatched three extra ammunition cartridges from the unconscious man's belt and sprinted off into the darkness.

Unaware of the attack on Ruiz, Miranda focused on trying to record every detail of the hidden launch facility. Now knowing exactly where to look, he could just make out what he believed to be a set of tracks running from the rock wall that had opened in the hillside to the center of the flattened valley floor.

"Get up," a voice said from the darkness.

Miranda froze in place. Two figures stood several yards away, their guns leveled at his head.

"I said, stand up," one of the figures repeated.

The college professor slowly got to his feet and raised both hands. "Who are..."

A single shot rang out, the loud report echoing through the mountains before slowly disappearing into the night.

From a hiding spot behind a low rock outcropping, Ruiz flinched when she saw the muzzle flash and heard the shot. She couldn't do anything for the rather naïve professor her superiors had sent with her into the Andes. And she knew it would take all of her extensive training and experience with the Argentinian Air Force Special Operations Command to survive the next few minutes – a fact driven home by a single shot ricocheting past her head.

Ruiz spun on her heels and sprinted away from where the shots came from, her boots barely touching the hardscrabble surface. Several more shots came from below and behind, but even if her attackers had night vision, she knew that she made a difficult target. She moved like a mountain antelope, fast, slim, and carrying nothing but the rifle she had just inherited.

After moving uphill a hundred yards, she paused and, using her night vision, looked behind her. She could see two soldiers, dressed identically to the gunman she had taken out, moving cautiously but steadily, confident that their target would have no place to go other than deeper and higher into the mountains.

She watched for another fifteen seconds, ensuring they were not losing her trail. To make things a bit easier for her pursuers, she kicked several good-sized stones down the hill. The two men pointed and continued their climb toward where she had concealed herself behind several boulders.

Now confident of the path the Chileans would take, Ruiz carefully skirted around the boulders and found a spot where she could remain undetected while she watched the soldiers hunting her approach. She didn't have long to wait. The sound of boots crunching over gravel and stones grew louder. When the two men passed within ten feet of where she knelt, Ruiz aimed at the closest soldier's back and pulled the trigger.

The gunshot sounded like a cannon in the frozen wasteland.

The man Ruiz shot landed hard on his face while his partner swung his rifle around in a wide arc, looking for a target.

"Drop it," Ruiz ordered, revealing herself.

Seeing Ruiz aiming an assault rifle, the soldier slowly lowered his weapon to the ground and raised his hands.

"Use your thumb and index finger to remove your sidearm and drop it on the ground. Do the same with the backup in your boot."

After doing what he was told, Ruiz's prisoner asked, "What do you want?"

"You're a lucky boy. You are going to show me the way into those tunnels," Ruiz explained.

"Are you crazy?"

"In a way. But here's the best part. After we get inside, you get to be a hero and take me prisoner."

# CHAPTER NINE

The Cause's Underground Complex

As soon as the remotely operated platform transporting the glossy black helicopter came to a smooth stop inside the tunnel, a set of stairs unfolded from the fuselage. A moment later, Dr. Dave Knox and Alexander Monroe, both wearing custom-tailored Saville Row suits and shoes of the finest Italian leather, stepped onto the polished concrete floor.

"Well, Knox, you outdid yourself this time," Monroe commented, looking up at the smooth ceiling of the tunnel, sixty feet above their heads.

"Thank you for saying so, Alexander. I hope the other Directors found it as impressive," Dave responded.

"Oh, they were impressed, all right. But as you suggested, our visit was limited to this entrance and the main conference room where we watched the sphere demonstration. They didn't seem to care about getting a grand tour. As expected, they were completely focused on the promised return on their investment."

Dave looked around, taking a moment to appreciate his handiwork.

"Don't worry so much, Alexander. They are always skittish. That's their job. Mine is to be bold," Dave responded dismissively before continuing his impromptu tour. "Allow me to show you the highlights. The scope of this project reaches far beyond what you can see here. We are standing at the entrance to the launch site. The entire tunnel runs over fifty miles to the west. In between, side tunnels branch off to either side, housing supply depots, living quarters, laboratory facilities, and testing stations. We can visit all of these using the tram system."

"Then lead on," Monroe responded, dropping the other Directors' concerns for the moment.

"This way," Dave said, stepping toward a wall of opaque glass.

A second later, one of the panels in the wall slid open, revealing a white, lozenge-shaped tram car. A gullwing-style door unfolded and rose, revealing a plush interior outfitted with four light gray leather seats.

"Nice," Monroe commented. "Maglev?"

"Of course," Dave answered. "Like the bullet trains in Japan, magnetic force lifts the car off the track and propels it forward. We limited the speed of this executive car to 200 mph. Supplies, parts, and personnel move through the tunnels at a crawl – only 130. We can be at the western entrance to the facility in central Chile, over 50 miles away, in less than 15 minutes. Our first stop today will be the final assembly station where our second launch vehicle is being fitted with the payload pod and the mother satellite that will deposit the next ten cubesats into orbit."

Monroe barely had time to perceive the tram's silky acceleration before the car came to a stop and the door opened. Following Knox, he stepped into another section of the tunnel, but this time, a massive missile lying on its side filled most of the space.

Dave reached up, placing one hand proudly on the launch vehicle's stainless-steel skin. With a smug grin, he lowered his voice and donned the full persona of President Cayo.

"Are you surprised to find that a humble country such as our beautiful Chile could produce a space program that can compete with NASA or Russia's RSA?"

Dave's uncanny ability to instantaneously switch personalities caught Monroe off guard, and he had to remind himself that he was still talking to the genius who conceptualized The Cause's space operation.

Monroe decided to play along. "Very impressive, Mr. President. May I be the first to ..."

An urgent ring on Dave's cell phone cut off Monroe's response.

Dave held up one finger as he swiped open his cell phone with his thumb and held the device to his ear. As Monroe watched, Dave listened for a moment, his brows knitting closer and closer together.

"How did they get through the security perimeter?" Dave barked into the phone.

Monroe stayed silent while Dave asked several more questions about what was clearly a report concerning a breach of the launch site's security.

"Keep the prisoner isolated in the detention cell. No one is to speak with her until I get there. And I want the entire sector scoured for any accomplices. Patrols are to be doubled from this moment forward."

Dave closed his phone and turned to Monroe.

"We had a visitor," he said casually.

"So, I gathered," Monroe responded. "Do you anticipate this interfering with our launch schedule?"

Dave laughed. "Not at all. We could not keep the location of our facility a secret from American satellites. I have our best teams canvassing the mountains for any more infiltrators. If there are, we'll have them shortly. Additionally, we are monitoring and vetting all foreigners entering the country. President Cayo will deal with anyone getting too close to our operation. Harshly."

The tour over for the moment, Monroe followed Dave deep into the bowels of the tunnel complex. A short elevator ride to the lowest level and a long walk down several corridors brought the men to a thick metal door.

"Wait here," Dave advised. "You can listen in through the intercom."

Dave stepped through the door and pulled up a chair to the table across from where Violette Ruiz sat with her wrists and ankles chained to eyebolts sunk deep in the concrete floor.

Monroe couldn't care less what happened to the Argentinian spy they plucked out of the mountains but could fully appreciate the Air Force officer's fit young physic and relaxed, almost disdainful, body language.

*She obviously doesn't fully appreciate the precarious situation she faces.*

Turning to the wall, Monroe flipped a switch on an intercom panel so he could hear the conversation that promised to be profoundly unpleasant for the Argentinian officer.

Dave said nothing as he sat down, lit a thick cigar, and exhaled a cloud of pungent gray smoke across the table, goading his prisoner into making the first move.

But it didn't work.

Ruiz sat quietly, looking steadily at Dave through the smoke cloud with impassive eyes.

Monroe found himself glad he had accompanied the leader of The Cause to interrogate an unexpectedly formidable prisoner. This promised to be a show he didn't want to miss.

For the next full minute, Dave stared at Ruiz, studying her expression and body language while patiently waiting for her to display frustration, anxiety, or any emotion whatsoever he could exploit. But he waited in vain. Ruiz didn't even wrinkle her nose when Dave intentionally blew the acrid smoke directly into her face.

Outside the room, Monroe began to wonder how long the stand-off would last. Dave possessed an IQ so high it could barely be measured. Yet, he had seen him lose his temper on several occasions – usually resulting in somebody getting killed. He hoped that wouldn't happen, at least not before they found out what this woman had been doing in the mountains.

The tension inside the room built until Monroe could feel it through the impenetrable steel door. A few seconds later, Dave stamped out his cigar under his shiny leather brogues. Monroe had to admire the young female officer's nerve in facing down the person she must have identified as the president of Chile.

"Identify yourself," Dave demanded.

Ruiz sat up just a bit straighter in the chair, leaned forward, and looked Dave directly in the eye.

"You first."

"You know who I am. I am Juan Mateo Cayo, president of Chile. And I don't think you understand..."

"No. You are not," Ruiz said coldly, cutting Dave off.

Monroe's eyes grew wide. Dave had convinced Cayo's closest advisors, the media, and the entire country he was, indeed, the president of Chile. *Did this woman somehow know the truth?*

To his credit, Dave didn't react to Ruiz's unexpected revelation. "Well, then, who am I?" he asked with a disdainful chuckle.

Monroe was glued to the window, fully enjoying the dramatic confrontation playing out on the other side of the door.

Then, with the revelation about Dave's identity still hanging in the air, Ruiz stood, the chains that should have kept her planted firmly in the metal chair falling to the floor with a long, sustained rattle against the concrete.

Dave jumped to his feet and staggered backward into the far wall. "Guards!"

Ruiz didn't advance toward Dave. Instead, she grabbed his chair and shoved it under the doorknob, effectively locking the door from the inside. When she noticed Monroe staring at her, she smiled broadly and waved.

Recovering quickly, Dave stepped forward. "Who are you?"

"You keep asking the same question, Dr. Knox," Ruiz responded, the shock of revealing she knew Dave's actual identity rocking him back on his heels. "Even an eggheaded prick like you really should be able to figure that out."

"I'm afraid you have me at a disadvantage," Dave managed. "But in less than ten seconds, my people will remedy that situation."

Ruiz snorted derisively and sat back down, this time leaning back in her chair and resting her boots on the tabletop. As if by magic, a thin knife popped out of the heel of one boot.

The woman's blatant contempt, lack of respect, and profanity suddenly reminded him of someone he used to know. *But who?*

Outside the room, three massive guards dressed in black combat fatigues and holding assault rifles ushered Monroe away. Two of the men tried to force the door open, but the heavy metal chair inside held fast.

Ruiz jumped to her feet and grasped Dave's neck with her left hand.

"If you want to go through the rest of your life with your balls still banging around between your legs, tell them to stand down," Ruiz demanded, raising the knife to Dave's crotch.

Dave's eyes grew wide.

"Back off! Now!" he shouted at the guards. "Damn you. Who are you? What do you want?"

Ruiz flashed a smile.

"You don't know me, but you knew my mother quite well. Without her, you would still be locked in some dark laboratory, toiling away in complete anonymity for the American government. And if that doesn't give away her identity, you must remember *murdering* her in cold blood."

# CHAPTER TEN

Santiago, Chile
The next day

Michael yawned loudly and shivered in the cold breeze that blew down the crowded streets of Chile's capital city. Sarah walked close to her tall boyfriend, using his body to block some of the wind that chilled her to the bone.

"Tell me again why we are out here trudging around and not snuggled up in our warm hotel room?" Michael asked. "I have a bad case of jet lag."

"You slept on the plane, you big oaf," Sarah said, playfully slapping Michael's arm. "Santiago is only an hour behind Washington time. You can't have jet lag."

"*You* slept on the plane leaning on my shoulder the whole time. I sat up, crammed into the cheap seats like a sardine."

"Yeah, I did," Sarah said, snaking one arm under Michael's. "Walking around will help get your blood moving."

"Where are we anyway? I thought you wanted to see the Presidential Palace and some park or another."

Sarah pulled out her cell phone and looked at the map.

"A few more blocks, and then we turn right," Sarah said.

The pair strode down the sidewalks, taking in the sights, sounds, and smells. Like many major cities around the world, the streets were clogged with cars, buses, and taxis while motorcycles, scooters, and bicycles weaved in and out between the larger vehicles with reckless abandon. Stores offering cheap electronics and cheaper clothes lined the sidewalks, and Michael noticed that every block seemed to have its own little shop offering pastries stuffed with pork, beef, or vegetables.

"This reminds me of parts of New York," Sarah observed.

"Yeah, if New York had been the battleground for riots, revolutions, and violence for the past fifty years," Michael griped. "You can tell this could be a cool city. Even beautiful. But it just looks beat up and tired. It's kind of a shame, really. Graffiti on everything, trash blowing around, and pollution so thick I can feel it in my throat. And did you see those big busted-up concrete barriers with barbed wire on top we passed a minute ago?"

Sarah smacked Michael's arm again. "Don't be so negative."

After another block, Sarah pulled her cell phone out of her pocket again.

"We turn here," she said, pointing down a cross street that looked considerably less congested than the major avenue they had been following for the last twenty minutes.

Sarah was still holding the phone when a red motorcycle jumped onto the sidewalk behind the couple. Without slowing down, the rider, wearing a dark blue helmet and brown leather jacket, expertly plucked Sarah's cell phone from her hand before speeding away.

"Hey! What the hell!" Michael exclaimed, picking up a beer bottle out of the gutter and launching it in a high arc down the street.

As the bottle landed harmlessly on the road, the thief made a sharp right turn while holding Sarah's phone triumphantly over his head. In seconds, he disappeared into the downtown congestion.

Sarah was still looking at her empty hand in utter disbelief when Michael turned to check on her.

"Are you okay?" he asked.

"He just.... how?"

"I don't know. That guy must have had a lot of practice," Michael responded. "Let's sit down a second."

"Goddammit!"

Michael led Sarah to a crusty green bench under a graffiti-covered bus stop shelter. Putting an arm around her shoulder, he noticed a tear run down one cheek. He said nothing, letting Sarah process what just happened.

"I'm okay," she said.

"You sure? That was weird."

Sarah stood and paced up and down the sidewalk. "Yeah. It was. And fast. My god, he just came from nowhere. I feel so stupid. After all we have been through with Deal and nearly finishing our FBI training, I let some stupid punk snatch my phone right out of my hand! Stupid."

Michael let Sarah vent a moment more.

"That was your personal phone, right?" Michael asked, already knowing the answer.

"Yeah, nothing important on it, I guess," Sarah answered, already thinking more clearly. "Let's call Bubba and get him to lock it down."

They used Michael's phone and called Bubba, who remotely disabled Sarah's phone, making it useless as anything but a paperweight.

A mile away, the motorcycle rider left his bike leaning against the wall of an alley filled with rotting garbage and strode into a police substation. The front desk clerk didn't even look up as the thief waved at a security camera. A moment later, a magnetic lock clicked loudly, and a solid metal door behind the front desk opened. After striding down a hall lit by ancient fluorescent lights, he knocked lightly on an office door.

"Come in," a man dressed in a suit and tie said from behind a well-organized but worn-out metal desk.

The motorcyclist reached into his pocket as he entered the office and tossed four cell phones on the desktop.

"This is it?" the man behind the desk asked as he pulled on a set of glasses and gathered the phones.

"Not many tourists strolling around town today," the thief explained, shrugging.

"All foreigners?"

"Of course."

The man at the desk pulled a wad of notes out of a drawer and handed them to the thief.

"My usual buyer wouldn't pay half this. Why are you so interested in buying used phones we, uh, borrow from gringos, anyway?"

"Don't get too curious, my friend," the man in the suit replied, without looking up from his desk. "Why the government does what it does is none of your business. Now leave."

The look on the other man's face made the thief raise his hands in mock surrender and take a step backward.

"No problem."

After the thief left, the man in the office picked up his desk phone.

"I'm sending four more to your laboratory. See what you can pull from them. Check them against arriving passports as usual. Let me know what you find. And I want this today."

Two hours later, the laboratory called back.

"Two of the phones belonged to European tourists and another to a Canadian mineral exporter. I was able to unlock each and confirm identities. But there's something strange with the fourth. I can't pull anything from it. I can only conclude it has been locked by a true computer expert."

"Nothing?" the man wearing the suit asked.

"Nothing at all. This has never happened before. If I cannot pry out its secrets, nobody can."

The man in the office hung up and pressed the intercom button.

"Get me Major Garcia. Immediately."

# CHAPTER ELEVEN

<br>

Highway 5
25 miles south of Santiago
The next morning

"How long will it take to get to ... what's the place called?" Michael asked.

"Talca, dumbass," Zach said from the bus seat across the aisle from where Michael and Sarah sat together.

"That's a weird name," Michael commented, pulling a tattered baseball cap bearing the faded logo of Southern University down over his eyes and stretching out his long legs. "Sounds like where they make talcum powder."

"Shush," Sarah scolded. "Be nice."

"Yes, dear. Wake me up when we get there, dear," Michael responded, his sarcasm drawing a sharp punch on his upper arm from his girlfriend.

"Sit up, you big ape," Sarah ordered. "Let's make sure we have our thoughts together before we meet the family we will be staying with."

Michael grunted but hauled himself upright in the surprisingly comfortable leather seat. The trio paid a little extra for first-class tickets on the bus's second level, giving them a panoramic view of the Andes Mountain range rolling past the wide front windows.

"Yeah, come on, buddy," Zach agreed. "Sarah, what do we know about these people?"

Sarah pulled out her laptop and opened the email from the organization that hired them as English teachers.

"Fernando and Rosa Valdez. A retired couple that now run a bed and breakfast out of their home," Sarah said, holding up her laptop so Michael and Zach could see the picture of a smiling couple in their late 60s or early 70s standing in front of their two-story yellow stucco house. A handmade sign on one wall advertised Hostal Casa Anita.

"And we're all staying with them? Two bedrooms?" Michael asked, hopefully.

"Yes. But you are bunking with Zach. Sorry, stud," Sarah teased. "You can still be my boyfriend, or novio, in Spanish, but we have to behave ourselves. These are traditional people, and we can get fired immediately if we mess up."

"Jeeeez," Michael complained. "Okay."

Sarah ignored him.

"Let's see," Sarah continued, scanning the Chilean couple's biographical information from the website. "Fernando and Rosa have one son, Fernando, Jr., and one granddaughter. No pictures of the rest of the family. They lost a second son not too long ago. No details there. They have run the bed and breakfast since Fernando retired from the Chilean government about ten years ago. No details there either."

"They look nice," Michael commented. "What do we know about our teaching jobs?"

Zach picked up the question. "We will all be teaching at different schools, and we should have plenty of time to look around. But I'd like to get some hiking in as quickly as possible."

Zach pulled his tablet computer out of his backpack and opened a detailed map of the Maule region. The entire country of Chile was only about a hundred miles wide, with the Pacific Ocean to the west and the border of Argentina high in the Andes Mountains to the east. Talca sat in a vast plain roughly halfway between the two.

"Looks like we're not far from the mountains. Maybe 20 or 30 miles. The trick will be getting up there without anyone getting suspicious," Michael commented, leaning over Sarah to take a closer look at the map.

Sarah pursed her lips and gave Michael a withering look.

Her boyfriend didn't understand Sarah's reaction at first, but then it hit him. The bus was full of people and surveillance cameras.

"You know, in case we can sneak away for a little one-on-one camping," he said quickly, snuggling up closer to Sarah.

Sarah rolled her eyes.

"Maybe. But don't get your hopes up," she said, pushing Michael playfully away.

Deal had been adamant about maintaining their cover. Ever since the unexpected rocket launch, the Chileans had been stepping up their surveillance of foreigners. Michael, Sarah, and Zach had to be careful despite appearing to be nothing more than college students looking for an adventure before confronting 'real life.'

"If that's all settled, can I get a nap now?" Michael asked, pulling his ball cap down over his eyes again and crossing his arms across his chest.

As Michael drifted off, Zach patted the empty seat next to him and motioned for Sarah to cross the narrow aisle.

Michael opened one eye and said, "I saw that."

Sarah pulled the brim of Michael's hat down over his face as she climbed over him.

"Maybe I like Zach better," she teased.

"Uh-huh," Michael grunted, pushing his hat up a bit with one finger.

Sarah chuckled and slid into the seat next to Zach.

"What's up?" she asked.

Lowering his voice, Zach asked, "Any news about your phone? I'm a little worried that someone might use it to, you know, figure stuff out."

"Yeah, I get it. It was just my personal phone, but I got Bubba to erase it completely and then lock it down anyway. And you know Bubba."

"If he says he took care of it, then we're good."

## Office of National Emergencies
### Santiago, Chile

Alberto Juan Jacinto squirmed in the hard wooden chair, his fingers fiddling with the chin strap of the dark blue motorcycle helmet sitting on his lap. The silent, windowless room deep inside Chile's infamous Office of National Emergencies contained only one other chair and a heavy metal table someone had bolted to the floor. A single dirty light fixture spit and crackled overhead, casting the interrogation room in lighting fit for a Hollywood gore fest.

Just an hour before, his contact at the police station where he sold stolen cell phones ordered him to report to the imposing stone building in downtown Santiago. The phone buyer hadn't told him the reason for the unusual request, but the long rusty steel bar welded to the tabletop did nothing to relieve the motorcycle riding thief's mushrooming anxiety.

After an hour of imagining what the ANI, Chile's rough equivalent of the FBI, could have in store for him, the door finally opened. Alberto turned in his chair to find a thin man with slicked-back black hair and wearing a severely conservative black suit slide past him and almost daintily take a seat on the other side of the table.

"I am Major Garcia of the ANI," the man said with an insincere smile. "Thank you for coming so quickly. We appreciate your cooperation."

Garcia's tone did not ease Alberto's nerves. Nobody in their right mind wanted to see the inside of an ANI interrogation room.

"It is my pleasure to be of whatever service you require," Alberto replied, hoping he sounded earnest but only managing to highlight his quaking nerves.

Without taking his eyes off the other man, Garcia cocked his head slightly to one side but said nothing.

After several tense seconds, Alberto added, "I came as soon as I got the call."

Garcia's eyebrows raised.

"I see. And you did not stop on the way here to eat?"

Alberto's heart seemed to leap out of his chest. He had, indeed, stopped for five minutes at his aunt's tiny hot dog cart. *They had been watching him? Why?*

"I...I did. Yes. I..."

"Save your excuses. You acquired a cell phone this morning from a female foreigner."

Alberto shifted in his chair.

"Yes. I believe so. I delivered three or four cell phones to Mr. Alverez. I recall at least one belonged to a girl."

Garcia placed a digital voice recorder on the table, pressed 'record,' and slowly turned its microphone toward Alberto.

"Describe the female foreigner and anyone with her. I want every detail of the encounter. Leave nothing out," Garcia ordered, fixing his eyes on Alberto and crossing his arms. "Begin now."

Alberto looked down at the recorder and then back up at Garcia. Below the table, his right heel pumped up and down like a piston, and a bead of sweat tickled the back of his neck before working its way under his collar.

"I...uh...let me think a moment..."

Garcia slapped an open hand on the table, causing Alberto to jump in his seat.

"Are you hesitating because you don't remember an event that took place less than six hours ago or because you are hiding something?" Garcia demanded. "I suggest that your memory improves very quickly. You already lied to me once. Why should I not conclude you are being evasive now? Maybe you would prefer I remand you to one of President Cayo's new rehabilitation camps."

Alberto had heard rumors that the government's supposed crackdown on crime was nothing more than a cover for Cayo's suppression of political dissenters. Alberto was too young to remember the concentration camps that murdered thousands during the terror-filled reign of Chile's last dictator. But some people quietly claimed Cayo was leading Chile back in that direction. Either way, Alberto didn't want to find out firsthand if the rumors were true.

"Yes. Yes. Wait. Let me think," Alberto pleaded, trying to pull his thoughts together even as Garcia's dark eyes seemed to bore into his soul. "I am waiting."

Alberto's fingers fiddled nervously with his helmet strap while he desperately tried to picture the people he had robbed earlier that day.

"Yes, there were three men, all obvious foreigners. But there was also a woman. A girl, really. She was holding her telephone up, probably using it for directions. That one was easy. I just popped onto the sidewalk and took it out of her hand."

Garcia slapped the table again. "That tells me nothing."

"Okay, yes. She was short, no more than five feet two or three inches," Alberto said, closing his eyes and picturing the scene in his mind. "A yellow knit cap she probably bought at a local vendor. But I didn't see any hair. So, I don't know the color, but it must have been short. She also wore a puffy coat. Dark color. Black or dark blue."

"Better," Garcia said. "Keep going."

With Garcia relieving some of the pressure, Alberto warmed to his task.

"She was with a man. He was very tall. Well over six feet. Medium build. I remember thinking I needed to stay clear of him. After I got the girl's phone, he threw something at me. He was also wearing a dark-colored coat, like the girl's. I don't remember a cap. His hair was light and not dark like ours."

"Anything else?" Garcia demanded.

Alberto desperately wanted to come up with something to satisfy the man sitting on the other side of the table.

"I don't think they had been in the country long," Alberto offered.

"And why do you say that?"

"They seemed, if not reckless, then at least ignorant. Walking through the middle of town, gawking at things, and using a phone to navigate. Everyone who has been in Santiago for more than a day knows to look out for people like me," Alberto said, shrugging.

Garcia studied the young man another moment. He was just the type of low-life criminal that sullied Chile's reputation with the rest of the world. He should be in jail. But today, he had served an important purpose and would be set free.

"You may leave now," Garcia said. "Take your things and go."

Alberto didn't have to be told twice.

After the petty thief's swift departure, Garcia picked up his phone.

"Review the footage of every person entering the country in the last week. I'll send you two descriptions. Find these people and identify them. I'll expect a report detailing who they are, where they are now, and, importantly, where they came from. I want this in six hours. Less if you want to keep your job."

# CHAPTER TWELVE

FBI Laboratory
Quantico, Virginia

Special Agent Stella Sims knocked on Agent Deal's open door before stepping into her boss's office. Deal waved her inside as he finished a telephone call.

"Yes, sir, the team is in place in Talca now. They will begin surveilling the area for the launch site and any support facilities as soon as possible," Deal said into the phone. From her boss's tone, Sims could tell Deal was reporting to FBI Director Glover.

Sims lowered herself onto one of the straight-back chairs placed in front of Deal's desk, settling herself on the edge of the seat so that her feet could rest on the ground. Though shorter than most people's idea of an FBI agent, Deal chose Sims as his second in command due to her leadership skills and weapons expertise honed by her service in the United States Marine Corps.

A moment later, Bubba appeared at Deal's door and was waved inside as well.

"Who's the boss talking to? He looks tense," Bubba asked, drawing a glare from Deal's steel blue eyes.

Bubba threw his hands up, earning him a withering look from across the desktop.

Sims suppressed a chuckle but said nothing. Only Bubba could get away with clowning around when the boss was present.

"It's Director Glover," Sims answered quietly. "Any idea why he summoned us?"

Bubba didn't get a chance to answer before Deal ended the call and swiveled in his office chair to face him and Sims.

"Looks like this thing is heating up," Deal began. "The British and French have demanded answers from the Chileans about the satellites hovering over northern Europe. The British prime minister and French president have called for an emergency meeting of the United Nations Security Council and put NATO on notice of a possible attack."

"Whoa!" Bubba exclaimed. "That's an enormous overreaction to a few cubesats in geosynchronous orbit. Have either country presented some evidence that they pose a discreet threat of some kind?"

"The British filled us in on one thing. Something happened to one of their drilling platforms in the North Sea. They are still investigating, but the entire rig was destroyed after some kind of unknown explosion," Deal reported.

"What kind of explosion?" Bubba asked, leaning forward slightly.

"Here," Deal said, punching a few buttons on his keyboard and turning to the monitor in his office.

A relatively serene video of a tall oil rig floating in the ocean appeared on the screen. The sea was calm, and the sky was clear, with only a few fluffy clouds hanging high in the air. Suddenly, the sea seemed to explode in a fountain of water and steam. Less than a minute later, the colossal steel oil drilling platform was just – gone.

"Wow. When did this happen?" Bubba asked.

"Less than an hour after those cubesats got dropped off over Europe," Deal responded.

"Yeah. No wonder everyone over there is nervous. The timing fits, but do they have any evidence the satellites did that?"

Sims partially answered Bubba's question. "The European Space Agency, or ESA, has been monitoring the satellites from the moment they were inserted into orbit. Our monitoring systems are better, but theirs are closer. I just received a report that ESA launched a high-altitude fighter to pick up any weak electronic emissions. Maybe they found something they didn't like."

Deal nodded. "Director Glover just told me that they found nothing."

"That doesn't make any sense," Bubba said. "Nothing still in use in space is just dead. There must be some kind of signal telling those things what to do. Did anyone think to compare the Chilean rocket to the flight characteristics and fuel signatures of Chinese, Russian, or any other country's launch vehicles? That might at least give us a clue about who is behind this."

"No idea," Deal responded. "But good thinking. That's your next assignment. We need to see if there is any corroborating evidence to back up the Europeans' suspicions. Is this something that the Chileans actually accomplished on their own? If not, who is helping them and why? Can we tell anything about what the spacecraft that dropped off the smaller cubesats is doing now?"

Bubba stood and punched a few commands into his ever-present tablet computer, causing Deal's monitor to display a map of the Earth. After a few more taps on the computer, lines depicting the Chilean spacecraft's orbit appeared over the map. Bubba pointed to a spot somewhere above Mongolia.

"As you can see, after depositing the cubesats over Europe, the vehicle continued its orbit. If it maintains this orbital path, the spacecraft will overfly the Chinese mainland. What it may or may not do when it gets there – or anywhere, for that matter – is pure conjecture. We just don't know."

Sims stood and joined Bubba as he stared at the screen. She could almost feel the wheels turning in his shaggy-hair-covered skull.

"Could that spacecraft carry more of those cubesats?" she asked.

"Sure," Bubba replied.

"Well," Sims said, thinking out loud, "the last time it placed cubesats, it was directly over Europe. That's a big economy with advanced military and civilian technology. Since then, it's been making its way across the Russian wastelands, Mongolia, and places like the Gobi Desert. But, like you said, in a few hours, it will be over East Asia. China, Japan, Korea, and Taiwan. I bet if anything else is going to happen, it will be when it gets there."

"Oh, boy. The finger-pointing is already beginning, and if Miss Stella is right, there's going to be a real shit show at the United Nations Security Council meeting."

Deal scowled at Bubba's colorful description but had to agree. "If something like that happens, the world is going to get a lot more dangerous in a very short time. The Chinese don't play games when it comes to satellites hanging over their territory. Their anti-satellite weapons are almost as good as ours. I could also see them accusing the United States of using Chile to pull the wool over the eyes of the rest of the world. Assuming Sims' theory is correct, how long do we have until our mysterious spacecraft is in a position to deploy more cubesats?"

Bubba entered several commands into his tablet. The lines crossing the map sped up, marching quickly to the east. When they reached the western provinces of China, Bubba paused the program.

"Twenty-six hours, twelve minutes, seventeen seconds," Bubba pronounced. "You know, approximately. You thinking about taking Blue and Red teams down to Chile, boss?"

Deal blew out a long breath.

"Not yet. The Chileans are getting dangerously paranoid. I'm working on a cover for me and Sims, but I don't want to risk an international incident until we have more information about who and what we're dealing with down there."

"Have we heard anything from Michael, Sarah, and Zach?" Sims asked.

"No," Bubba answered, worry creeping into his voice. "By now, they should be close to getting set up in Talca."

"We're running out of time," Deal said, running one hand over his head. "They need to get us something quick."

# CHAPTER THIRTEEN



The aromas of freshly baked bread and hearty roasted pork greeted Michael, Sarah, and Zach as soon as they stepped into Rosa and Fernando Valdez's bed and breakfast.

"Empanadas," Rosa said with a hint of pride when she saw Michael's nose turn toward the door between the front sitting room and the kitchen. "We will eat in a little while. Before, you can get settled in your rooms."

While almost seventy, Rosa looked a decade, maybe even two, younger than her actual age. Strands of gray that streaked through her once-black hair lent an air of wisdom, and her smile could put even the most overwrought traveler at ease.

A tile-covered set of stairs led to the upper floor, where four bedrooms shared two bathrooms. Rosa showed Michael and Zach into a large bedroom with two full-size beds and a window that looked out over a courtyard. She assigned Sarah a smaller bedroom with a high window overlooking a tiled roof and the front yard. At least five blankets covered her cozy bed, making her wish she could climb inside for a long nap.

"Dinner will be at 6:00. Make yourselves at home. Please let Fernando or me know if you need anything," Rosa said cheerfully before making her way back to the kitchen.

As soon as Rosa disappeared down the stairs, the three friends gathered in Zach and Michael's room.

"Nice place," Michael commented, falling backward onto his bed and rolling over on his side.

Sarah plopped down next to him. "I just love Rosa. She is so strong and confident. But, you know, sweet too."

"Fernando kinda scares me," Zack said while beginning to unpack the fastidiously folded clothes from his suitcase. "He's like a soldier from back in the day. He's seen some stuff but won't talk about it. I had a great uncle who fought in Vietnam. Great guy but always seemed to be looking over his shoulder."

"Oh, I don't know," Michael chimed in. "He has a backyard with a couple of old trucks and a tractor. I'm not sure why he needs a farm tractor in the middle of a city, but I bet he likes mechanical stuff."

Sarah changed the subject and lowered her voice. "We have a few minutes until dinner. Let's go over our plan."

Zach pulled up their work schedule on his tablet.

"It's Friday. We're not supposed to start classes until Tuesday, so we have a few days. The question is – how do we use the time? Our first priority is getting into those mountains."

Michael sat up. "Sure, but how? If we take off on our own the minute we get here, someone is bound to notice. We're supposed to be English teachers, not mountain climbers."

"Let's keep our eyes and ears open tonight," Sarah suggested. "For now, we're just naïve college students on an adventure in an exotic country."

"That won't be hard to fake," Michael laughed.

Thirty minutes later, Sarah stood in the kitchen watching Rosa assemble empanadas. After stretching out a ball of homemade dough, she spooned on a heap of fragrant roasted pork and onions, folded the dough over the top, and transferred it to a baking sheet.

"They look delicious. You have done this before," Sarah commented in Spanish, obviously impressed.

Rosa chuckled. "Empanadas are my family's favorite. All of Chile's favorite. And mine are the best. You're Spanish is quite good, Sarah."

"Thank you. Chileans have a distinct accent that is fairly challenging, but I'm working on it," Sarah replied. "How many people will be at dinner? Your empanadas are bigger than Michael's hand, and it looks like you have already made three dozen! I think I could only eat one."

Rosa laughed. "You are too skinny. You will eat three tonight. Our son Fernando, Jr., we call him Junior, and his daughter Flor will also be here."

As if on cue, the back door opened, and a man of about 40 wearing a puffy black jacket stepped into the kitchen, walked directly to Rosa, and embraced her as if he hadn't seen his mother in months. With a thick head of wavy dark black hair and wide-set eyes that looked as if they laughed constantly, Sarah could instantly see the newcomer's resemblance to Rosa and Fernando.

"Empanadas! This is what I was hoping for tonight, Mamma," Junior exclaimed, picking up one of the pastries from the overflowing tray and taking a mighty bite.

Rosa playfully slapped his hand away when he reached for another. "Did you bring the beer your father wanted?"

With his mouth still full, Junior hefted a case of bottled beer onto the counter.

"This is one of our American guests, Sarah. She and two of her friends are here to teach English," Rosa said.

"Excellent!" Junior exclaimed. "Welcome to Talca, Sarah. There's not much to see or do here, but I hope you enjoy your stay."

"Thank you," Sarah responded. "Just being in Chile is a big adventure for us."

Rosa slapped Junior's hand again, preventing him from absconding with a second pastry.

"Where is Flor? Dinner will be in thirty minutes. Do not keep your father waiting."

Junior plucked two beers out of the carton. "Where is the old man? Outside fiddling with his tractor?"

"Yes, of course," Rosa responded, not looking up as she expertly assembled another empanada. "One day, he might even get one of those things running, although I have no idea what he will do with that dirty old tractor if he does."

"Michael loves to work on old cars. Could he join you?" Sarah asked quickly.

"Send him out," Junior answered. "My father can use all the help he can get."


Fifteen minutes later, Michael pulled his head out from under the ancient, rust-covered tractor's hood.

Fernando handed him a greasy red rag to wipe his hands on and asked, "What do you think?"

With Junior interpreting, Michael said, "Well, she's getting plenty of gas, and the carburetor looks good. But, for some reason, the spark isn't getting to the cylinders. Would it be okay if I pull the distributor cap off and take a look at the points?"

Fernando just shrugged.

"That's his way of saying yes," Junior explained with a grin.

Michael dived back under the hood and appeared again, holding the black plastic distributor cap and the rotor that spun around inside. He closely inspected both parts in the fading evening light while Fernando and Junior looked over his shoulder, trying to see whatever Michael was looking at. After a moment, Michael found an old piece of sandpaper in Fernando's toolbox and went to work cleaning the tiny metal contact points inside the cup-shaped distributor cap. After just a few more minutes, he had the parts reinstalled.

"Okay, crank her over," Michael said, wiping his grimy hands on the rag.

Fernando looked skeptical but climbed into the driver's seat, made sure the transmission was in neutral and turned the key. The engine whined as it spun and then coughed twice before roaring to life.

Fernando triumphantly threw both hands into the air, his grin lighting up the entire yard. Waving for Michael and Junior to move out of the way, he put the old monster into gear and took off, shouting at Junior to open the gate in the wall that surrounded the bed and breakfast.

After they lost sight of Fernando happily piloting the old tractor down the suburban street, Junior slapped Michael on the back.

"My friend, you have made my father as happy as I have seen him since we lost my brother six months ago. Thank you."

"Just some dirty points," Michael replied. "No big deal."

"Oh, no. You are mistaken. This means the world to him and to our family. My father and Rodrigo spent many hours together working on these old wrecks. He will want to repay you many times over."

"That's not necessary," Michael answered self-consciously. "I'm sorry about your brother."

Michael could see Junior's eyes glaze over as if staring into space.

"It is hard to think about. He was an engineer working on a construction project just a few miles out of town. He couldn't tell us much about it."

Junior's answer piqued Michael's interest.

"Did he say why?"

Junior studied Michael's face for a moment before deciding to open up to the American.

"The entire thing was being kept secret. He suspected President Cayo was allowing some big corporation to illegally build something massive on the vast ranch Cayo owns outside of town. He wanted to tell me more, but he said he couldn't. I knew my brother well, Michael. He wasn't only a brilliant engineer. He served almost ten years in the army's special forces. But Rodrigo looked frightened that night. The next day, we were informed he died in an explosion. Nobody ever explained what happened, and his body was never recovered."

"That's horrible. I'm sorry. Where exactly was this construction project?"

Junior turned and looked Michael in the eye.

"Why do you want to know?"

Rosa's call to dinner saved Michael from having to answer.

"Let's talk later."

# CHAPTER FOURTEEN

After Fernando finally returned from driving his tractor all over the neighborhood, Rosa's dining room quickly filled with guests and family.

"These are delicious!" Michael exclaimed, holding up one of Rosa's empanadas.

Without hesitation, Fernando picked up the platter, handed it to Junior, and pointed to Michael. Junior stood from his chair and carried the platter like a waiter to the head of the table.

"I told you my father would be grateful," Junior said, placing three more empanadas on Michael's plate. "If you can't tell, he has deemed you to be a special guest. This was where my brother sat when he was alive. He has only allowed family to sit in this spot since he died."

"That is very kind. But I don't think I can eat three more," Michael objected.

Junior laughed. "You don't really have a choice, I'm afraid. You could have done nothing more to earn his respect than fixing his tractor. And please don't say it wasn't important again because it was."

Michael accepted the food and looked at Rosa and Fernando. "Gracias."

Fernando beamed back at Michael and nodded.

"Will you stay for a while after dinner?" Michael asked Junior. "I may want to discuss something important if you can spare the time."

Junior nodded. "Yes, I think we can stay. Anyway, it looks like Flor and your friend Zach have found things to talk about."

Michael looked up to see Zach in an animated conversation with Flor. He was showing her pictures on his phone, and the two were laughing together as if they had known each other for years instead of minutes.

After dinner, Zach, Michael, and Sarah met back upstairs.

"We don't have much time," Michael began. "I'll cut right to it. Junior told me that his brother died during work on some secret construction project on a ranch owned by President Cayo. I asked him where, but he got a little suspicious and asked why I wanted to know."

"Oh, boy. I don't know, buddy. That doesn't sound good," Zach said warily. "Deal doesn't want us doing anything that could blow our cover."

"I know. I know," Michael said, holding up one hand. "But hear me out. We're looking for a launch site somewhere in the Andes. A launch site with no roads, buildings, or anything. Bubba thinks there's an underground facility up there and a tunnel system for supplies and stuff. Junior's brother told him the project was being built secretly on land owned by President Cayo. He also suspected some big corporation or something was financing it. This could be our best lead."

"What do you suggest?" Sarah asked.

Michael took a deep breath before throwing out an idea that sounded a little crazy, even to him.

"For whatever reason, I've hit it off with Junior and his father. They're good people. I want to see if they will help us find the tunnel and launch site."

"Whoa!" Zach exclaimed under his breath. "We haven't even been here a day. Don't you think that's taking one hell of a big risk? We don't really know these people. They might just report us to the authorities as spies for all we know. I say let's give it some time before we start recruiting the locals into our little spy ring."

Sarah put a hand on Michael's shoulder. "Maybe Zach's right."

Michael stood and ran a hand through his hair before turning back to his girlfriend and best friend.

"Yeah. Well, I might have already got the ball rolling on that."

Zach fell backward onto his bed while Sarah stood and clamped her hands around her hips.

"What did you do?" she demanded.

"Not too much, really. I asked him to wait around for a little while tonight so I could talk to him about where his brother was killed. I guess I got a little ahead of myself," Michael explained sheepishly.

Zach slowly rose back to a sitting position.

"So, what you're saying is this is kind of a done deal? You really should have run this by us first," Zach said, obviously irritated.

"I know. You're right. But it was a spur-of-the-moment thing. Anyway, Deal also made it clear we needed to move as quickly as possible."

Sarah softened her stance. Her boyfriend could be impetuous and tended to leap before considering all the consequences. Yet, it was that very boldness that had attracted her to him in the first place. Plus, his instincts had proved to be utterly dependable. If nothing else, he had certainly earned the benefit of the doubt.

"Okay. It would be worse to try and explain your way out of wanting to know more now. If you think you can trust him, I will too," Sarah said, taking her boyfriend's hand in hers.

Michael turned to Zach who just threw his hands into the air.

"I'm not about to take on the dynamic duo. I guess we can all go to prison together if this goes sideways."

A few minutes later, Michael followed Junior out into the backyard.

"You have been a little mysterious, my friend," Junior said, leading them to an iron bench against the wall that surrounded the property.

"I know. And I apologize. I'm not trying to pry into your family's business or anything. What I'm about to tell you could get me and my friends into a lot of trouble. Serious trouble. Like with the government."

Junior didn't react other than to take a sip of his beer.

"My government or yours?"

"Yours."

"I guess you better tell me what is going on. Then I'll decide what to do next," Junior replied.

"Okay. Here goes. My friends and I work for the FBI..."

Before Michael could finish the sentence, Junior spit beer out of his mouth and howled with laughter. After a moment, he stood and continued to laugh so hard he doubled over and held his stomach. Suddenly, the back door swung open, bathing the yard in yellow light.

"What is going on out there?" Rosa called.

"Nothing, Mamma," Junior responded, catching his breath. "Michael was just telling me a joke. We'll be back in shortly."

The door closed, once again plunging the backyard into darkness.

Junior took a long pull on his beer, allowing him to recover.

"Michael, that was excellent. The *FBI*. You should be a comedian."

In response, Michael looked Junior directly in the eye.

"I'm not joking around, Junior. This is real."

Junior studied Michael's face. When he didn't detect any deception, he sat back down.

"Alright. You aren't joking. I have to say, you don't look like an FBI agent. Do you have a badge or something?"

"No. No badge or gun or anything like that. They sent us down here to gather information about the space launch from the mountains. Specifically, where the rocket came from and who is behind it," Michael explained, pointing vaguely toward the west.

"And your friends, too?" Junior asked.

Michael nodded.

"Michael, you have to know this is hard for me to believe. But you seem sincere. So, I'll take you at your word. I am not the police or ANI. But if you are here to spy on my country, maybe you should tell me why you decided to reveal this to me."

Michael stood and paced back and forth for a moment, trying not to let the pressure that was turning his stomach upside down show. He was placing a lot of trust in a brand-new relationship. But he knew in his gut that the location of Rodrigo Valdez's death and the rocket launch facility had to be one and the same. On top of that, the fact that President Cayo was somehow involved made the possibility seem even more ominous.

"Two reasons. First, that rocket launch has caused a lot of concern for the rest of the world. We know that the rocket put a satellite into orbit that has already deployed several smaller devices over Europe. We don't know their purpose or who put them up there. They could be weapons. Since President Cayo flatly denied Chile had anything to do with the launch, we have to assume he is lying, or some unknown country or organization is using Chile for their own purposes," Michael explained.

"That makes some sense. But why didn't your government just get permission to investigate the launch? Do Chile and the United States not have decent relations?"

"That would have been better, for sure," Michael agreed. "But President Cayo has denied every request to do just that. He's keeping his own people and the rest of the world in the dark. That's why we had to come down here under cover."

Junior rubbed at his chin a moment. Michael was right. Cayo had been elected as a conservative, but recently, he cracked down on political dissent, placed his cronies in positions of power, and threatened to curb constitutional rights. His family did not support Cayo's policies, but Michael was still taking a big chance by asking for his help.

"Let's assume for a minute I have even the slightest interest in helping you. You said there were two reasons why I should do so. What's the second?"

Michael had carefully considered his response to this question.

"Your brother. You said he died working on a mysterious underground project near here. We think the launch from the mountains could only take place by bringing the rocket, satellites, and everything else they needed to support the operation to the site by using a tunnel or complex of tunnels and underground facilities. There are no roads, railways, or landing strips anywhere near where we think the launch took place. Your brother's suspicion about Cayo and the tunnel may have been right. If we can uncover whatever is going on, maybe we can also answer your family's questions about his death."

Junior looked down at the ground, scratched his head, and paced away a few steps.

"I apologize if I completely overstepped," Michael added.

He had no intention of opening old wounds.

"No. No. It is alright," Junior responded, wiping a tear from one eye. "My family desperately needs to find the truth about what happened to Rodrigo. But I do not want to involve my parents. I will help you. But I will not betray my country. And if you try to harm Chile in any way, I will make sure the authorities know about what you are doing."

Michael held up both hands. "Agreed."

"Now, how can I help?"

"First, we need to get into the mountains and confirm the exact location of the launch site," Michael answered, pulling out his phone and opening a map of the Andes Mountains. "This is where we believe the rocket came from. Any idea how we can get up there without raising a bunch of suspicion?"

Junior studied the map and mulled the question over for a moment.

"Yes. Let me work on it tonight, and I'll come by in the morning. But remember, my friend, whoever built your supposed tunnels must be bold, intelligent, crazy, and very, very dangerous."

# CHAPTER FIFTEEN



"I'm glad you came to your senses, Mr. President," Violet Ruiz cooed sarcastically, lifting a glass of Dom Perignon champagne in a mock toast.

The woman who could infiltrate an ultra-secret facility, free herself from handcuffs, and hold the leader of The Cause at knifepoint now sat across from Dave and Monroe in the facility's luxuriously furnished conference room just outside Dave's office. Several heavily armed security guards waited just outside the door.

Dave and Monroe ignored Ruiz's quip and sipped on their glasses without taking their eyes off the intruder.

"Still a little confused about who I am?" Ruiz asked, enjoying the men's discomfort.

"Not since you held a knife to my genitals and insisted we run your DNA," Dave replied. "You are, indeed, Margie Franks' biological daughter. That is no longer an issue. If it were, you would not have left that interrogation room alive."

Ruiz just sniffed derisively.

"Mr. President, Lieutenant Ruiz is our guest," Monroe said, placing a calming hand on Dave's forearm before turning to Ruiz. "It's your appearance here and how you came to be so knowledgeable about our little organization that remain mysteries."

"Then let me enlighten you," the Argentinian lieutenant responded, snatching the champagne bottle from the wine chiller and topping off her glass.

"As you will recall, Margie used every tool available to her to get ahead, including sex. I am the product of a short-lived tryst between my mother and an Argentinian general. They met while she was, shall we say, brokering a deal to sell military equipment to Argentina without the U.S. government's knowledge. She could have had an abortion, but she was a member of the Texas assembly at the time and pontificated a staunchly pro-life position. She couldn't risk a scandal if she got caught. So, she simply disappeared for several months until I was born and promptly shipped me south to become my father's problem."

"That doesn't really explain how or why you are sitting here now," Dave prodded.

"My father raised me in Argentina and led me to believe I was adopted. After I finished at the top of Argentina's special forces training class, Margie reappeared in my life. Apparently, she retained some twisted form of maternal instinct. At least enough to see if I had grown up to be someone she could use. And guess what? I did!"

Dave stood and walked to a leather-covered bar and made a show of choosing a three-inch diameter sphere of ice from a black bucket, placing it in a crystal tumbler, and slowly pouring two fingers of Blanton's bourbon over the ice. As the amber liquor slithered around the frozen globe, Dave considered his next move. One thing became immediately apparent – he needed to know more.

"Perhaps we got off on the wrong foot," Dave said, dropping his confrontational tone. "You seem to know a lot about us. Would you care to elaborate?"

Ruiz didn't hesitate.

"Good old Mom. She was nothing if not proud of her work. My family, like the Monroes and ten others, created The Cause back in the 1920s. The founding members, if you like. They came together with an antiquated vision of forming a new country out of the American South. Almost a hundred years later, thanks to you, Dr. Knox, The Cause got its hands on a fancy new fighter that allowed you and my mother's organization to come close to achieving that misguided aspiration. But by then, you didn't expect, or even want, to have a whole new country in your hands. Your actual goal was to destabilize the United States, and as the world got nervous, you would step in and sell more weapons of war in two years than in the entire history of mankind."

Dave looked at Monroe, who raised his eyebrows.

*She knows.*

Not quite finished flaunting her knowledge and enjoying the looks on the men's faces, Ruiz continued.

"Then, Doctor David Knox, who is now impersonating President Juan Cayo, pulled off a major coup by transporting a vintage nuclear bomb into the heart of the Strait of Hormuz and detonating it. That little stunt netted The Cause many billions in profits when oil prices quadrupled."

"Really?" Dave asked.

"Oh, yes. Very impressive. So impressive, in fact, that your rich cock-heavy, crony club made you their leader. There was only one little thing in the way. Margie Franks wouldn't step down. But that was no problem for a man like you, was it Dave? No. You simply had an assassin shoot her in the head during one of your meetings. Probably the same lovely young lady that blew away the real President Cayo.”

Dave narrowed his eyes and glared at the woman smugly sipping champagne as she revealed The Cause's deepest secrets.

“Her name is Amina, and she didn't shoot Cayo; she strangled him with a piano cord. And yes, we do what is necessary to whoever stands in our way. Even children of past members.”

Ruiz sat back in her chair and smiled.

“Oh, my. Back to threats. Fine. Let me explain my position clearly so it penetrates your hyper-conceited, misogynistic brain,” Ruiz began, looking Dave dead in the eye. “I'm here to claim what you stole from my mother. I'm now one of you with all the rights, privileges, and money due my family. I could have killed you the moment we met or at any time since. But while simple cold revenge would have been quite satisfying, it wouldn't make me rich. Your people, including Mr. Monroe here, would have become upset, and my plans would have been delayed. So that you know, I've compiled a complete dossier on The Cause, its members, and past exploits. Names, places, bank accounts – everything. If I disappear, that information will be sent to the American FBI and CIA, Interpol, Mossad, and every other intelligence service in the world. You and The Cause would be dead in a day, maybe even hours. So, in case it escaped you, I'm metaphorically holding a dead man's switch.”

Dave just rolled his eyes. “And do you think that revelation will save your life now? A dead man's switch! That's ridiculous.”

Ruiz slowly stood and said, “Fine. I guess you need more convincing. Please check your Cayman Island account. The one that had $750,000,000 in it this morning. The account ends with 0284.”

While Ruiz and Dave competed in a contest of wills, Monroe pulled out his phone and entered a long series of numbers and letters. A moment later, he held the phone up so Knox could see the screen.

The balance of the account stood at zero.

"How did you ... ?!" Dave exploded, moving toward Ruiz.

In a flash, Ruiz's fist shot outward, striking Dave in the throat.

The leader of The Cause collapsed to the ground, both hands wrapped protectively around his neck, gasping for air. At once, three men burst through the door with guns aimed at Ruiz.

Dave held up one hand and croaked, "No."

"I missed one check-in. That was just a taste, a demonstration if you like, to get your attention. Did I succeed?" Ruiz asked, backing away with both hands raised.

As he slowly regained the ability to draw breath, Dave nodded and waved the guards back outside.

Monroe stood and helped Dave back to his feet before turning to Ruiz.

"Welcome to The Cause, Ms. Ruiz. Could I pour you another glass of champagne?"

Just as Ruiz held out her glass, Dave and Monroe's phones flashed a message.

"Intruders approaching Pad 1."

Dave showed Ruiz the message.

"Prove yourself."

# CHAPTER SIXTEEN

"Hey, Junior! ... Dang!... Does this thing have any, you know, shock absorbers?" Michael asked in the few seconds between potholes that threatened to swallow the ancient van Junior had borrowed from his church that morning.

"I hope you enjoyed the ride," Junior responded as he wrenched the steering wheel to the left to negotiate yet another hairpin turn just before stepping on the brakes. "We are as close as the road can take us."

As the van rolled to a stop, Sarah shook her head and took a long pull from her water bottle.

"You okay?" Michael asked.

"Those last few miles did a number on my stomach," Sarah explained. "I'll be fine. Just give me a minute."

While Sarah recovered, Michael stepped out of the van and took a moment to appreciate the peaceful silence that descended on him after the loud, rough ride into the mountains. As he looked around, the scenery made him catch his breath. Just past several lonely mountain peaks, Chile's central valley spread out to the north and south as far as the eye could see. Beyond the valley, he could just make out the much lower coastal mountain range.

A minute later, Zach and Sarah appeared and handed Michael his backpack.

"Ready?" Zach asked. "Junior says we have a hard five-kilometer climb to reach the place Bubba identified as the launch site. We better get going. I want to get back to Talca in time for Rosa's dinner."

Junior climbed out of the van and, after walking around it looking for any damage or deflated tires, joined the group of friends.

"Are you sure you do not want me to show you the way?" he asked. "I have brought Flor's youth group to this area several times over the years."

Michael put one hand on Junior's shoulder.

"No, my friend. We have asked too much already. Your idea was awesome. Nobody would look twice at a church van heading into the mountains for a day hike. But stick around. I don't want to walk all the way back to town."

Sarah, Michael, and Zach left Junior sitting in the van. When they looked back, the tall Chilean had stretched out his legs in the back seat and pulled his wide-brimmed hat down over his eyes.

"At least he looks comfortable," Michael quipped.

The trio quickly found the trail that Junior had described. They followed the relatively easy, if steep, path until they came to a dead-end.

"This is as far as Junior's directions can take us. From here on, we'll be following the GPS," Michael said, pulling out his cell phone and opening a GPS app that Bubba had installed along with an independent Global Positioning Signal receiver.

"We don't need it yet. The only way forward I can see is through there," Sarah said, pointing at a narrow slit in what, at first glance, looked like a solid rock wall.

"Can't argue with that," Zach responded, adjusting his backpack to a more comfortable position. "Let's go. But keep that thing on."

"That's the right direction," Michael agreed, looking at his phone.

One by one, the three Americans slipped past the opening and found themselves in a tight ravine between high rock walls. Sunlight spilled into the miniature canyon, highlighting horizontal layers of rock in a multitude of colors and textures.

"This is cool," Zach exclaimed. "I wonder what made this place."

"Are we still going the right way?" Sarah asked. "It's hard to tell."

"Not sure," Michael replied. "I'm not getting a good signal down here. Let's keep going. This can't go on forever."

Michael was right. Just a few minutes later, they emerged from the slit canyon.

"Wow," Sarah said, pointing. "Look up there!"

High above, winds they couldn't feel pulled sheets of snow off steep mountain peaks and curled it into what looked like massive angel wings. They seemed to have entered a different world – one where the land seemed to stand almost on its side rather than lying flat under their feet.

Michael ignored the astounding landscape, looked up from his phone, and pointed to the east. "We're getting closer. About a mile over that ridge."

The Cause's Underground Complex
The same time

Ruiz and Monroe rushed to the facility's security office.

"What have you got?" Monroe asked. "Also, this is Lieutenant Ruiz. She has Director authority."

"Yes, sir," a man dressed in black fatigues responded. "Our seismic sensors first picked up footsteps three clicks from the launch site. We now have visual confirmation of three individuals. They have entered the security perimeter."

"Show me," Ruiz ordered.

The screen in front of the security man changed from a topographical map of the area to a somewhat grainy view of Michael, Sarah, and Zach making their way across a rocky slope.

"Hikers," Monroe concluded. "Kids. Probably on a day hike from Talca. We've seen groups like this before."

"Yes, sir," the security officer said. "But not this close. And they look like they are headed directly toward Pad 1."

Ruiz had remained silent as she studied the image closely. Something didn't look right to her.

"I don't think they are Chilean," she said. "Their packs are brand new and an American brand that is not sold in South America. And their hair is too light. They are either American or European. My bet is American."

"What do you want to do, Lieutenant?" Monroe asked.

"I'm going to take a closer look. Who can I take for backup?"

"After you injured two of my best men, I can only release the four remaining members of Condor squad. But be aware. They don't like you."

"*Condor?* Cute name. They don't have to like me to obey my orders," Ruiz replied. "Have them meet me at the west end of Pad 1 in three minutes."


"Hey, hold up a second," Zach called to Michael and Sarah. "This altitude is getting to me. Let's take five."

Michael and Sarah didn't admit that they, too, were feeling the effects of a hard hike at nearly 10,000 feet above sea level. But they gratefully plopped down next to Zach.

"You okay, buddy?" Michael asked.

Zach took another drink of water and laid back on the ground.

"Man, I don't know. All of a sudden, I felt dizzy, and I'm getting a headache."

Sarah scrambled around Michael and felt Zach's pulse.

"Too fast," she reported. "None of us are acclimated to this kind of altitude yet. I think we have to go back down."

Zach objected as he sat up. "We still have a job to do. I'm fine, but I think I better head back. If you guys are okay, go on. Don't worry. I know the way. I'll meet you on the far end of the slit canyon."

"Are you sure?" Michael asked. "If so, Sarah and I will take a quick look. We'll be back in no time."

"Yep," Zach said, getting to his feet. "Go."

From a position a half mile away at one of several security overlooks, Ruiz watched her three targets take a break and then split up. This was her chance.

"Condor seven, get down to coordinates 37-44-23 and grab the single hiker when he gets to the top of the trailhead just after the split in the rocks. Don't kill him. I want to know what the hell they are doing. We'll monitor the others from here."

"Copy."

"And make yourself look less like a soldier and more like a criminal of some kind. If they are just hikers, they can report being robbed. I don't want anyone to launch a whole search and rescue operation for lost American tourists."

Zach felt better every step he took down through the narrow canyon. Relieved it was only the altitude but feeling a little guilty about not being able to continue with Sarah and Michael, he slipped back through the opening in the rock wall.

"Freeze, gringo."

Zach froze in place as a semi-automatic shotgun barrel touched the side of his head.

"Damnit!" Michael spat, just minutes after Zach disappeared down the mountain. "Zach has the GPS."

"Alright," Sarah said. "Don't beat yourself up. He's not that far back."

As they entered the slit canyon, Michael jogged ahead, hoping to catch up to his best friend and quickly retrieve the GPS without wasting any more time. As he passed through the entrance to the canyon, he was confused to find Zach sitting with both hands on top of his head and his eyes as big as saucers.

"What the ...?"

Michael's question was cut short by the sight of a shotgun aimed at his face.

# CHAPTER SEVENTEEN

"Hey, hey! Okay, buddy! No need for guns!" Michael shouted, hoping Sarah would hear his warning before popping out from the canyon entrance. When she didn't immediately appear, Michael turned back toward the heavily muscled man holding the shotgun. A few jerks of its barrel in Zach's direction gave Michael all the instructions he needed.

With a weapon tracking his every move, there wasn't much he could do but comply. The gunman wore a dark green sleeveless t-shirt and what looked like black combat pants. Despite the cold wind whistling through the mountain passes, he had no jacket, and his hiking boots looked like he had laced them up for the first time that morning. Strangely, he wore a camouflage-patterned bandana over his nose and mouth like an old-time Western bandit.

Michael was about to make a snide comment to distract their captor when Sarah suddenly screamed from the other side of the rock wall.

"Help! Michael! Zach! Help!"

Sarah's panicked call barely made their captor turn his head.

"Hey, man. Come on. Let me go see what's wrong," Michael pleaded.

"Yeah, it sounds like our friend is hurt," Zach added, looking in the direction of Sarah's voice. "Please."

"HELP! Please, oh God, help!"

"She can't hurt you. Please let me get her," Michael begged.

"MICHAEL! Aaaaaa! MICHAEL!"

It sounded like Sarah was being torn apart by wolves.

At that moment, a rock came bouncing through the narrow gap between the boulders. The unexpected sound, combined with Sarah's screams, made the Chilean soldier turn and raise his weapon.

At that moment, Michael shot to his feet and charged into the gunman's back, slamming him into the ground. A fraction of a second later, Zach sprang into action, grabbing the shotgun and jerking it out of the bandit's hand. Zach pumped a shell into the shotgun's chamber and leveled it at the masked man's face.

"Sarah?" Michael called. "You okay?"

Sarah appeared a few seconds later, completely unharmed.

"How did you like my horror movie screams?" Sarah asked, taking in the scene.

"Had me convinced," Michael replied, throwing his arms around his girlfriend. "How did you think to do that?"

"Easy. I heard what you said about a gun. I just kinda improvised."

Michael turned to Zach. "You're pretty comfortable with that thing. Where did you learn to wrack a shell into a shotgun?"

"Movies, of course," Zach replied. "Now, what do we do with this guy? He seems upset about laying on the ground with his own gun aimed at his head."

Just as Zach made that comment, the bandit tried to push himself off the ground, but Michael's boot on his back quickly convinced him to keep still.

"Thank you," Zach said. "He was waiting for me. I didn't even think..."

"We got lucky," Michael responded.

"Who is he?" Sarah asked. "Some kind of robber or something?"

Michael shot Sarah a sideways look. She was acting ignorant. He and Zach played along.

"They said be careful up here. Outlaws hide in the mountains and prey on tourists and hikers. We should have listened," Michael said.

"What should we do?" Sarah asked.

"Tie him up, and get the hell out of here," Zach suggested without hesitation.

Half a mile away, Ruiz watched the entire encounter with high-powered binoculars. She had made a play to question one of the intruders and lost. Yet, she had gained invaluable information. The Americans who looked like college students were not so naïve as they appeared. They marched into the mountains and somehow knew where to look for the launch site. Most telling, they managed to take down a highly-trained special forces operator.

Michael, Sarah, and Zach wasted no time securing the man who attacked them and disposing of his weapon. It only took them an hour to make their way back down the series of trails they had followed earlier and find Junior, who was sound asleep in the back of the rickety old van.

Back on the mountain, the three friends had agreed to keep the surprise attack to themselves. Michael didn't want to involve Junior more than he already had, and they all agreed they didn't want to worry Fernando and Rosa – or get involved with law enforcement.

After another of Rosa's sumptuous, family-style dinners, Michael, Sarah, and Zach met in Michael and Zach's room to discuss their next move.

"That was no lone mountain criminal, no matter what he looked like," Sarah began, keeping her voice low. "He was military all the way and probably dumped some of his uniform and equipment to disguise that fact."

"Yeah," Michael agreed. "It was almost like he didn't expect to have to confront anyone and had to come up with something on the fly."

Zach stood and paced a moment, his mind obviously turning.

"So, here's what I think that tells us. First, he had to be watching us. That means we were close to the launch site. Second, whoever was giving the orders decided not to kill us. Would have been easy enough to take us out and dump our bodies somewhere up there."

"That gives me the creeps," Sarah added with a shiver.

"Yeah, but he or whoever was in charge wanted something. But what?" Zach asked, scratching his chin.

"Maybe," Sarah said. "But my guess is they wanted to find out who we are. If they killed a Chilean, someone from here, the police would be all over that place."

"And killing American students, or even if we went missing, would draw media attention and diplomatic problems. The whole operation was obviously thrown together, probably after whoever is guarding the launch site saw us climbing up there," Zach concluded. "We got too close. We need to call Deal."

"Yeah, but not from here. Let's go for a walk," Michael suggested.

Deal answered on the first ring.

"This line is secure. I have Bubba and Agent Sims in my office. We've been waiting for your report. What is your current status and location?"

"We are a block and a half from the house," Michael responded. "Our status is fully operational. Hey Bubba. Hey Stella."

"How's Chile?" Michael heard Bubba ask.

"Save the chit-chat," Deal barked. "What have you found?"

Michael handed the phone to Zach.

"Our cover is intact. We haven't seen anything that makes us think we are under suspicion, at least here in Talca, as anything other than three poorly paid English teachers. More importantly, we managed to get up into the mountains today. We didn't lay eyes on the actual launch site, but there's no doubt someone up there doesn't want anyone snooping around."

Zach described their sightseeing hike and the attack by the lone gunman.

"Is everyone alright?" Deal asked.

"Michael took the guy down with a major league tackle," Zach said.

"Team effort," Michael responded.

"I'll want to hear more about that another time. For now, it sounds like you have confirmed the location of the launch site. Have you dug up anything about the other end of the tunnel? Should be somewhere close to Talca," Deal wanted to know.

"We may have something on that soon," Michael responded.

"Good. Sims and I are on the way," Deal reported. "We'll have to take the long way into the country, so it will be 48 hours or so before we arrive. We'll be in contact."

"Excellent," Michael said, relieved the boss would be joining them. "Whatever is happening in Chile is bigger than just a surprise missile launch."

Sarah held out her hand, and Zach gave her his phone.

"Bubba, I know you locked my phone down. You haven't gotten any indication someone was able to break into it, have you?"

Sarah heard Bubba laugh.

"No. No way," Bubba said after a minute. "My protocols not only lock the phone, but they also wipe every bit of data. Just to be sure, I also implant a device that physically smokes the memory chips with a tiny electrical charge. Nobody will be able to find or trace you. At least not by using that phone."

# CHAPTER EIGHTEEN



Major Jaime Garcia studied the video footage the technical division had sent him only hours before. Ever since interrogating the low-level thief responsible for stealing the perplexing cell phone that couldn't be hacked, Garcia had known that whoever brought that phone into the country was more than just a tourist. With enough knowledge and expertise, any phone would eventually spill its secrets. But not the nondescript light rose-colored device sitting next to his computer. The phone rested on top of a report describing the efforts his experts made to break into it using advanced hacking software. When that failed, the technicians cracked into the phone itself and discovered the reason its data couldn't be retrieved. Several tiny devices had been hard-wired to the memory chips that fried whatever data remained.

Garcia picked up the dead phone and held it in one hand as he watched the surveillance videos of passengers arriving at Santiago's airport on international flights. Reviewing videos of thousands of passengers passing through customs had been a monumental task. But finally, Garcia felt certain he and his team had identified the phone's owner.

The video depicted three college-aged Americans walking down the long, wide ramp leading from the international terminal to the customs stations. A tall male walked next to a second darker-haired male of average height. A second later, a shorter female caught up with her two friends. The trio looked to be chatting amiably as they waited in line to present their passports.

As they moved slowly along the line, the girl reached into her jacket pocket, pulled out a cell phone, and held it to her ear. The cell phone in the picture was the same rose color and model as the dead device he now held in his left hand.

Passport records showed that the girl in the video was Sarah Marshall. A quick search of hotel records shows she and the two males – Zachary Self and Michael King – had stayed two nights at a youth hostel in Santiago before buying bus tickets to Talca. A little more digging uncovered that the three Americans would be working as temporary English teachers.

"Who are you, Sarah Marshall? And what were you doing with such a special phone?" Garcia asked the girl on the computer screen.

### The Cause's Underground Complex

Dave Knox hung up the secure telephone line and pressed the intercom button.

"Find Lieutenant Ruiz and send her in."

While he waited for the newest member of The Cause to knock on his office door, Dave stood and walked to a wide bank of windows that overlooked the vehicle assembly area. Below, three gleaming rockets sat end to end on massive frames. Workers in white jumpsuits and wearing matching white hardhats swarmed over the next three vehicles that would carry The Cause's cubesats into low Earth orbit. Meanwhile, another dozen men in light blue work clothes maintained the ingenious carriages and rail system Dave designed that moved the missiles through the assembly process and served as the launch platform.

"You wanted to see me?" Ruiz said, startling Dave.

Dave turned and cocked his head at the tall, dark-headed, and incredibly physically fit woman standing in the middle of his office.

"You really are your mother's daughter," Dave commented.

"What do you mean by that? A compliment, I hope?" Ruiz replied, not missing a beat.

Dave gave a short laugh. "Of sorts, I suppose. She didn't give a crap about social niceties either."

"Do you want me to go back out and knock, or do you just want to tell me what you want, *Mr. President?*" Ruiz asked sarcastically.

Dave took a deep breath and turned back to the windows.

"You might show at least a little respect. I designed this facility, those rockets, and developed the plans for when and how we will use the cubesats they will place in orbit."

"Yes, I know all about your impressive intellect. Bravo," Ruiz responded, clapping her hands slowly with insincere applause. "Just what do you plan to do with those things anyway? I doubt you have the public's best interest in mind."

"Well, probably not," Dave admitted. "But as its chairman, I always have The Cause's best interest in mind."

"Oh, don't sell yourself short," Ruiz remarked. "You're also a ruthless and cunning dick who looks out for Dr. Dave Knox above anyone or anything."

"Ha! Well said," Dave countered, sitting down behind his desk and gesturing toward a comfy armchair placed at a slight angle across from him. "Those rather simple launch vehicles that look so impressive lined up out there are merely delivery trucks. The real miracle lies in what they carry into low Earth orbit."

"And just what is that?"

"Those," Dave said proudly, "will put the majority of the world's population under our thumb."

Ruiz laughed out loud. "Wow. You want to rule the world? Who do you think you are? Genghis Kahn? Alexander the Great? Hitler?"

Dave let Ruiz laugh a moment.

"Perhaps you're right," The Cause's leader agreed. "That sounded a bit megalomaniacal. Perhaps not so much under our thumb as susceptible to our, uh, gentle influences. But I will have to fill you in on the details later. We have more pressing matters to attend to at the moment."

Ruiz decided not to press the treacherous and excentric genius further and took a seat, making sure she had a clear view of the door. She didn't trust the mastermind behind The Cause and its growing empire of oil holdings, weapons manufacturing and sales, and aerospace companies. And she hadn't yet learned how deeply The Cause's tentacles reached into the halls of governments, the boardrooms of financial institutions, and the military headquarters of several countries. Despite Dave Knox's welcome into The Cause after she revealed her relationship to Margie Franks, she still had a lot to learn while also watching her own back.

"I have news about your little encounter with those hikers," Dave said, not hiding a satisfied smirk.

"Okay," Ruiz responded warily. "I don't know why you look so self-satisfied, but go ahead."

"You remember the college students who managed to stop your half-assed plan?"

"They got lucky."

"No, they didn't. We don't have all the details yet, but they are not what they appear to be. We have solid evidence they are American intelligence operatives," Dave explained.

Dave's news didn't catch Ruiz by surprise. She had suspected the three young people were not just common American students. She just didn't think it necessary to share that fact with Dave.

"Fine. Good information. But what am I supposed to do with that?"

Dave leaned forward in his chair and looked Ruiz in the eye.

"They are staying at a bed and breakfast in Talca. You let them escape from the mountains. So, this is your mess to clean up."

"What do you want me to do?" Ruiz asked, unfazed by Dave's attempt at looking intimidating.

Dave stood, placed his hands flat on his desk, and leaned threateningly into Ruiz's face.

"Take care of the problem. Obviously. I could care less how you do that. We can't have spies from America or any other goddamned place lurking around. You want a real piece of the pie? Earn it. For all we know, they are not the only American spies trying to infiltrate the country at this very moment."

# CHAPTER NINETEEN

Maneuvering the massive Range Rover SUV up the tight switchbacks of Argentina's Route 7 required all of Special Agent Stella Sims' concentration. The two-lane road that began 500 miles to the east in the balmy capital city of Buenos Aires now snaked its way up through a barren mountain landscape. She might have described it as the most desolate place on Earth except for the miles of truck traffic crawling along the road in both directions, shipping goods across one of the only passes through the Andes between Argentina and Chile.

"Where are we now?" Deal asked from the back seat.

"Only a couple of miles from the Paso Internacional Los Libertadores. The Chilean customs station is on the other side of the tunnel at the top of the pass," Sims reported.

Deal sat up in the deeply cushioned, smooth leather back seat and poured himself a glass of red wine. After placing the crystal glass in a holder built into a fold-out tray, he straightened his tie and donned a set of black-framed glasses. A neatly trimmed gray beard and a copy of Wine Spectator magazine placed casually in the seat beside him completed his disguise as a wealthy wine buyer.

"How far is it to Santiago after we get into Chile?" Deal asked.

"Not far as the crow flies, but we'll have to navigate out of the mountains, and the road on the Chilean side twists and turns even more than this one. With this traffic, we're still several hours from entering the city – if we don't get sidetracked by customs," Sims answered.

"I don't think we'll have any trouble. Bubba and the rest of the tech team did a great job building our identities as Canadian wine buyers. Even if they run a deep background check, which they probably won't, they will find a legitimate company that buys wine from all over the world. And even though President Cayo has warned the rest of the world not to interfere in Chile's affairs, he can't risk damaging the market for one of his country's major exports," Deal explained.

"And we haven't received any information that security has been beefed up at this port of entry?" Sims asked.

"Our contact cleared customs just 24 hours ago. He reported that getting into Chile this way would be slow due to the amount of traffic using the tunnel. But the border security forces are stretched thin up here and don't have the time or resources to do much more than scan passports and conduct cursory cargo inspections. So, we should sail through. That's not the case at the airports. The government has become paranoid and is closely monitoring every single foreigner arriving by air. I'm certain they vetted Michael, Sarah, and Zach closely. But college-aged English teachers shouldn't have raised any eyebrows," Deal said, taking a sip of wine.

"If you say so, boss," Sims said into the rearview mirror. "I didn't know you even drank wine."

"That's why we've been studying up on Chilean grape varietals," Deal replied, lifting his glass to the dim light filtering in through the tinted windows. "Like this Carignan. I find this one a bit light on the pallet but with good legs and excellently balanced tannins."

Sims didn't know if her boss was kidding or not. Since Deal rarely cracked a joke, she decided not to respond.

A few minutes later, the entrance to the two-mile-long tunnel connecting Argentina and Chile came into view. After climbing 10,000 feet into the Andes, they followed a long line of dirt-caked tractor-trailer rigs into the rectangular entrance. Once inside, Sims found herself forced to creep along behind the truck in front. The dark, two-lane road kept the traffic packed together, and she had no idea when they crossed over the border into Chile. After almost 20 minutes, they emerged on the western side of the pass. Ahead, she could see the vehicles in her lane forming several lines at the border station.

Another thirty minutes passed before a customs officer, wearing a bulky uniform coat, approached the car and signaled Sims to roll down her window.

"Passports," the officer said, barely looking inside the big SUV.

Sims handed over both passports and watched the officer place the documents on some sort of portable scanner.

"Your purpose for visiting Chile?" the officer asked perfunctorily.

"We are wine buyers," Sims answered, trying to sound bored and tired, which wasn't far from the truth.

The officer took a moment to hold up the passports and compare the photos to the FBI agents' faces. Without another word, he handed back the documents and waved Sims through the checkpoint.

"You were right, boss. That was easy," Sims said, looking over her shoulder for approaching traffic before pulling out onto Chile's Highway 60, which would take them out of the mountains and into Santiago.

In the basement of the Office of National Emergencies, the FBI agent's passport information and pictures had already been dropped into a file that included every foreigner entering the country. As each came in, advanced AI-driven facial recognition software scanned the images, compared them to information already in the national database, and then conducted an internet search for pictures matching each passport. The program searched social media sites, commercial websites, photo databases, online news sites, newspapers, magazines, and television stories to confirm each person's identity.

A few seconds after the software uploaded Sims' photo, a notification appeared on Major Jaime Garcia's phone and desktop computer. An obscure little opposition newspaper in the United Arab Emirates had run a story entitled: "The Prince's New Concubine?" Under the headline, the article included a picture of Special Agent Stella Sims standing at the railing of a massive yacht with a handsome Mideastern man.

When Garcia finally looked at the notification ten minutes later, he snatched the phone off his desk.

"We have a problem. I'm sending you pictures, vehicle identification, and location now."

For several long seconds, Garcia waited for a response from the other end of the line.

"We'll take care of it."

# CHAPTER TWENTY

Thirty minutes after pulling away from the border, the long line of trucks thinned out as the drivers scattered across the country to make their deliveries. Sims breathed a sigh of relief. For the first time in over eight hours, she didn't have to steer the big SUV around tight mountain switchbacks or worry that one wrong move could send her and her boss plummeting into a deep gorge. They were nowhere near civilization, but the road toward Santiago now wound gently down through the foothills of the Andes.

Only a few cars passed them headed in the opposite direction. After the sun completely disappeared from the western sky, Sims flipped on the vehicle's bright lights. She had once driven across the southwest deserts of Arizona and New Mexico. Those barren landscapes were beautiful at night. But this was different. The moon had disappeared behind low clouds, leaving only the two slim headlight beams to pierce the inky darkness that enveloped the entire car.

"Are you getting tired?" Deal asked from the back seat.

"I'm okay," Sims answered. "But I'm not going to write a glowing trip review about this part of Chile. I'll be happy to get back to civilization."

"Me too. A nice glass of whiskey and a steak would go down pretty good about now," Deal commented. "I hope the hotel...."

Suddenly, Deal's phone beeped insistently, cutting off the FBI agent's wish list.

The message on his screen read: "You have been identified. Run."

"What the hell?" Deal blurted.

"What is it, boss?" Sims asked.

Deal leaned up between the front seats and showed Sims the message.

"That didn't come through the secure link with Washington, did it?" Sims asked.

"No..."

Before Deal could respond further, the car lurched to the right as the rotor wash from a massive helicopter crashed into the vehicle's left side. Sims wrenched the steering wheel to the left, trying to keep the car from bouncing off the road and onto the hard, rocky shoulder.

Deal hauled himself back into his seat and looked out the windows on the right side. "They're coming back around."

Sims planted her right foot down hard on the gas. The big V-8 engine roared in response, catapulting the three-ton vehicle forward. But even as they rocketed down the road, the FBI agents both knew they couldn't outrun a military helicopter.

"What do we do, boss?" Sims asked calmly. "These guys mean business."

"Keep going," Deal responded. "Let's see just how serious they are."

As they watched, the big Airbus H215M swung back in their direction, its nose dipping menacingly, like a bull getting ready to charge, just before it hurtled back in their direction. A moment later, the fifty-caliber machine gun mounted in the helicopter's nose came to life. Bright yellow tracer rounds flashed across the windshield and chewed into the tarmac.

"I'd say they are fairly serious," Sims called out as she threw the car into the opposite lane. "Somehow, I don't think they're too concerned with arresting us."

As the helicopter pirouetted in the sky to their left, setting up for another run, Deal's phone dinged again. This time, the message read: "Take the next left."

Deal didn't have time to worry about who was giving the advice. They were about to get torn to pieces.

"Go left!" Deal ordered.

Sims saw a small road appear, and she cranked the wheel in that direction. The SUV nearly spun as it jumped onto the dirt and gravel path. The FBI agent expertly counter-steered, pointing them toward a high chain link fence. Without lifting her foot from the gas pedal, Sims blasted through a gate secured by a rusty chain and padlock.

"Where are they?" Sims shouted into the back seat.

Deal craned his neck, looking out the side windows.

"Coming around from behind. Our little detour threw them off for a second, but we're a long way from losing them."

Sims didn't have time to look. She suddenly found herself driving between what looked like petroleum storage tanks. The tall white tanks that whizzed past her window would make it harder for the helicopter pilot to get a shot, but she felt like a rat trapped in a maze with a hungry tomcat.

Suddenly, tracers appeared overhead, punching a long line of ugly holes in the tank just to their left. Almost instinctively, Sims jerked the wheel to the right, narrowly missing some piping that connected underground lines to the tanks.

"What now, boss?" Sims called over her shoulder. "We can't play hide and seek with these guys much longer."

Deal stuck his head between the front seats and saw more rows of rusting white tanks on both sides. When he glanced behind, he could see the helicopter carefully lining up for its last lethal attack. Sims was right. They needed a new plan. And right now. Then Deal's phone beeped again.

"Turn off your lights and take the next right," Deal ordered.

"Gonna make it hard to see, but okay," Sims replied, dousing the headlights, hitting the brakes, and throwing the SUV into a sharp right turn. "I've got some kind of metal building ahead."

Deal turned and squinted through the windshield. Sure enough, he could just make out a large storage building. But its massive, corrugated sheet metal doors were closed.

The helicopter followed their move and now rushed toward them from behind. In seconds, it would unleash a hail of bullets that would shred the car and its occupants. Sims looked left and right, trying to find an opening she could use to jink away from the chopper. But none appeared. With no other choice, she aimed the SUV's grill at the building and hoped they could crash their way inside.

Then, as if by magic, the two doors opened just wide enough for the SUV to slip through. A second later, they closed again, even as a swarm of fifty caliber rounds turned the sheet metal into Swiss cheese.

Enveloped in complete darkness, Sims reached over and flicked the vehicle's lights back on. Almost immediately, she slammed her foot down on the brake pedal.

Ahead, three men and one woman stood in a line – all armed with assault rifles aimed directly at Sims' head.


"Lion Flight to Control," the helicopter pilot said into his helmet-mounted microphone. "The subjects entered a storage building on the west side of the old petrol storage facility off Highway 60. Request instructions."

"How long can you stay on station Lion flight?"

The pilot checked his fuel situation. It didn't look good.

"I'm into my reserves. I need to return to base."

The pilot studied the corrugated metal structure displayed in his night vision goggles while he held the chopper in a hover thirty yards from the building's doors.

"Lion Flight. You are clear to destroy the building. How do you copy?"

"Good copy Control…"

Before the pilot could confirm his orders, the building suddenly blew apart. A massive flare in his night vision goggles temporarily blinded the pilot, even as the explosion's shock wave smashed into the hovering aircraft, swatting it out of the air. When one of the chopper's blades broke free and pierced a petroleum storage tank, a fireball seen for miles rose into the sky like a miniature nuclear mushroom cloud.

# CHAPTER TWENTY-ONE

FBI Laboratory
Quantico, Virginia

Bubba sat in Deal's office chair outside Washington, D.C., his fingers flying over the desktop's keyboard as he desperately tried to reacquire the signals from Deal and Sims' secure cell phones. He had successfully tracked the two agents during their trip across the border and into Chile. Then, an hour later, they inexplicably turned off the main road just minutes before the signals from their phones completely disappeared.

Now, he was checking surveillance footage, hoping to find a satellite that covered central Chile. The surprise launch, several hundred miles to the south of where Deal and Sims disappeared, had prompted the CIA to retask several of their classified assets to keep an eye on the country. But even they could not cover every square inch.

After thirty minutes of furious searching the feeds from several satellites, he finally found a surveillance platform that had overflown Santiago at the same time he lost Deal's signal. Scanning northeast toward his boss's last known location, Bubba found what he didn't want to see – a massive explosion that lit up the night sky. Bubba's calculations conclusively showed the blast came from an oil storage facility next to the highway Deal and Sims had been using when they disappeared.

He knew that didn't necessarily mean Deal and Sims had been killed or even injured. But the fact remained – he had no idea where they were. And until they contacted him or at least turned on their cell phones, his hands were tied.

As of that moment, the Special Agent in Charge of the FBI's WMD Fast Response Team and his second in command were, at best, missing.


"Who are you people?" Deal demanded for the tenth time from under the black hood that covered his entire head. "Where are you taking us?"

After being unceremoniously pulled from their wrecked SUV, blindfolded, and shoved into the back of an old four-wheel-drive Land Rover, Deal and Sims had been ignored by their captors for the last hour. For most of that time, they had bounced down rough dirt and gravel roads that twisted and turned so much they lost all sense of direction. Then, fifteen minutes ago, the ride had smoothed out. The sounds of heavy traffic and stop-and-go driving could only mean they had entered a city.

"This is ridiculous," Sims pleaded in Spanish. "We are here to buy wine. Why have we been attacked? What do you want? Money? Let us go. We can pay."

"We have American dollars..." Deal tried to add before a gun barrel on the back of his head cut off the FBI agent's offer.

"No talking," a gruff male voice ordered in heavily accented English.

"Why are you...?" Deal responded.

Suddenly, a hand holding a rag soaked in chloroform clamped down over his face.

Deal struggled for a moment, but with his hands cuffed behind his back and sitting in the cramped back seat, he could do little to resist. He didn't feel Sims' head fall onto his shoulder when she blacked out a few seconds later.

# CHAPTER TWENTY-TWO

<br>

Hostal Casa Anita
Talca, Chile

"Wake up. It's Bubba," Zach whispered, shaking Michael's shoulder and holding up his cell phone.

"What?" Michael responded groggily. "Bubba? He's not supposed to call us."

"Not unless there's an emergency. He sent a secure text," Zach responded.

"Well, what's it say?"

"Should we get Sarah?" Zach asked.

"Not unless we have to. I don't want to get in trouble with our hosts for having a girl in here after hours."

Zach entered a code that would unlock the second level of security Bubba had insisted on adding to all such communications.

"Wow," Zach exclaimed quietly.

"What?" Michael asked.

Zach held up the phone so Michael could see the message.

*Deal and Sims' location lost after they crossed the border. No contact since 1800 local time. Will update.*

Zach and Michael looked at each other.

"What the hell are we supposed to do with that?" Michael asked, throwing both hands in the air. "It's not like they filled us in on their travel plans."

Zach shrugged. "I guess Bubba thought we should know."

Just then, the bedroom door cracked open, and Sarah stuck her head inside.

"What are you two doing? I could hear you through the wall."

Zach and Michael showed Sarah Bubba's text.

"That's not good," she said. "If they got caught, we could be next. The real question is – what do we do now? We came to Talca to confirm the launch site. We did that. Bubba's theory about that was dead on."

As usual, Sarah's clear-headed analysis cut to the chase.

"But we haven't found out anything about how they pulled off transporting an entire rocket, payload, fuel, and everything else into the mountains. Like Bubba said, there must be a pretty serious underground tunnel or something," Michael reminded them. "Until he or someone gets us more information about Deal and Sims, I think we should stick to our original mission. We don't know if we have been compromised yet. I think our next move is to look into the facility where Junior lost his brother."

Zach sat on the edge of his bed, staring at the floor. After a moment, he said, "Look, I know you believe Junior is solid. He sure helped us out when he didn't need to. But, whoever built that launch complex saw us coming, or someone tipped them off. I wouldn't be the least bit surprised if they had all of us on camera and identified us by now."

"And you're worried about whether we can trust our hosts' son?" Sarah asked, completing Zach's thought.

"Yeah. I don't want to be suspicious, but I think we have to be."

Michael stood and paced around the room, stepping over open suitcases he and Zach had left at the foot of the beds.

"What if we split up?" Michael asked.

Zach and Sarah looked at each other with raised eyebrows.

"What are you talking about?" Sarah asked.

Michael stopped pacing.

"It was my idea to tell Junior about our real identity and what we are doing in Chile. I'll stay here and keep looking for the tunnel or whatever kind of entrance that leads into the mountains. You guys take the next bus back to Santiago and see what you can do for Deal and Sims," he said.

"Hell no!" Sarah blurted a little too loudly. "If you think for one second I'm leaving you here, you've lost your mind."

Zach didn't respond immediately. Michael's idea made some sense. If the Chilean authorities knew about their mission in Talca, it could be only a matter of hours before they were arrested as spies. But they had no idea if that was the case or not. On top of that, if Deal and Sims needed help, they were the only other American assets in the country, and there was very little they could do from a backwater city hundreds of miles to the south.

"I think Michael has the right idea," Zach said, earning a scowl from Sarah.

Zach held up the palm of his hand to keep Michael's girlfriend from shooting daggers into him with her eyes before he could get his idea off the ground.

"Go ahead," Michael said, putting a calming arm around Sarah's shoulders.

"Okay. Hear me out. Let me stay. Whoever goes looking for Deal and Sims will have to have an excuse to leave. Some emergency back home, for example. It doesn't make sense for Sarah and me to leave together. That would raise way too much suspicion. You guys take off in the morning. I can stay here and see what Junior knows."

Michael and Sarah knew their friend was right. But they didn't have to like it.

"Okay. Agreed. I think Junior is a standup guy," Michael said. "But keep your eyes open."

# CHAPTER TWENTY-THREE

Deal pressed his eyelids together, trying to keep out the brilliant white light that seemed to stab deep into his skull. It took him a minute to open both eyes, and when he did, he was intensely surprised by his surroundings. After being kidnapped and chloroformed, he expected to wake up in a prison cell or interrogation room. Instead, he sat propped up on a comfortable brown leather couch. Someone had placed a throw blanket over his legs, and a steaming cup of fragrant coffee sat on the table in front of him.

As he oriented himself to his new surroundings, he saw Sims curled up on the other end of the couch, sipping from a matching ornate cup.

"I'm sure you have questions," a slim man said from an armchair placed across from the couch.

Deal studied the other man for a moment. He sat with his legs crossed, a coffee cup held delicately with only his thumb and index finger. Dark hair seemed to race up from his forehead and cascade back over his head. Hard, shiny black eyes matched a form-fitting black suit and a highly-polished pair of plain black oxford dress shoes.

"My guess is you won't believe we are wine buyers," Deal said casually, reaching for his coffee.

"Oh, no. I'm afraid not, Special Agent Frank Deal. I must say, it is a pleasure to have the world's most renowned tracker of weapons of mass destruction sitting in my living room. But please allow me to introduce myself. I am Major Jaime Garcia of the ANI, if I may be so bold, Chile's FBI."

"I have heard of the ANI. But, I'm confused, Major," Deal said, gesturing to his surroundings. "This is your home?"

"Indeed, it is."

"May I ask how we came to be here? Given your president's current attitude toward foreigners, particularly those working for governments such as Agent Sims' and mine, I would have expected to be in, well, less pleasant surroundings."

Sims placed her cup on the side table beside an antique brass lamp and joined the conversation.

"Let me guess, you identified us at the border crossing?" she asked. "Advanced facial recognition?"

Garcia nodded. "Not just advanced, I'm told it's the best in the world. I'm not privy to how it works exactly. Some kind of artificial intelligence linked with a web-search function. But yes, when your true identities didn't match your passports, I had no choice but to notify my superiors. They decided to send one of their new helicopters to eliminate you."

"But it was also your decision to save our lives?" Sims asked.

"And you sent the messages to my phone leading us into that tank farm," Deal added.

"Yes. My computer technicians are quite good. I didn't know if you would follow the instructions or not. Luckily, you did. We had a team nearby that could intercept you there," Garcia responded. "They just had time to set the charges that destroyed the facility and get you out before the aircraft could fire a missile. I've already reported your deaths."

"You said 'we'"? Deal asked.

"I'll explain later. For now, you should know Chilean security services know about your team in Talca and that they are in danger."

"Who identified them?" Sims asked.

"I did."

# CHAPTER TWENTY-FOUR

Garcia's apartment
Santiago, Chile

Deal didn't react to his host's revelation other than to sit back on the couch, take a sip of coffee, and take stock of the man who had just saved his life but also put him, Sims, and his team in Talca in mortal danger. Deal knew he had much to learn about Garcia and that his current, admittedly confusing situation could be nothing more than an unconventional method to elicit information from him.

"Major Garcia, we appreciate your hospitality, but as you might imagine, we have urgent business..."

"I am well aware," Garcia said, interrupting the FBI agent. "You are here to investigate the spacecraft launched from the Andes several days ago. When my government denied any knowledge of that incredible incident and then refused any assistance to find out who was behind it, our security services, particularly the ANI, knew the United States and other countries wouldn't just let the matter drop."

"Couldn't let the matter drop," Deal corrected. "And, not to be impolite, but we won't let it drop until we have a reasonable explanation. So, where does that leave us, Major? Sims and I have a job to do. You can take us into custody and hand us over to Cayo's goons or let us know what's really going on here and help us avoid what is quickly developing into a dangerous international crisis. The decision is yours."

Garcia sipped at his coffee and smiled for the first time. "Yes. It is. And I appreciate how you didn't feel the need to add vague threats of repercussions from American intelligence services should anything happen to you."

Deal found he actually enjoyed sparring with Garcia. During the course of his career, the FBI agent had interrogated international arms dealers, fanatical terrorists, and heads of rogue states. He had come to rely on his gut to judge someone's true character. It wasn't as simple as labeling them "good guys" or "bad guys." The key to getting every scrap of useful information from a subject came down to understanding their motivation – what made them tick. And Garcia was proving to be a real challenge.

Deal leaned forward and looked Garcia in the eye. Most people withered to some degree when caught in Deal's steely glare. But not this officer. Whether or not it was because Garcia held all the cards, the man's poise was unshakable.

"Okay, Major. Where do we go from here?" Deal asked.

"I propose we cooperate. President Cayo has placed Chile in the crosshairs of international scrutiny while clamping down on political dissent. The last time this happened, my country endured decades under an iron-fisted dictator. Thousands of pictures of his victims, Chile's own citizens, now hang in Chile's Museum of Memory and Human Rights right here in Santiago. Countries seem to spend money on such museums after their people throw aside democracy and bow to one man. But let me be clear. I will not betray Chile. I am talking to you now only because I have information that Cayo has sold out to some other powerful country or corporations who wish to, once again, take control of my country and steal power from the hands of its citizens."

Deal could see and feel Garcia's conviction. The man was a patriot walking a fine line between protecting his country and defying its laws.

"And where does the rocket launch fit into Cayo's plans?" Deal asked, still probing for information.

"We are not sure. My people do not have the technical resources to track the spacecraft in orbit. I have made discreet inquiries with the military, but they claim they knew nothing about the launch before it took place."

"Do you trust your sources?"

"My own brother is the general in charge of the Central Operations Theater for Chile's Air Force. So, yes. I can trust my sources," Garcia replied without a hint of sarcasm.

Sims asked, "Let's assume for a moment President Cayo is either in charge of this rogue space program or has been manipulated, maybe paid off, to allow it to exist here in Chile. Who else in the government would he need to loop into his plans?"

Garcia thought for a minute. The rocket launch's remote location suggested Cayo would need the cooperation of at least some members of his cabinet who would be willing to overlook the massive construction program, payoffs, and financial coverups needed to pull off such an incredible feat without attracting too much attention.

"Minister of the Interior, Sergio Aybar," Garcia answered. "Whoever has done this should not have been able to build the needed infrastructure without Aybar knowing about it."

"Can we talk to Minister Aybar?" Sims asked.

Garcia didn't answer Sims' question. Instead, he turned to Agent Deal.

"Are we working together? Or do I need to arrange for you two and your team in Talca to be picked up and escorted out of the country? I hear the Peruvian deserts on our northern border are particularly hot and desolate this time of year," Garcia said.

Deal chuckled just a bit. Garcia already knew his answer. He didn't have a choice. But that didn't mean he would take his eye off the obviously brilliant Chilean intelligence operator.

"We are," Deal responded. "And I'll continue to refrain from making any, how did you put it, 'vague threats of repercussions' from other American intelligence agencies should you not prove trustworthy."

Now, it was Garcia's turn to chuckle.

"I think we understand each other. I'll set up a meeting with Minister Aybar. He is a reasonable man. Perhaps he will talk to you."

# CHAPTER TWENTY-FIVE



Sarah and Michael's departure from Talca went as smoothly as possible. Sarah had come up with a story that her mother had suffered a minor stroke back in the United States. While not life-threatening, Rosa and Fernando understood when she explained that she couldn't stay in Chile. And Michael wouldn't let his girlfriend travel home all by herself. To show their support, the entire close-knit Valdez family drove the couple to the bus station.

When they got back to the bed and breakfast, Zach pulled Junior outside for a quiet conversation. He could immediately tell the other man wasn't happy.

"Michael claims you are with the FBI," Junior began before Zach could say anything. "I suspect they didn't leave because Sarah's mother is sick. And I don't like keeping information from my parents or anyone lying to them. I listened to Michael because my father believed him to be a fine young man. But I won't let my family be used by you, the FBI, or anyone. So, out of respect for my father, I'll listen to you once. If I don't like what I hear, you will leave their home and not return."

Zach couldn't blame Junior for protecting his family. He would have to be sincere and convincing to win his trust and convince him to help find the entrance to the suspected tunnel system. Luckily, the young American student of diplomacy had a knack for this sort of challenge.

Zach sat with his elbows resting on his knees, looking thoughtfully out across the Valdez's backyard. He didn't respond immediately, letting the other man's words soak in. Finally, he sat up and looked at Junior.

"You're right, of course. Yes, we are with the FBI. I know Michael told you we are investigating the rocket launch. Michael, Sarah, and I meant no disrespect to your family. You have been nothing but kind to us," Zach said, meaning every word. "Michael and Sarah returned to Santiago because two of our colleagues may be in trouble there. He wanted to talk to you before they left, but there just wasn't time to do that."

Junior seemed to accept Zach's story. But he didn't look totally convinced.

Zach continued. "Have you ever heard that Chile had any ambitions about starting a space program?"

Junior huffed. "Of course not. Chile isn't a rich country like yours. A space program would be a waste of badly needed resources."

"So, doesn't that make it more likely that your president would want the world to know if Chile had done something impressive, like start a peaceful space program of some kind? Instead, he's blocked any release of information and kept his own people in the dark. If this was all above board, why would he try to hide it?" Zach argued.

"I don't know," Junior said, agreeing. "We thought it was a good thing when my brother went to work at the big project north of here. The pay was good, but he claimed he couldn't tell us anything about it. Classified by the government or something. When he died, they told us almost nothing – just claimed it was some kind of explosion. They couldn't even find his body. The bastards just ignored my family's pain."

Junior stood and walked a few steps before wiping away tears from both cheeks.

Zach sat silently, letting the other man work through his feelings.

After a minute, Junior came back and sat down.

"I'm sorry," Zach said.

Junior turned and looked directly into Zach's eyes. "I want to find out what happened to my brother. I have done some looking around but haven't been able to uncover anything. Can you help me do that?"

Zach took a deep breath. That wasn't his job, but he needed Junior's help.

"I can't promise anything," Zach answered honestly. "But if you'll help me get to where your brother worked, I'll do my best to find out what I can."

"That's all I can ask."

Zach spent the next few minutes recounting the details of their earlier hike into the Andes that they had decided to withhold from Junior. When he was done, he could see Junior's mouth pulled into a tight line and his eyes hidden by full dark brows knitted together in deep thought.

"Does that change your mind?" Zach asked. "Whoever is in charge up there is deadly serious about keeping whatever they are doing secret."

"My brother died working for them. I will show you where he worked. We can't get in, but I think that's our first step."

"When can we go?"

"Twenty minutes. I need to go home and get my truck."

# CHAPTER TWENTY-SIX

Ruiz pulled a set of earphones away from her head, set them on the old white van's dashboard, and handed the ex-special forces soldier sitting casually in the driver's seat the small parabolic mic she had just used to listen in on Zach and Junior's conversation.

"Do we know what happened to Junior Valdez's brother?" she asked.

The driver opened a laptop and scrolled through several menus. Eventually, he handed the computer to Ruiz and pointed at the screen. Ruiz sat back and took her time reading the report.

"What are your orders?" the driver asked in a flat, bored voice.

Ruiz didn't have a set plan when she took the high-speed tram to the camouflaged entrance to the tunnel complex and headed toward Talca. The three agents posing as students had foiled her first attempt to stop their investigation. Then, two of the students had left unexpectedly, bound for Santiago. This complicated her job significantly, and now she had to deal with Junior Valdez and his stubborn curiosity about what happened to his brother.

After the ANI informed Dave Knox, posing as President Cayo, about the identities of the three young people, Ruiz decided to learn as much as possible about the American spies. Her simple stakeout of the Valdez bed and breakfast quickly netted useful information. She had confirmed that they worked for the FBI. She also knew that

Zach Self and Junior Valdez were headed toward the tunnel entrance several miles out in the country. Like the excellent chess player that she was, Ruiz considered her next several moves.

"Follow them," Ruiz ordered. "And get the rest of Condor Squad moving in that direction. We're going to stop playing nice."

Ruiz's driver acknowledged her order with an indifferent grunt and picked up the radio.

Talca wasn't a big city, and it didn't take long before Zach and Junior found themselves on country roads that didn't so much twist and turn as ungulate over the rolling landscape. At first, they passed small farms and tiny towns consisting of a few houses and small businesses. Soon, Zach could tell they had entered what he thought of as open ranchland. Every few minutes, cows would appear near the road, lazily munching on the thick, tough grass. But Zach wasn't wholly focused on the scenery. He had been keeping one eye on a single vehicle that appeared and disappeared as they crested one small hill after another. Not wanting to unduly worry Junior, Zach didn't mention that someone might be following them.

Before leaving Talca, Ruiz had ordered a surveillance drone to track Junior's truck. A mile behind Junior and Zach, she watched a green dot indicating her target's position march across a map displayed on her laptop.

"They will be stopping near the tunnel entrance. Have your men intercept them here," Ruiz said, showing the map to the driver. "They will apprehend Zach Self and take him into custody. He is to be taken alive."

"And the other one?" the driver asked.

"Make him wish he never met the Americans. But let him escape. We don't need the police looking for a missing Chilean or the Valdez family making trouble over another missing son."

"Copy that," the driver said before relaying Ruiz's orders.

"How far are we from this place?" Zach asked.

"We are here," Junior said, pulling the truck to the side of the road.

Zach couldn't see anything that looked like a warehouse or buildings, only rolling hills that seemed to stretch from where they sat to the foot of the Andes.

"Really?" Zach asked. "Here?"

"Yes. Have faith, my friend. I am about to show you something amazing."

Zach jumped out of the truck and followed Junior to the other side of the road. They hopped across a shallow drainage ditch and climbed a steep rise covered with prairie grass. Zach slipped once and caught himself with one hand before joining Junior, who motioned for him to stay low near the crest. Zach crawled up the last few feet and lay down in the grass next to Junior.

After Zach joined him, Junior asked, "What do you see?"

Zach peered over the hill and down into a vast, low-lying plain. He cocked his head to one side and looked again. Finally, he turned to Junior.

"I don't see anything."

"Look again. This time, don't believe what your eyes tell you."

Zach shook his head but did as Junior suggested. Again, he saw quiet, empty grassland. Then, as if he was looking at one of those pieces of art that reveal an image only when you stare at it long enough, the valley slowly revealed its secrets.

A few seconds later, he could discern the outlines of a long building with a gently rounded roof. On one end, he could just make out a massive set of doors, at least sixty feet wide and thirty feet tall. The rest of the building tapered off in height, seemingly disappearing into the Earth several hundred yards behind the doors. Grass and shrubs, matching the surrounding landscape, covered the entire structure. The disguised building wouldn't fool the best surveillance satellites or trained military pilots looking for a target. Still, it effectively hid the entrance to a massive underground complex from the few people who traveled across the area – either on the ground or through the air.

"How do they get deliveries?" Zach asked. "If there's a road leading to the entrance, I can't make it out from here."

"Rails," Junior explained. "They are hard to see from this position. A few months after my brother's death, I came to this very spot. I didn't dare to go closer. Rodrigo told me how the work site had security monitors planted in concentric circles radiating out a kilometer from the entrance. So, I stayed here and watched for almost two days. On the second day, I could hardly believe my eyes when a train appeared coming from the west and seemed to roll over the open countryside. As it approached that building, the doors opened, and I counted twenty cars behind the locomotive. The entire train disappeared inside and did not come out again."

"Did Rodrigo ever tell you anything else about what he was doing?" Zach asked.

"No, he said he couldn't. I knew him better than anyone. He was worried, but he refused to tell us anything. I know it was because he didn't want to put us in danger."

After studying the area and snapping several shots on his phone, Zach and Junior wormed their way back down the slope.

"I have to get in there," Zach said, almost to himself. "But if security is that tight, I have no idea how."

"*We* have to get in," Junior corrected. "I'm going to find out what happened to Rodrigo. They owe my family an explanation."

Zach didn't respond to Junior's bold announcement. While he didn't know if he could help, Zach had volunteered to take on this part of the investigation by himself. He didn't speak Spanish and he needed a guide and a means of transportation to get around the countryside.

"What do you suggest?" Zach asked. "Could there be some access inside without just walking up and ringing the doorbell?"

Junior pulled himself up to the top of the hill again.

"I don't see any other way in. Ventilation shafts, utility junctions, and even emergency exits must be camouflaged. We have no choice. We'll have to get closer to find out more," Junior said, rising to his feet.

"Wait," Zach said, waving for Junior to get back behind cover. "If we walk out into the open, we'll just be inviting a response. We can't just storm the castle in broad daylight."

Junior sat back down. "Do you have another idea?"

Zach took another look into the valley. "I'm not sure yet. Let's go back and...."

Suddenly, the roar from several engines pierced the quiet countryside as if vehicles of some sort had just materialized out of thin air. Junior peered over the crest again, immediately jumped to his feet, and began running toward his truck.

"Let's go, Zach!"

Zach didn't have to see what or who was coming. The terrified look on Junior's face told him everything he needed to know.

The two men sprinted down the short hill toward the ditch that separated them from the truck. At the last moment, Zach's foot landed on a large stone, violently twisting his ankle under him. A distinct 'pop' accompanied by a lightning bolt of pain threw Zach to the ground.

"Go!" Zach shouted through clenched teeth as Junior jumped into the truck.

Seeing Zach on the ground holding his right ankle, Junior started back toward his new friend.

"Go! Damnit!" Zach shouted again. "Find Michael and Sarah!"

Junior ignored Zach until three bullets slammed into his truck's front fender. A moment later, a motorcycle flew over the hill, jumped the ditch at the edge of the road, and spun to face Junior's truck. Within seconds, a four-wheeler carrying two more men crested the hill and pulled up next to Zach.

Now completely cut off from Zach, Junior jumped into his truck, fired up the engine, and executed a near-perfect skidding U-turn back toward Talca.

As Junior sped away, Zach looked up to see two men in black combat fatigues standing over him with weapons aimed at his head. He was relieved to see Junior's truck speeding away without anyone in pursuit.

Zach slowly raised both hands. "I don't suppose you guys have an ice pack I could borrow?"

Junior had never been so scared. The first time getting shot at has that effect on people. For the next few minutes, he let his instincts take over. He kept his right foot planted hard on the gas while keeping one eye locked on his mirrors. After fighting off his initial panicked reaction, and with no one on his tail, Junior's breathing finally slowed down. His hands shook from the massive dose of adrenalin coursing through his system, and he had to force himself to think clearly.

He knew he couldn't have helped, but he still had to wrestle with a growing sense of guilt about leaving Zach behind.

He tried to convince himself he should go home and try to forget what happened. But even as he entertained that thought, he knew he couldn't. He had no idea how he would find Michael and Sarah. But he owed it to Zach to try.

Five miles further on, he turned right and joined the never-ending flow of traffic heading north toward Santiago.

# CHAPTER TWENTY-SEVEN



Bubba opened the window on his desktop that displayed a map of Chile for what seemed like the hundredth time, looking for signals from Deal and Sims' phones. He could see the icons that showed Michael and Sarah on the highway between Talca and Santiago. Zach now seemed to be well outside the smaller city. But finally, after almost giving up hope, the icons for both Deal and Sims glowed brightly on the screen. He found Sims' phone in a high-rise apartment building in the heart of Santiago while, curiously, Deal's signal showed him inside Chile's Presidential Palace.

Bubba silently pumped a fist in the air even as he moved his cursor over the icon and hit the left button twice. Immediately, he could hear Deal's phone ringing in his wireless headset.

"Hey, boss! Man, I'm glad I found you," Bubba said when Deal answered. "Are you visiting the president or something?"

"We're fine, Bubba," Deal said without other niceties.

"I thought we lost you guys in that oil tank explosion outside the city," Bubba responded. "What happened?"

"I'll fill you in on everything later. Right now, we have another problem," Deal responded. "So, listen up."

"Okay."

"We believe that another launch from Chile is imminent. Don't worry about how we know right now. What do we have that can take a close look at the launch vehicle."

Bubba's fingers flew over the keyboard, looking for surveillance assets that could monitor a second launch.

"Looks like we don't have anything in the air to watch this one, boss," Bubba reported. "Our brothers and sisters in the other agencies aren't letting us play with their toys right now. Something about lack of available assets."

"I thought that might be the case," Deal responded. "Screw them. Get down to Kennedy Space Flight Center in Florida. I've talked to the head guy down there. He owes me a big favor."

"You sending me into space, boss? I've always wanted to be an astronaut."

Bubba could almost hear Deal trying not to get mad at him for kidding around.

"Bubba, shut up," Deal growled. "He's got something down there we can use to keep an eye on the next launch. You leave in thirty minutes on the Gulfstream. When you get there, you won't have much time. Get up to speed and keep me informed about what you find."

Deal hung up abruptly, leaving Bubba wondering just what NASA had that could get him into a position to watch the next launch. Looking at his watch, Bubba headed back to his laboratory to grab the bag he kept packed for just such an occasion and find a ride out to the airstrip.

Minister Sergio Aybar sat up in his chair and looked directly across his opulent desk at Garcia. He had remained silent while Deal ordered Bubba to get NASA's help identifying the mysterious launch vehicles. But his eyes narrowed at the mention of some kind of surveillance flight.

"Explain," the minister ordered.

"What do you have in mind?" Garcia asked after Deal hung up the phone with Bubba. "You may not just order an overflight of our country without our permission."

Deal put up one hand. "Absolutely not. I wanted you to hear my orders in person. Please allow me to assure you and Minister Aybar that we won't come anywhere near your borders. Bubba is our best aerospace engineer and a certified genius. We need his eyes on the launch vehicle. Its configuration will tell us a lot about what kind of vehicle they are using – Russian, Chinese, North Korean, or something else."

Minister Aybar stood and paced around his office, his highly polished black wingtip shoes echoing off the parquet floor. He reached into a jacket pocket with one hand, retrieved a long cigar, and jammed it between his teeth. Instead of lighting up, the minister vigorously gnawed on the end.

Deal and Garcia sat quietly as the third most powerful politician in the country literally chewed over allowing Deal and Garcia to investigate nothing less than President Cayo's secret pet project. The minister stopped to look out one of the fifteen-foot-tall windows that overlooked the wide piazza in front of the palace. Tourists and Chileans casually walked under a bright sun, sipping coffee or chatting on their phones. Across from the piazza, businesspeople spilled onto the streets for the long lunch hour and enjoy what had turned out to be a glorious day.

Despite the idyllic scene, Aybar's eyes remained shaded under knitted brows as he turned to look at a low wall across the plaza.

"On September 11, 1973, I was only ten years old when I hid behind that wall for almost two hours while right-wing military officers attacked the palace and killed the new president. I saw our own aircraft come in low and drop bombs on this very building," Aybar said before turning and looking directly at Deal. "I also saw one helicopter circling the palace and strafing people inside. That helicopter was American."

"I know those things happened," Deal responded. "But I'm not here as an apologist for what my government did over fifty years ago. I'm here about Chile's surprise space program. The rocket launched a few days ago placed several stationary satellites over Europe. My analysts have just informed me another ten satellites have just been deployed over eastern Asia. We need information. Are they a threat? If not, what is their purpose? We have asked your government for an explanation, but President Cayo has blocked every diplomatic and back-channel request for information."

Aybar held up one hand. "I didn't explain about the coup to open old wounds. I need you to know why I am choosing to help you. Cayo has kept everything about his space ambitions to himself and bribed and threatened his cabinet and military officers to stay away from the issue. I've made discreet inquiries with the head of every agency I can trust, but nobody seems to have reliable information. Cayo's disregard of the law and cavalier use of Chile's resources cannot continue."

Aybar walked to his desk and opened his laptop computer. He studied something for a moment, wrote a long series of numbers on a sheet of paper, and handed it to Garcia.

Garcia tucked the paper into his jacket pocket.

"Now, thank you both for coming," Aybar said, standing. "You might find that particular place of interest. But allow me to be clear. The United States will not attempt to interfere in internal Chilean matters or attempt to infiltrate any governmental or private facility. This meeting was about land available for vineyard expansion and nothing else."

As Deal and Garcia walked into the broad plaza outside the palace a few minutes later, Deal asked, "What now? How do the minister's orders affect what we are doing here?"

Garcia grinned. "I didn't hear any orders. Even if he had, I don't work for him. He made a rather broad admonishment to the United States, but nothing official."

"What's on that?" Deal asked.

Garcia unfolded the paper and showed it to the FBI agent.

"Latitude and longitude coordinates," Garcia said.

Deal opened his phone and entered the numbers into a mapping app.

"What is it, my friend?" Garcia asked, seeing the profoundly confused look on Deal's face.

Deal held up the phone for Garcia. Instead of rock-covered mountains or a vast open area of farmland, the map showed a spot just outside the center of Santiago.

"Where is this?" Deal asked.

"I think I can show you," Garcia said, walking down the block to the next intersection.

When Deal caught up, Garcia raised an arm, pointing to a massive building high on a mountain.

"What is that?" Deal wanted to know, puzzled.

"The Pacifico Hotel."

# CHAPTER TWENTY-EIGHT

Castillo Rojo Hotel
Santiago, Chile

"Is this it?" Michael asked, surprised.

Sarah looked out of the cab's window and chuckled.

"Well," she said, "the name of the place is Castillo Rojo. That means Red Castle. So, yeah, this is it."

"Okay," Michael replied, hoisting both backpacks and carrying them inside.

Opulent old-world Spanish flair softened the distinctly medieval interior. At the small front desk, a smiling young woman greeted the Americans as if they had been friends for decades and took them up a narrow flight of stairs to their room.

"I hope you enjoy your stay. My name is Daniela Montego. I am the day manager. Please call the front desk if you need anything at all. Ms. Smith left a message asking you to meet her in the lounge as soon as you get settled."

"Thank you, Daniela," Michael said. "I hope you don't mind me saying so, but your English is excellent."

As Daniela left the couple alone, Sarah smacked her boyfriend on the shoulder.

"What was that for?" Michael asked.

"*Your English is excellent....*" Sarah cooed, mocking Michael's tone.

"Not as good as yours," Michael said with a lascivious grin, grabbing Sarah and pulling her to him.

"Not now," Sarah chided, slipping out of his grip. "We have to meet Sims and Deal."

Ignoring Michael's pout, Sarah took stock of their new home. The room had only one window that looked out onto the street four floors below. Though small, the room's comfortable heavy wood furniture and slanted ceiling that followed the building's steep roofline added a cozy feel.

"How did Sims find this place?" Michael asked, starting to unpack a few things from his backpack. He had not anticipated a hotel with such odd décor and striking red exterior.

"No idea," Sarah said. "After Bubba got in touch with her and Deal, this is where she told us to meet. I like it. It's unusual."

"Yeah, for a weirdo vampire movie or something," Michael kidded.

Sarah ignored her boyfriend's attempt at comedy.

"Daniela's nice," Sarah mentioned. "Pretty, too."

"You can't date her," Michael joked. "You're taken."

"Oh my gosh, Michael!" Sarah laughed. "Okay, I'll stop teasing you."

Twenty minutes later, the couple walked down to the second floor. The lounge was empty, except for Daniela, who was busy setting up the bar and a small buffet table.

"Welcome!" Daniela said as soon as Michael and Sarah came in. "What can I get you?"

"Probably just some water for now," Sarah replied. "We have to meet our boss."

"Ah, yes. Mr. Darrow," Daniela replied, using Deal's assumed name. "I'm sure he and Ms. Smith will be down shortly."

"This is a beautiful hotel. Unique as well," Sarah said, climbing onto a barstool next to Michael. "Working here must be interesting."

"Oh, I love it," Daniela answered with a smile.

"I saw a textbook on the front counter," Michael said. "Are you also a student?"

"I am. I have a degree in business from the university, and I'm working on what in the U.S. would be considered a master's degree in hospitality management," Daniela replied, setting down the towel she had been using to wipe down the bar. "I'll be back in five minutes. Later, I'd like to buy you both a glass of one of our famous wines. When you are free, of course."

"Where are Deal and Sims?" Michael asked quietly.

As if on cue, Sims came down the stairs, followed closely by Deal. They both wore casual but expensive clothes, perfect for a wealthy Canadian wine buyer and his assistant.

The lounge was long and narrow, stretching from the staircase on one end of the building to the opposite wall. Deal gathered his team in a comfortable seating area near the back of the bar. While Deal and Sims dropped into two armchairs, Michael and Sarah found seats on a bright red couch.

As soon as they were settled, Daniela appeared once again.

"May I get you something, Mr. Darrow and Ms. Smith?"

"Yes, please," Deal replied. "I'm here looking for Chile's best wines. Please bring us whatever you enjoy. Some of my favorite discoveries have come from recommendations made by hotel staff, waiters, and bartenders."

Daniela didn't hesitate. "I just got in a new Carignan blended with a Syrah. I like it because the deep character of the Carignan pairs perfectly with the Syrah."

While Daniela went to retrieve and open the wine, Deal filled Michael and Sarah in on the attack that occurred after they got into the country and their eventual rescue by people working with Officer Jaime Garcia.

Before Michael and Sarah could report about their investigation in Talca, Daniela returned and poured them all a glass of wine from a plain bottle bearing only a handwritten label to identify its contents.

Deal held the glass to his nose and took a deep sniff before swirling the wine around his glass, holding it up to the light, and taking a sip. After rolling the lush red liquid around in his mouth, Deal looked at Daniela.

"What do you think?" Daniela asked.

"Delightful!" Deal gushed. "Full fruit, enough tannins to make it interesting without getting in the way of the rich flavor. Excellent."

"Thank you," Daniela said, obviously relieved the wine buyer had approved of her choice. "I'll tell my uncle Javier. He grew the grapes on his vineyard and made this wine himself. He will be pleased."

Daniela left to attend to other guests, leaving the foursome alone in the lounge.

"Okay, report," Deal ordered. "What did you find in Talca? And where is Zach?"

Sarah recounted their hike into the mountains and how the unsuccessful assault by a soldier rather poorly disguised as a mountain bandit proved they had come as close as possible to the launch site. Michael explained how he had become close with their host family and the tragic loss of their son at a massive construction site outside of Talca. Zach had remained to investigate that site with Junior Valdez.

"I appreciate why you two decided to return to Santiago," Deal said. "But I'm not sure leaving Zach alone in Talca was the right call. We don't know what or who we are dealing with down there. Do you know what he's planning to do?"

"Junior is going to show him the facility where his brother died," Michael replied. "We should be hearing from him any time."

Deal looked up and saw Daniela headed back to their table.

"Hold that thought."

When Daniela arrived, she poured the remainder of the wine into the four glasses on the table.

"Anything else I can offer?" she asked. "We have a small dining room downstairs run by a talented chef. I'd be happy to get you a table."

"Thanks, Daniela. I will take you up on dinner in a little while. You are an excellent host," Deal remarked as he sipped his wine.

"Daniela is working on a master's degree in hospitality management," Sarah added. "I'm not sure she shouldn't be teaching that class."

"That's very kind," Daniela replied.

As the hotel manager turned to leave, Deal said, "Daniela, I'm looking into partnering with a friend of mine down here to wholesale local wines to hotels and restaurants in Santiago. Could I ask you for a few minutes of your time later? Perhaps you would meet with my associates to discuss one hotel he mentioned as being the best."

"What hotel?" Daniela asked with a polite smile.

"The Pacifico."

# CHAPTER TWENTY-NINE

The Cause's Underground Complex

Zach tried to raise his hands to his head but found he couldn't seem to move his arms. And the glaring overhead light pierced his eyeballs every time he dared to lift his eyelids. Disoriented and in significant pain, Zach struggled to sit up but failed, which only added to his blossoming anxiety.

Remembering his training under Agent Deal and some alarming terrorist kidnapping scenarios the State Department required its diplomacy students to experience, Zach forced himself to relax and take several deep, measured breaths. Deal once told him that a human cannot be both calm and panicked at the same time. Thankfully, it worked.

Better able to think, Zach realized he was lying on a hard bed. Thick leather straps bound his hands and feet to steel bars. Above, he could see a smooth concrete ceiling. To his right, he found a solid wall. To his left, he could see the rest of his tiny cell and a thick metal door.

"Hey!" Zach shouted. "I have to pee!"

He waited a minute or two and then tried again.

"Hey! Sorry to be a problem. I don't want to mess up your nice dungeon, but I'm really serious here!"

Zach had no real hope anyone would show up. But there wasn't a reason not to try something. Then, to his surprise, the door opened, and a tall, slim, dark-haired woman stepped into the cell.

"Good afternoon, Zach. I'm Lieutenant Violette Ruiz."

Ruiz's matter-of-fact manner came as another surprise.

"Nice to meet you, Lieutenant," Zach replied, trying not to wince at the pain in his head that seemed to explode with every word. "I'd shake your hand, but you seem to have me at a disadvantage here."

"If I release the restraints, do you promise not to try and escape?" Ruiz asked, looking Zach in the eye.

"No," Zach answered.

Ruiz turned and motioned for two more men to enter the room. Both stood over 6 feet tall, wore the same black combat gear as the men who attacked Zach earlier, and carried matching submachine guns that hung across their chests on black leather straps.

"How about now?" Ruiz asked.

"Since you insist, I gladly agree to your terms," Zach replied.

One of the two guards unbuckled the heavy restraints, allowing Zach to sit up. He couldn't help putting both hands to the side of his head.

"God! What the hell did you drug me with?" Zach asked.

"Weren't drugs," the guard that released him said with a sneer. "Just a light tap from the butt of me rifle did the trick, boyo."

"East London?" Zach asked, recognizing the accent.

"None of your concern, mate. And if you keep acting like a wanker, you'll have more than a love tap," the guard snapped.

"That's enough. Wait outside," Ruiz ordered, dismissing the guards. "I'll be fine."

Ruiz leaned her back casually against the closed door and raised one leg so that the sole of her boot rested against the metal. Without saying anything, she crossed her arms and studied Zach closely.

Zach just sat on the bed rubbing his head. He couldn't help but notice Ruiz's tight-fitting military-style bodysuit and utility vest that masked what he imagined to be a stunning body.

As he openly admired Ruiz's shoulder-length hair and smokey eyes, the Argentinian finally chuckled.

"See anything you like?" Ruiz asked.

"Well, yeah. Except for our first date being in a prison cell. How about we get out of here?"

Ruiz had to admit that she admired Zach's completely inappropriate bravado.

"Maybe later. For now, why were you and Junior Valdez spying on the facility in the valley?"

Zach shrugged and told a half-truth.

"He likes to visit the spot where his brother died. Like visiting a gravesite, I suppose. He and I hit it off at his parent's bed and breakfast, and he asked me to go along. He didn't tell me we could get in this much trouble by just looking at a building," Zach lied. "How about I don't sue you guys for bashing in my skull and kidnapping me, and you let me go. We'll call it even."

"So, you are going to stick to the story that you and Michael King and Sarah Marshall are in Chile to teach English?"

Zach didn't blink an eye. "I'm not sure why you think that's a story. And I doubt Chile's government wants to create a problem with the United States by covering up the disappearance of one of its citizens."

"They probably wouldn't. But I don't give a shit," Ruiz answered. "You and your friends are here to spy on our space program."

"Well, lady. You got me. I'm just freakin' James Bond. Could you have someone bring around my Aston Martin? I left it outside."

Ruiz laughed. Then stepped forward and slapped Zach hard across the face. The blow triggered a lightning bolt of agony.

"You have a sharp tongue for someone in your position," Ruiz taunted.

The pain in Zach's head slowly subsided enough for him to form a response.

"Okay, Lieutenant, you have my attention. What do you want from me?"

She could just eliminate the American spy. But then she realized that while bringing Zach into the heart of the facility posed its own risk, it also presented her with an unexpected opportunity.

"Maybe something. Maybe nothing," Ruiz answered. "I don't think you are going to admit being employed by the CIA or one of your other overly intrusive government agencies. But keeping you here could invite a more, shall we say, direct intervention against this facility."

"I see," Zach said, not understanding where Ruiz was going with this at all.

"I don't think you do," Ruiz said, plucking a small walkie-talkie from her belt and stepping out of the room. "Wait here. I'll be right back."


"This is Ruiz. Where is Supervisor Manuel Mancha now?" Ruiz asked into the radio after shutting the cell door.

A moment passed while someone checked through the day's work schedules. "He and his crew are performing maintenance on the sled for launch vehicle TS3, ma'am. TS3 is currently stationed at assembly area 4."

Less than a minute later, Zach limped heavily as he followed Ruiz out the door and down several long, brightly lit hallways. Stepping through another door, Zach almost forgot about the throbbing pain in his head and ankle. His mouth opened slightly, and his eyes grew wide as he gawked at his surroundings. A massive tunnel, over thirty feet high, stretched out to his left and right. Lights embedded in the concrete walls provided near-daylight levels of illumination. But most astounding of all was the massive rocket lying on its side right in front of him.

"Wow," he said almost involuntarily.

"This is TS3. It is nearly complete. TS2 is complete and being loaded with its payload. Several others are in various stages of assembly."

"What does TS stand for? And what payload?" Zach asked, not actually expecting an answer.

"That's classified. But I wanted you to see this. Please take your time and study it as much as you like."

The rocket was perched on a metal frame mounted on what looked like a massive flatbed train car riding on tracks in the floor. Zach wasn't an engineer or overly mechanical, but he could infer that materials and parts arrived at the tunnel entrance Junior showed him. From there, these people assembled the rocket as it moved along the tunnel. When it was ready to launch, it emerged from the other end – high in the mountains.

Zach estimated the launch vehicle to be about 12 feet in diameter and approximately 150 to 200 feet long. Trying to ignore his painful ankle, he hobbled to the back of the rocket, where he counted seven bell-shaped exhaust nozzles and a complex web of tubes and pipes – what he knew must be engines. The other end lacked a nose cone or other structure. All he could see was the top of what he assumed to be a fuel tank. He tried to take in as much detail as possible, but he would need Bubba's expertise to fully understand what he was looking at. Just behind the massive spacecraft, several men in light blue jumpsuits knelt next to the tracks, running some kind of test on the rocket's mobile platform.

Zach noticed that the three workers studiously avoided looking in his and Ruiz's direction.

"What are those guys working on?" Zach asked Ruiz.

Ruiz shrugged and turned to the group of men.

"Who is in charge there?" she asked.

A tall dark-headed man stood and removed his cap before addressing Ruiz.

"Supervisor Mancha, ma'am. Sled bearing maintenance. We should be done in a few minutes."

Zach's eyes flew open when he saw the maintenance supervisor's face. The other man clearly noticed Zach's surprise and recognition but turned back to his task without reacting.

"Very well," Ruiz replied. "Carry on."

"What now?" Zach asked quickly, turning away.

"Now you go back to your nice dungeon, as you called it, while I decide what to do with you."

"Why did you show me this?" Zach asked, truly confused.

"I have my reasons."

Ruiz didn't notice the leader of the maintenance crew watching her march Zach back into the lockdown area.

# CHAPTER THIRTY

Junior had no idea what he would do when he got to Santiago. Michael and Sarah had not told him where they would be staying or the real reason why they left Talca. Then he remembered Zach's phone. Keeping his eyes on the busy highway, Junior reached for the glovebox. When he lifted the latch, the door swung open, and Zach's cell phone fell to the floorboard.

Although knowing the device would most likely be locked, Junior grabbed the phone and tried to swipe it open, hoping he could at least find Michael or Sarah's number. Nothing. More in frustration than anything, he pushed the buttons on the side of the phone several times. Except for displaying the time, the screen, as expected, remained stubbornly blank.

Junior shook his head at his own foolishness.

Then it rang.

Startled, Junior nearly dropped the device, juggling it with one hand before getting it under control.

"Hello?" Junior answered.

"Who is this? You are not the owner of this phone," a stern voice challenged.

"No. No. My name is Fernando Valdez, Jr. This is Zach Self's phone. He's in trouble. I'm trying to reach Michael King or his girlfriend, Sarah."

Junior didn't have any idea who he was talking to or how they knew he had tried to use Zach's phone. Suddenly, the screen came to life, and the picture of a large young man with scraggly brown hair and a jovial smile appeared on the screen.

"You are Junior Valdez. Zach, Michael, and Sarah were staying with your parents at their place in Talca. My name is Lawrence Adcock, but my friends, well everyone really, call me Bubba."

Junior remembered Michael talking about their friend and colleague with the unusual name of 'Bubba.'

"How did you...the phone...know..."

Bubba put up a hand.

"I designed that phone especially for my friends. Nobody can get it to work or pry information out of it without me knowing. If someone tries, I can zap the important parts of the insides remotely. Had to do that with Sarah's phone after someone swiped it in Santiago," Bubba explained.

Junior decided to pull off the highway so he could talk without crashing.

Bubba looked away from the screen for a second before continuing.

"It looks like you stopped on Highway 5 near Curico. Where is Zach? And why are you so far from Talca?" Bubba asked, his voice turning serious.

Junior didn't hesitate to describe how, after Michael and Sarah left for Santiago, he and Zach had tried to investigate the gigantic facility where his brother lost his life.

"Whoever attacked us had advanced military training. I know it sounds loco, but they seemed to appear from underground. We were alone and exposed. Zach fell as we tried to get back to my truck. He made me leave without him. I...there wasn't anything I could do."

"Fell?"

"Yes. Yes. Just fell. Not shot. He was alive the last time I saw him."

"So, you took off toward Santiago, hoping to find Michael and Sarah?" Bubba concluded.

"I didn't have Michael's phone number," Junior explained. "As I sit here now, I guess rushing off like that was foolish."

"Don't worry about it," Bubba said. "Let's get Michael and Sarah on this call, and we can discuss what to do next."

Junior waited in a dark parking lot while Bubba added Michael and Sarah. After Junior once again recounted the attack on him and Zach, Michael slammed his fist down on what looked like a table in a hotel room.

"Did you see what happened to Zach after he fell?" Sarah asked, placing a calming hand gently on Michael's arm.

"No. I'm sorry," Junior replied.

Michael took a deep breath and said, "Okay, Junior. There wasn't anything else you could do, and I really appreciate you trying to find us. But I think you should head home. Zach can take care of himself. I'm sorry I got you and your family mixed up in this."

Junior had to agree with Michael that he should return to Talca. But he was also more convinced than ever that whoever built the tunnels knew what happened to his brother and might be responsible for his death.

"I will go home," Junior said. "But my family and I stand ready to help you find Zach while we try to determine what really happened to Rodrigo."

## The Cause's Underground Complex

Zach couldn't sleep. Ruiz and her guards didn't give him so much as an aspirin, and the pain in his ankle kept him from finding a comfortable position.

A quiet knock on his door made the young American sit up. Someone had turned out the lights, leaving the cell in perfect darkness. Questioning whether he heard anything at all, Zach sat perfectly still, staring in the direction of the sound.

A second knock, not much louder than the first, confirmed that he wasn't hearing things.

Zach stood and followed the wall around to the door.

"Yes?" Zach said through the door. "Who is it?"

The observation window suddenly slid open, admitting a blinding bright light. When his vision cleared, Zach saw the same maintenance supervisor Ruiz had questioned earlier in the day. But his name wasn't Mancha.

"Good to see you, Rodrigo. Your family has been worried sick."

# CHAPTER THIRTY-ONE

Castillo Rojo Hotel
Santiago, Chile

After what turned out to be a truly excellent meal, Deal sat down with Michael and Sarah to explain why he needed them to continue building a relationship with Daniela. Well aware that they would rather rush back to Talca to help Zach, Deal ordered them to remain in Santiago. Until they knew a lot more about the tunnels and launch facility, any attempt to extract Zach by force was doomed.

Zach's two best friends knew that Deal was right, but they didn't have to like it.

With Michael and Sarah working on the Pacifico angle, Deal and Sims got a cab over to Jaime Garcia's apartment building. The ANI officer ushered the two FBI agents quickly inside.

"Thank you for coming. I have news you need to hear," Garcia began.

"You look flustered, Jaime," Sims said, intentionally using Garcia's first name.

"Ah, Stella," Jaime replied, "that is because I am. We have a problem. No. Let me correct that. We have two problems."

"Then you better fill us in," Deal said, taking a seat.

Garcia picked up a tablet computer and opened a messaging app.

"One of our operatives unexpectedly made contact just an hour ago. He reported that the next launch will take place in less than ten hours. 9 hours 55 minutes, to be exact," Garcia said, looking at his watch. But he had more news. "One of your investigators, Zach Self, has been kidnapped and is being held in the underground tunnel system by Cayo's people."

Deal studied Garcia for a moment but couldn't detect any hint of deceit in his voice or mannerisms. To the contrary, he appeared truly concerned about both the launch and Zach.

"You didn't tell us you had undercover people inside the launch facility," Deal said, not revealing that he already knew about Zach's capture.

"Until an hour ago, we didn't believe so either. Some time ago, after learning about a massive and apparently classified construction project on Cayo's land in the 7th District, I assigned several of my best people to apply for jobs at the site. Whether Cayo knew who they were or just got lucky, none came close to getting hired, much less being able to infiltrate the construction project. Except one," Garcia explained.

"Who?" Deal asked, confused.

"His real name is Rodrigo Valdez. He is a mechanical engineer. We haven't heard from him in months. The shell company building the facility reported an industrial accident, an explosion, that took five lives – including Valdez's. We are not sure what happened, but my best guess is that Valdez managed to change places with one of the men who died. If nothing else, it certainly helped him remain undetected. This was his first communication."

"How did he contact you? Can you confirm his identity or information?" Deal asked, not convinced.

"He's using a chatroom function installed on a handheld game of some kind," Garcia explained. "And he included a message to Agent Sims."

Sims leaned forward. "What did it say?"

"I shall just quote it verbatim," Garcia replied, a bit embarrassed. "It said, 'Bubba still has the hots for Stella.'"

"That's Zach, alright," Sims laughed, shaking her head. "I'll send Michael and Sarah a secure text. They should know."

"Okay. I agree. Only one of our team would use something that cryptic," Deal said. "Is there any way to confirm your guy's information about the next launch?"

"No. But Valdez risked his life to get us that information. I advise we act on it."

Fifteen minutes later, Deal had Bubba on a video call.

"What's your status?" Deal asked.

Instead of answering, Bubba pointed his phone's camera down at the yellow and black pressure suit that barely fit over his substantial beer belly.

"These guys are good, boss. They had our ride on standby status when I arrived, and we've been in final flight prep since you sent the secure message about the next launch window. I'm all suited up and about to squeeze my big butt into the back seat of this ER-2," Bubba said, pointing the camera at a huge white aircraft.

"Brief us on your plan," Deal ordered.

"Okay, boss. Hi, Stella," Bubba responded, waving at the camera. "Okay, this plane is like the grandchild of the old U-2 spy plane. Like the U-2, this little baby has a wingspan of 104 feet, while the fuselage is only 67 feet long. This configuration gives the plane the ability to fly in the ultra-thin atmosphere above 65,000 feet. Usually, NASA uses this to test satellite cameras and sensors before they spend the big bucks shooting them into space. Tonight, we'll be using some of those cameras and other really cool sensors to take a very close look at this rocket launch."

"This flight will not cross into Chile, will it?" Garcia asked. "Our Air Force has been ordered to intercept any unauthorized aircraft."

Bubba laughed. "That won't be a problem. I'll be able to collect all the data I need, including detailed photos of the launch vehicle from well off the coast of Argentina. I've looked at our flight plan, and after we leave Florida, we won't be over land at all until we return."

"You have 9 hours, 33 minutes until launch," Deal noted. "Can you make it in time?"

"We're making final preparations now," Bubba said. "We'll be in position at least 30 minutes ahead of time."

"That's your genius aerospace scientist?" Garcia asked skeptically when the call ended.

"He may drink too much beer, care too much about football, and drive a pickup truck in the city, but he's the smartest person I've ever known," Deal replied.


9 hours thirty minutes later


"How are you doing back there, Bubba?" NASA pilot Colonel Ron Massey asked over the internal intercom of the ER2.

Behind the pilot in the tiny passenger cockpit, Bubba pressed the intercom button.

"I feel like a big, fat sardine jammed into a tin can. And that turbulence over the Gulf of Mexico challenged my ability to keep my dinner down," Bubba replied. "But I'm good to go now, and I've reprogrammed the cameras and sensors. We'll collect all the information we need to study the launch vehicle in excruciating detail."

A few minutes later, Massey's voice came back over the intercom.

"We're at our cruising altitude of 65,000 feet, so feel free to use your large electronic devices. I'm going to leave the fasten seatbelt sign on in case we encounter any unexpected turbulence. I'd like to say the flight attendants will be serving drinks soon, but there aren't any," Massey quipped.

"Ha, ha. Very funny," Bubba responded. "Are we on schedule?"

"Right on time. If your information is correct, we should be picking up the launch out your left window in three minutes and thirty seconds."

Bubba entered a series of commands into his instruments, double-checked every setting, and sat back with a set of binoculars to watch for the rocket to appear. He would study the close-up footage captured by the high-tech surveillance cameras and sensors mounted in the plane's nose while they returned to Florida and later back at his laboratory. As the rocket climbed higher and higher into the atmosphere, the aircraft's infrared, high-definition visible light, high-speed video, and several highly classified instruments would capture enough images and data to present Bubba with a complete picture of the rocket and its capabilities. The binoculars would just confirm when the rocket left the ground and give Bubba a cool view of a space launch from their unique vantage point in the stratosphere.

Massey's voice came over the intercom. "Launch scheduled in 15 seconds. If it takes place on time, the vehicle will clear the cloud cover in approximately 20 seconds. We should pick it up visually 5 seconds after that."

Bubba looked out his small window and brought the binoculars to his eyes. He had to remember to look down. From 65,000 feet, he could see the curvature of the Earth and the darkness of outer space that seemed to loom in the distance.

"Visual contact. Ten degrees off the left wing," Massey reported in a near-emotionless monotone.

Bubba swung his binoculars forward and immediately picked up the rocket's fiery plume and trailing engine exhaust. The spacecraft looked like a bright orange dot moving upward in a gentle arc.

Bubba turned to his instruments and pulled up a map overlaid with the vehicle's trajectory. After overflying Argentina, it cleared the South American coast and was now heading northeast over the Atlantic Ocean. Bubba would later calculate the precise orbit of whatever payload it carried, but he could already see this launch looked similar, if not identical, to the one that took place less than a week before.

Bubba tracked the rocket as it climbed past their altitude. A moment later, he could see the orange dot disappear for a moment, followed by a bright flare.

"Staging," Bubba said. "Looks like we have everything we can get. Let's go home."

Bubba sat back and tried to relax for the rest of his exclusive flight high above the Earth. He would have enjoyed it more if he could stretch his legs or even move them around more than an inch or two to either side.

Suddenly, Bubba felt a disturbing jolt, accompanied by a single loud *POP* from somewhere to his right. Before he could even turn his head, the aircraft lurched alarmingly in that direction, throwing Bubba against the opposite side of the tiny cockpit.

"Close your helmet!" Massey shouted over the intercom. "Prepare to eject."

# CHAPTER THIRTY-TWO

Bubba's hands shook as he pulled the visor down on his helmet and made sure it locked even as he felt the aircraft rolling over on its right wing. Bubba looked down between his legs and found the yellow and black striped strap that would trigger his ejection seat.

Before they left Florida, Massey had pointed at the strap and said, "Don't touch that. But if you hear me say, 'EJECT, EJECT, EJECT,' you pull that thing up hard. If you wait even one second, you'll be looking at my ass because I'll be gone."

Bubba had no illusions about his chances if they had to eject. Even if his ejection seat and parachute worked perfectly, the extreme cold could kill him in less than a minute. If his emergency oxygen system failed, he would suffocate. And if he made it all the way back to Earth, he would be all alone in the middle of the Atlantic Ocean.

Bubba did his best to push such thoughts aside. All he could do was hold on, try not to vomit, and let Massey fly the damaged aircraft.

After several minutes of pure terror, the plane seemed to come back under control, and he heard Massey's voice over the intercom.

"Well, that was interesting. Are you okay back there?"

"All good," Bubba replied, trying to match Massey's casual tone – and failing. "What happened?"

"Best I can tell, something hit the right wing. Can you see the damage?"

Bubba turned and examined as much of the long, thin wing as he could see from his seat. "Not from this angle. But we are definitely leaking. Something must have punctured the wing and internal fuel cell. I can see liquid escaping from the top of the wing and from somewhere underneath. It's like something either shot up through the wing or, less likely, came from above."

"Alright. We'll have to put our theories on hold. I've got control of everything except the right secondary aileron. Whatever it was must have severed the hydraulic lines. We have just enough fuel to make it back to the cape. But we'll have to slow way down."

"I'd complain about the lack of space back here in economy class, but right now, I'm just thrilled to still be sitting inside the airplane and, you know, breathing."

Far below, sixteen-year-old Alejandro Alfero and several of his friends chose to spend the afternoon drinking beer and lighting up some local island weed instead of attending class. Nobody spent much time at the secluded beach on Puerto Rico's south shore, and that day was no different. The group of friends had just planted their cheap Styrofoam cooler in the sand when, without any warning, a column of water and steam a quarter mile offshore blasted hundreds, maybe even thousands, of feet into the air.

The terrified youngsters spun on their heels, raced across the beach, and plunged into the thick jungle. As they ran, great floods of seawater fell through the canopy, soaking them to the bone. Just seconds later, a ten-foot-tall wave crested just offshore before crashing into the sand, washing away their precious stash.

"What was that?" one of the boys shouted breathlessly as they dashed through the undergrowth. "Maybe an old bomb? Like from a war or something?"

Neither Alejandro nor any of the other boys had a clue, and they weren't going to hang around to find out.

But two fishermen who witnessed the same event from almost a mile away radioed the Coast Guard station and reported the odd explosion.

Several torturous hours later, Massey eased the aircraft onto the long runway originally built for the space shuttle. The extremely long wingspan of the ER-2 provided immense lift, allowing the plane to fly high in the atmosphere. But they also made it difficult to land. Even after Massey cut the power completely, Bubba could feel the plane fighting to stay in the air.

When they finally rolled to a stop, special vehicles surrounded the plane, opened the sealed canopy, and pulled Massey and Bubba out of the cockpit. Several men had to hold Bubba upright while blood rushed back into his legs. When he could walk on his own again, he found the pilot looking up at the right wing.

"I'll be damned," Bubba remarked.

"Agreed," Massey said. "What do you think could hit us at 65,000 feet and make a perfectly round hole like that?"

"No idea," Bubba replied. "But here's another brain twister – what could shoot at us at that altitude *from above?*"

"What? Nothing!" Massey responded. "That's just impossible."

"Well, if you look carefully, you can see the metal pushed outward ever so slightly under the wing. I have no doubt that on the top side, we'll see a convex puncture," Bubba concluded.

Massey just shook his head and had to accept the only logical conclusion.

"Then it came from space."

# CHAPTER THIRTY-THREE

The Cause's Underground Complex

At their first encounter, Zach thought he had seen a ghost. Rodrigo Valdez was supposed to be dead. But then he appeared standing in front of Zach's cell door, unquestionably alive and full of questions.

Zach quickly explained how he and Junior had been attacked and how Junior had escaped. He didn't immediately reveal why he was investigating the tunnels or that he worked with the FBI. But Rodrigo could put two and two together. An American snooping around the remote facility after the first rocket launch had to be attached to one of their intelligence agencies. Zach didn't try to convince him otherwise.

Rodrigo asked Zach for something he could use to prove his identity, and Zach responded with a joke about Bubba and Agent Sims.

Then, the Chilean disappeared.

That was several hours ago, or as close as Zach could estimate without a watch, a clock, or a view outside. He couldn't sleep, so he sat on the cot until the lights came back on, and a plate of cold scrambled eggs slid through a slit at the bottom of the door.

Time seemed to stand still. Other than a soft humming noise from a single vent high above his head, very little sound penetrated the cell's thick walls. After what seemed like hours, Zach started wishing they would turn off the brilliant overhead lights that bore relentlessly into his skull. Every so often, he would stand and hobble around the cell, testing his ankle. It hurt like hell but wasn't broken.

The day dragged on hour after hour. Nobody even opened the window to see if he was alive. Without the sound of a human voice or the sight of a blue sky, Zach began to wonder about that himself. When the narrow slit opened again, and a tray with three small tortillas and a tablespoon of beans appeared, Zach didn't know if this was supposed to be lunch or dinner. He got his answer a few minutes after eating when the cell went black.

The darkness and stillness weighed on Zach's psyche. He had no sense of time, and he had to fight becoming completely disoriented. So, he didn't immediately believe his ears when he heard the door unlock and open.

Zach stood and tried to see the face of whoever opened the door, but the backlight from the hall obscured any detail.

"We have to go."

"Rodrigo?" Zach asked.

"Yes, put these on and come now. We have only a short time while the entire complex is busy with the second launch."

Zach pulled on a set of light blue coveralls and hardhat, matching Rodrigo's work outfit.

"Okay, not my style, but it's your party," Zach agreed. "Let's go."

Rodrigo led Zach quickly through the security lockdown hall, pausing at the door leading into the main tunnel where Zach had seen the rocket – what was it? A day ago? Two?

"There are cameras everywhere," Rodrigo warned. "So, keep your head down and act like you're reading this."

Zach took a clipboard from Rodrigo, noting it held only a blank sheet of paper.

Without further instructions, Rodrigo walked into the main tunnel with Zach close behind. A group of workers stood near the top of the rocket that Zach remembered Ruiz calling TS3. Rodrigo walked purposefully but casually in the opposite direction.

"What are those guys doing?" Zach asked, already guessing the answer.

"Payload and nose flaring installation," Rodrigo replied.

"What's the payload?" Zach asked.

"Not now. Just keep your pace up and your head down."

They walked along the side of the transport tracks for almost a hundred yards. Zach tried not to limp while occasionally flipping the paper on his clipboard over as if studying its nonexistent information.

"Here," Rodrigo said, stopping at a red-striped door marked 'Emergency Exit' in English and Spanish. "We are on Level 1. Take the stairs on the other side of this door up to Level 8. You'll find an access hatch up there. It's camouflaged from the outside. Unlock it by spinning the wheel on the door counterclockwise. An alarm will sound when you push the door open. Get out and head downhill. Move fast and use this as soon as you have a signal."

Rodrigo pushed a cell phone into Zach's hand.

"What about you?" Zach asked.

"I'll be fine. Tell my family I love them. Maybe I'll see them again. But right now, I have a job to do. Listen, this is important. Tell whoever you are working for that the fourth launch cannot happen. Do not forget. It *cannot* happen. Now go!" Rodrigo said, physically pushing Zach through the door and closing it.

Zach stood in an open stairwell. The metal stairs that rose high above his head reminded him of an old-fashioned fire escape. Above, he could see several yellow doors, each marked with a number corresponding to the level they accessed.

Following Rodrigo's instructions, Zach started climbing using the handrails to relieve the weight he had to put on his injured leg and tried to keep from thinking about what would happen if one of the black-clad soldiers appeared on the stairs above him.

Zach kept himself in excellent shape. If he hadn't been injured, scrambling up the escape stairs wouldn't have caused him to even breathe hard. But getting up over sixteen flights on what he hoped was only a badly sprained ankle quickly became excruciating. As he neared the Level 8 platform, Zach found he had to hop up the stairs one at a time.

Exhausted, Zach rested his leg and caught his breath for a minute before finding the locking wheel mounted in the center of the door Rodrigo had described. He could see how turning the wheel would withdraw heavy metal bars that kept the door solidly locked from the inside. He could also see the armored alarm system control box mounted directly over the entryway.

Zach had no idea what he would find on the other side. Already sweating and in significant pain, he didn't look forward to what would happen next. But as he considered the alternative – going crazy in a windowless cell, or worse, he reached up and spun the wheel hard to the left and pushed.

# CHAPTER THIRTY-FOUR

A blaring alarm so loud Zach thought the entire country could hear it announced his escape.

Once outside, a cold wind cut straight through his blue jumpsuit while he took a moment to get his bearings. He found himself standing on a narrow but smooth path next to a rock wall. To his relief, it appeared the track was used often enough to remain open and free of obstacles. Behind him, massive peaks rose into the sky. Far below, he could see where the mountains ended, and the vast central valley stretched out into the distance.

Not wasting any more time, Zach began his painful descent down the path at the best pace he could manage. He leaned on boulders for support and put as much weight as he could stand on his bad leg while keeping an eye out for a large stick or anything he could use as a crutch or cane. But the arid mountains offered only rocks, rocks, and more rocks.

Zach moved with a single-minded purpose – to get as far away from the tunnels as possible. He had no idea why the Chileans had constructed such a massive complex high in the mountains other than to keep a fully functional missile manufacturing plant away from the eyes of the rest of the world. He didn't need to rely on his training or be an expert on foreign policy to know that countries tended to hide their most secret and dangerous weapons underground.

Somehow, Lieutenant Ruiz knew the United States sent him to investigate the rocket launches. Then why, he wondered, had she taken him out of his cell to openly display the rocket, tunnel, and assembly area? It didn't make sense.

The thought brought him to a dead stop. He looked behind him and listened carefully. He expected to hear the thump of helicopter blades echoing across the mountains or vehicles of some sort racing down the trail. Nothing. He couldn't detect any sign of pursuit. He might have had a head start, but as slowly as he traveled on an injured ankle, a determined contingent of those security soldiers would surely have caught up to him in the hour he had been on foot.

*Why not?*

"Where is he now?" Ruiz asked, standing over one of the consoles in the underground complex's Operations Center.

The technician typed in a few commands. A moment later, a window opened, showing a live shot of Zach sitting on a rock, rubbing his ankle and looking around.

"Excellent," Ruiz said. "I want him left alone."

"The drone will keep a visual on him for another hour. After that, the nano-sized trackers he ingested will take over," the tech noted, pointing to a red pin that marked Zach's exact location on a map.

"Good. I want hourly updates. If he stops or meets anyone, I want to be informed immediately," Ruiz ordered.

Five minutes later, Ruiz sat in Dave Knox's office sipping a glass of expensive tequila.

"You're taking a big chance letting that kid walk away," Dave said, lifting his heavy crystal tumbler to his lips.

"You knew when you built this facility and started shooting things into space that other countries would want to know what's going on," Ruiz responded. "Zachary Self is working for the Americans – as are Michael King and Sarah Marshall. We got lucky to eliminate the FBI's top investigators when it comes to weapons of mass destruction, Frank Deal and Stella Sims, just after they entered the country. We need to know what the other Americans are doing and whether they have more people in Chile. Mr. Self will lead us to the rest of his accomplices."

"Are the nano trackers I designed working properly?" Dave asked, already knowing the answer.

"Just like you said. A truly ingenious design innovation, programming them to seek out cellular or WIFI signals."

Dave just nodded. "One of my better inventions, if I do say so myself. Without using built-in radio transmitters like other tracking hardware, they are undetectable by usual methods of sweeping for such devices. Even X-rays would be useless because of their microscopic size. And, maybe best of all, they can't be removed."

"How long will they stay active?" Ruiz asked.

"They will relay Mr. Self's position for about seven days before the body slowly rejects them. And just how does he think he managed to escape?" Knox asked. "You didn't just open the door and let him run away."

"No. He thinks that he was helped by Junior Valdez's brother, Rodrigo Valdez."

"Rodrigo Valdez? That name sounds familiar."

"I looked him up. Rodrigo Valdez was one of the men killed during the blasting operation. Another one of our men looks just like Valdez, Manuel Mancha. I took Zach on a short tour of the rocket assembly area, making sure he saw Mancha. I immediately knew he believed Manuel was Rodrigo. So, I ordered Manuel to help Zach with his 'escape,'" Ruiz explained. "And it went just as planned. Manuel turned out to be a pretty good actor."

Zach shivered as the sun fell below the coastal mountains far to the west. The hours had passed slowly, and the miles even slower as he limped down the trail. He had stopped looking over his shoulder hours before. And he still didn't understand why the alarm had not triggered a full-scale hunt. But there had to be a reason – something to do with why Ruiz showed him the rocket and facilities.

For the hundredth time, he checked the phone Rodrigo had given him. Finally, he could see one bar of cell service.

One was all he needed.

# CHAPTER THIRTY-FIVE

Thirty minutes later, Zach sat huddled under the clear plastic roof of a remote bus stop. His lightweight jumpsuit provided almost no protection from the cold wind rushing down from the mountain passes. He shivered, blew on his hands, and periodically stood long enough to wave his arms around, trying to warm up.

When he heard the pounding beat of an approaching helicopter, Zach stood and looked into the northern sky. Sure enough, he could see an aircraft headed in his direction. He didn't worry about where the chopper could land – the graffiti-covered old bus stop seemed to be the only structure built by humans as far as the eye could see. And he hadn't seen a car, much less a bus, in the almost two hours since finally being able to contact Michael.

The helicopter flew directly over Zach's head before swinging around and landing in the vast open fields on the other side of the road. Michael and Sarah immediately jumped out of the wide side door and ran to their friend's side.

"Wow. Am I happy to see you guys," Zach exclaimed with a wide smile.

"Yeah, nice jumpsuit. The color really sets off your eyes," Michael kidded.

Sarah smacked Michael on his arm before embracing Zach in a warm hug.

"Can you make it to the helicopter?" she asked.

"If I can lean on you the whole way," Zach answered, giving Michael a smug look.

"Uh, no way," Michael objected, knowing his best friend was joking. "You can lean on me."

"Where are we going?" Zach asked. "I'd like to get back to Talca and talk to Junior and his parents."

"No can do right now, buddy. Deal wants us all in Santiago to regroup," Michael said as he helped Zach limp over to the helicopter.

"Where did you get the ride?" Zach asked. "Deal's too cheap to charter a helicopter just for me."

"Deal and Sims made some new friends."

"Are any of them hot?" Zach asked.

Sarah laughed out loud, glad to see Zach's little adventure hadn't dampened his spirits.

Two hours later, Zach sat on the comfortable couch across from the same chairs Deal and Sims had used earlier that night. His foot, now wrapped in Ace bandages and covered with an ice pack, rested on several pillows. Earlier, a doctor had confirmed the ankle was badly sprained but not broken.

"This is nice," Zach said to Michael and Sarah, who had just returned from the bar with three glasses of wine. "My last accommodations sucked."

"We have a nice room for you upstairs. But don't get used to it. Starting tomorrow, we're back on the streets," Michael replied. "You've had a long day, but we still need to talk."

Zach sat up. "Yeah. No problem. What's the plan? Where are we with this thing?"

Michael took a few minutes to fill Zach in on how Agents Deal and Sims made it into Santiago and their suspicions about the Pacifico Hotel.

"Hold on a second," Michael said, seeing someone enter the bar. "Stay here and just go with the flow."

Sarah stood and started to walk toward the front of the bar with Michael but first turned to Zach and pointed a finger at his face.

"You. Behave yourself."

Zach gave a hurt look. "What?"

Michael laughed. "Just do what she says. You'll see."

A moment later, Sarah returned with a tall, slim girl with luxurious black hair and dark eyes, which flashed around the room before falling on Zach.

For once, Zach couldn't produce one of his patented opening lines. The girl who just walked in had struck him dumb.

"Daniela," Sarah said cheerfully, "this is our friend Zach Self. He's part of Mr. Darrow's company."

Daniela walked confidently over to Zach and stuck out her hand. "You're hurt?"

"Stupid accident. No big deal. I sprained my ankle stepping off a curb," Zach explained, taking Daniela's hand, his voice betraying uncharacteristic nerves. "Sorry, uh, nice to meet you, Daniela."

Michael and Sarah gave each other a surreptitious look. They had never heard Zach stumble over his words in the presence of a beautiful girl. Or anyone, for that matter.

"Daniela manages the Castillo Rojo," Sarah explained.

She might as well have been speaking in Klingon. Zach couldn't take his eyes off the sultry young hotel manager – or let go of her hand.

Daniela flashed a brilliant smile. "I'd be happy to bring us all another glass of wine. But I'll need both hands."

"Oh, sorry," Zach said, dropping her hand like it suddenly burned his skin.

"No worries," Daniela responded with a vivacious smile.

When Daniela had walked out of earshot, Sarah couldn't help herself anymore.

"What is wrong with you?" she asked. "You're acting like you've never talked to a girl before."

Zach didn't have time to answer. Daniela returned with a bottle of wine and four glasses. After performing the usual ritual of opening the bottle, Sarah took the lead and got down to business.

"Like Mr. Darrow said, his company is looking to expand into the wholesale wine market here in Santiago. We are, for lack of a better term, his advance sales team. We check out an area that looks promising, make contacts, and sort of pry open the door to a new market. We aren't familiar with the high-end hotels in the city and were wondering if we could hire you as a consultant."

Daniela sat back with her wine.

"Interesting. What do you think of this wine?" she asked.

Sarah, Michael, and Zach all took a sip.

"Not bad," Michael commented, holding the wine up to the bar's lights. "Is it from this area?"

"Yes, it is. Can you tell anything else about it?" Daniela asked, turning to Zach.

Zach looked back at Daniela, and two thoughts popped into his head. First, Daniela's mere presence took his breath away. Second, she was testing them.

"My friend Michael's famously poor palate never fails. This wine ghastly," he answered.

"Yes, it is," Daniela agreed. "This bottle came from a case left outside on a hot day by accident. It's cooked. In other words, it got too hot and died. Now, maybe you better tell me why you are here. I like all of you, and Zach here is cute in a wide-eyed, dopey American sort of way, but I don't like being deceived."

Sarah, Michael, and Zach exchanged glances, silently communicating the same question – *should we tell her?*

The three friends had known each other for years, so they didn't need to openly discuss the answer.

Zach sat up a little higher on the couch and looked Daniela in the eye.

"We're with the FBI and in your country trying to find out the purpose of the surprise rocket launches. From what we have learned so far, the answer to that question isn't good."

They didn't yet know just how bad.

# CHAPTER THIRTY-SIX



Bubba stood next to a bright orange frame specifically designed to transport and maintain one of the ER-2 aircraft's immense wings. Shortly after they landed the damaged aircraft, NASA engineers removed the over 50-foot-long right wing and mounted it on the service frame so they could inspect and repair the damage.

For several hours after returning, Bubba had analyzed the footage and other data he and Colonel Massey recorded of the launch vehicle as it lifted off from the Chilean Andes. What he found didn't surprise him in the least. The rocket itself was a conventional design. Two stages of powered flight using several liquid-fueled engines. Further analysis showed that the rocket's first stage used seven engines identical to those designed and currently used by one of the private space companies owned by eccentric billionaires. Whoever had designed the Chilean launch vehicle had opted to purchase off-the-shelf, well-proven rocket engines.

Bubba had reported his initial findings about the rocket to Deal hours ago. Since then, he had been engrossed with examining the ER-2's wing and trying to determine what could have punched a hole straight through it while they were traveling 500 mph 65,000 feet above the ground.

NASA's engineers and scientists theorized they had been hit by a meteor even though no aircraft in the history of aviation had ever recorded such an event. Bubba wouldn't write off the incident that quickly. Instead, he took minute samples of the wing's skin and interior components. Using several instruments, including an electron scanning microscope, Bubba looked to see if kinetic friction between the object and the aircraft had transferred microscopic amounts of material to the plane's wing. What he found snuffed out the meteor theory.

Bubba knew that several countries had anti-aircraft missiles that could have reached their altitude. But he was convinced that whatever hit them came from above and was not fired or launched from the ground. Plus, the two neat holes punched in the wing measured exactly 100 millimeters, or 3.937 inches, across – far too small to be an air-to-air missile of any kind.

The projectile had sliced through the wing's skin, support structures, hydraulic lines, and fuel cell as if they didn't exist. Bubba realized the object must have been moving at an extreme velocity to make such a tidy wound.

Next, the aerospace engineer measured the angle at which the projectile entered the wing. As he predicted, the shot came in from several degrees to the left and slightly ahead of the plane. Bubba traced the projectile's path back to its point of origin using their precise position at impact, airspeed, altitude, and heading. Those calculations led to even more questions.

Next, following the object's path after it punctured the wing, Bubba estimated where the projectile would have impacted – if it had survived passing through the atmosphere. A quick search of police, fire department, Coast Guard, and aviation reports around the island of Puerto Rico revealed an anomalous explosion just offshore.

The results of his investigation turned his stomach to ice.

Bubba picked up his phone and called Deal's number.

"We have a big, big problem, boss," Bubba said as soon as Deal answered.

Bubba could hear one of Agent Deal's patented grunts of exasperation.

"Just tell me what you found," the gruff FBI agent ordered.

"Have you ever heard of the Rods from God?" Bubba asked.

"Yes, of course," Deal answered. "Some hair-brained idea from the 60s. The Air Force wanted to put telephone pole sized titanium rods into orbit and drop them from space onto a target. The project never got off the ground, so to speak."

"Correct," Bubba replied. "But the idea was sound. If you could get that much material into orbit and drop it precisely, the kinetic energy generated would annihilate most of a city just from the speed at which the titanium rod hit the Earth – around 17,000 miles per hour. Most of the destruction of an atom bomb without the messy radiation."

"Yeah, great. We both already know that. Now, tell me something I *don't* know," Deal said, trying not to sound as annoyed as he felt.

"Sure. Okay. I was just getting to that. Our plane was unquestionably struck by a manufactured sphere of titanium alloy."

"A what? What are you trying to tell me, Bubba?" Deal demanded.

"Someone took a shot at our very nice airplane from space and managed to put a hole in one wing as we flew along at over 500 miles per hour twelve miles above the Earth's surface," Bubba responded, his voice betraying admiration for the technical feat despite the fact the shot almost ended his life.

Deal had vast experience with all types of advanced weapons, but a space-launched hyper-accurate, for lack of a better word, cannonball was a whole new threat.

"Okay. So, go ahead with the really bad news," Deal responded in the emotionless, all-business tone he used when a situation took a hard turn toward insane.

"Yeah. It's not good. So, this technology isn't designed to take out a city. It's more targeted. I've run the numbers, and a sphere of titanium that size would weigh right at 4 pounds. If it hit the ground at 17,000 miles per hour, it would unleash enough kinetic energy to take down a small skyscraper. The damage would be severe, and we would have no early warning. Our first indication of an attack like that would be when something on the ground simply ceased to exist. Plus, whoever designed this weapon has worked out the orbital dynamics and other variables with such precision that they can target something as small as an aircraft wing."

Deal ran a hand over his close-cut gray hair. The implications of such a weapon hanging over the Earth suddenly made his skin crawl.

"What else do you have?" Deal asked.

"I'm sure you'd like to know where the one that hit us came from," Bubba stated.

"Our new constellation of Chilean satellites," Deal answered. "I suppose you could supply me with the math that would explain how satellites orbiting thousands of miles away could discharge such a thing and have it hit a moving target. But I'll just let you work out those calculations."

"I already did," Bubba replied. "And there's a simple answer. They couldn't. The projectile made several powered maneuvers before descending through the atmosphere. In other words, the titanium sphere is not just a solid dumb ball of metal. It's capable of powered maneuvers in space. Someone flew it into our plane. I don't have the full picture yet. But from everything I've seen so far, this could be bad. Like worse than a stolen nuke bad. A lot worse."

# CHAPTER THIRTY-SEVEN

Castillo Rojo Hotel
Santiago, Chile

Daniela sat back in her chair and held up her wine glass to the fading light coming through the expanse of windows that overlooked the bustling street below. She took her time digesting what the three Americans had just told her. She wanted to dismiss everything they said, and, truth be told, she probably should have. However, working as the daytime manager of a small boutique hotel, while rewarding, did not offer much excitement. And the appearance of three people her own age claiming they worked for the American FBI intrigued her enough not to throw them out on the street. At least not yet.

And she couldn't help being incredibly attracted to Zach's good looks and near overwhelming charm.

"Let us say for a moment I believe you," Daniela began. "You want me to help you investigate the Pacifico Hotel? What does that mean? And more importantly, why?"

Daniela could tell Zach had a lot of confidence around women, but she could also sense that he had dropped whatever banter and persona he usually relied on to impress the opposite sex. Now, his eyes seemed to search hers, looking for any glimmer of hope that she might be attracted to him. She might have used Zach's interest in her to her advantage, except that she wanted to believe everything he said just to keep him nearby.

"Yeah, I know that's a big pile of information to drop on you just like that," Zach said. "But it's really important we figure out what's going on. Like we said, President Cayo has kept Chile's apparent space program hidden from the world and even his own people. He couldn't do this thing alone, and we have good information that whoever is helping him or, maybe, whoever he is working for, has some connection to the Pacifico. Yes, we are posing as wine buyers from Canada. And, as you found out, some of us have only a pedestrian knowledge about wine."

"Hey!" Michael objected. "Who are you calling 'pedestrian'?"

Sarah laughed and kissed Michael's cheek. "Don't worry. You're mostly not pedestrian. At least with some important things."

"Well, I know this wine is better than the first one," Michael said with a confident smirk before taking a sip from his glass of the new bottle Daniela had opened.

"Anyway," Zach continued. "You have two things we could really use – actual knowledge of the local wines and hotels."

Daniela didn't respond immediately. Her instincts told her she could trust Zach, Sarah, and Michael. And only very poor spies would so openly reveal their plans. But she wouldn't risk being branded a traitor, even for someone as appealing as Zach Self.

"Sorry, guys," Daniela said. "I like you all, but I'm no spy and certainly no secret agent."

Sarah set down her glass, plucked Michael's cell phone out of his hand, and made a call. After a short, hushed conversation, she turned back to Daniela.

"Can you hang out with us a while longer?" she asked. "There's someone who wants to meet with us and answer any questions you have."

"I'm off work, and we haven't finished our glasses," Daniela replied, looking at Zach. "It's late, but I don't mind sitting a while longer."

Less than 15 minutes later, Garcia pulled a chair up to the little group.

"I'm so pleased to meet you, Ms. Montego. My name is Major Jaime Garcia of the ANI. You know of us?" Garcia asked, presenting his official identification.

"Everyone knows the ANI. Am I in some kind of trouble?" Daniela asked with an understandable amount of trepidation.

"No. No. Not at all," Garcia assured her. "I'm only here to explain why the FBI is in our country and to request your help. There is no requirement whatsoever for you to do so. And if that's your decision, we only ask you not to discuss what you've been told so far. But I can assure you that you would be helping your country if you decide to work with us."

Daniela looked relieved.

"I will leave you with this," Garcia added, standing. "I have only worked with this team for a short time, but they have proven themselves to be professional, trustworthy, and competent. You will be in good hands."

Garcia shook Daniela's hand and turned and walked away without waiting for an answer.

Daniela turned back to Zach, Michael, and Sarah.

"Wow," she exclaimed quietly, her dark eyes wide open. "Did that just happen? Did the ANI just ask for my help?"

Zach gave Daniela a knowing smile. "Exciting, isn't it?"

Daniela stood and walked over to the couch where Zach lounged.

"Move over," Daniela said, gently lifting Zach's injured leg, sitting down, and placing it on her lap. "I'm in. What do we do first."

"That's awesome!" Sarah exclaimed. "I guess tell us whatever you know about the Pacifico."

With one hand resting protectively on Zach's leg and the other holding her wine glass, the hotel manager gathered her thoughts.

"The Pacifico Hotel has been a fixture here in Santiago for many decades. It stands high on the side of the mountains just to the west of the city. You can see it from almost anywhere in Santiago. It is no exaggeration to say that it is the finest hotel in Chile, if not all of South America. I once applied for a job there and studied everything about the hotel I could find. I tried several times to get an interview, but I had no luck."

Michael asked, "So, it's a nice place. Let's start with its guests. What do you know about who stays there? Rich people?"

Daniela chuckled. "Oh, yes, Michael. Very, very rich people indeed. And only very, very rich people. The grounds, hotel, and restaurant are closed to the public and protected by a security force made up of heavily armed ex-military guards. To say the Pacifico is exclusive would be a gross understatement. One does not look it up on the internet and make a reservation. Oh no, one of the owners must invite you. If you are lucky and wealthy enough to receive such an invitation, you are treated better than royalty."

"Really?" Zach asked.

"Yes," Daniela answered, favoring Zach with a vivacious smile and topping off his glass of wine. "Service there makes our little hotel look quite quaint."

"I'd like to meet these owners, but I wouldn't change places with any of them right now," Zach responded, obviously enjoying Daniela's attention.

"I bet you wouldn't, buddy." Michael kidded.

"Behave yourself," Sarah said, rolling her eyes. "Go on, Daniela."

"Yes, well, most guests are picked up at the airport and flown to a helipad on the roof in the hotel's private helicopter. The staff greets the guests like arriving heads of state and escorts them to their suites, which are uniquely decorated by different world-famous interior designers. There is a magnificent three-star restaurant that is only for guests. A butler and two other staff are assigned to each suite, and a personal chef is on duty at all hours of the day or night. The staff fulfills anything a guest wants, from tickets to concerts or sporting events to trips to Chile's beautiful coast, mountains, or deserts. The level of service is unequaled anywhere in the world."

"Sounds nice," Zach remarked. "I can't believe they didn't hire you on the spot."

Daniela smiled at Zach. "You're sweet, but now I know I had very little chance of ever getting hired. Later, one of the restaurant's line cooks told me that most employees are the sons and daughters of former workers. Apparently, you have to be born into the Pacifico family or have very close ties to one of their people to get a job there."

Michael leaned forward and poured himself another splash of red wine. "So, do you happen to still know this guy?"

Daniela tensed just enough for Zach to notice.

"What is it?"

The Chilean girl hesitated a moment before admitting she had dated the employee for a short time.

"Lucky guy," Zach responded, causing Daniela to blush just a bit.

"Are you still in touch with him?" Sarah asked, meaning whether Daniela and the Pacifico employee had parted on good terms.

"Oh, yes," Daniela answered. "We have several mutual friends, and we run into one another when everyone goes out to clubs and such. He has been dating another girl for some time."

"Do you think there's any chance he would help us take a look around the Pacifico or get us a meeting with whoever buys the wine or whatever?" Michael asked.

Daniela thought for a minute. "Maybe. He once took me there. He showed me the restaurant and pool area. I think he wanted to impress me. But what would you be looking for inside?"

"People who launch suspicious rockets into space," Zach replied.

# CHAPTER THIRTY-EIGHT



Deal paced back and forth across Garcia's living room as he tried to calmly convince the ANI officer that they needed an intense and robust response to the new, dangerous threat his team had uncovered over the past 24 hours.

"Whoever is behind this operation openly and violently kidnapped one of my people. And Zach reported that the people inside the tunnels employ heavily armed and highly trained mercenaries. We must also take into consideration the warning from Rodrigo Valdez about not allowing the fourth launch. We don't really know what he meant, but we have to take it seriously, especially after what happened to Bubba during his surveillance flight. Jaime, the weapon Bubba described is worse than a nuclear warhead on top of a ballistic missile. At least with a nuke, we have some warning before it strikes. But with what Bubba has called 'spheres,' we have no defense at all. This is no longer just an investigation into unexpected launches into space or mysterious satellites. We now have evidence someone has placed weapons of mass destruction into orbit and has demonstrated their willingness to use them. Bottom line, I want to bring in my operators. They are standing by in Panama and can board a plane ten minutes from now."

Garcia shook his head. "As I said, I cannot condone armed American forces inside Chile. I have highly trained and dedicated people if we must use force. But at this time, even with Mr. Self's experience and your man Bubba's theory about what struck his plane, this is impossible."

Deal had to restrain himself. Garcia could kick him and his team out of Chile at a moment's notice. And he didn't have enough diplomatic cover or authority from his own superiors to take unilateral action.

"Alright. I'll leave them on standby for now in case things get out of hand. You have my word they will not enter the country without your knowledge and invitation," Deal reluctantly agreed.

"Thank you, Frank," Garcia responded, using Deal's first name. "Now, what more do we know about these spheres your man Bubba described? Does he have any tangible evidence of their existence? Or is this just a theory?"

"Well, he doesn't have one he can hold in his hand yet. He's working on that. But his analysis is sound, and I've come to rely heavily on his conclusions," Deal replied.

Sims added, "And, not to pile on, but Bubba also theorizes that the cubesats have capabilities beyond just firing these spheres."

"Such as?" Garcia asked, trying to digest the frightening implications of Deal and Sims' new information.

Sims looked at Deal before responding. Deal nodded.

"Our best people have been studying the rare electronic emissions from the four groups of cubesats now in orbit," Sarah began. "The consensus seems to be they could serve as communications platforms."

"But that isn't confirmed yet?" Garcia asked.

"Correct. The Europeans and Japanese have been cooperating with NASA, but they don't have enough data yet to solidify a conclusion."

"I understand," Garcia replied, absently massaging his temples. "How many cubesats were deployed from the second launch?"

Sims opened her laptop to display a map of the world.

"The first launch deployed 16 satellites over western Europe and another 16 over east Asia. NORAD has just confirmed that 16 new satellites have been deployed over North America – 8 over the United States' west coast and another 8 over the east coast." Sims explained, pointing to red dots on the map depicting the pattern of orbiting objects. "The fact that the U.S. has apparently drawn the most attention is ominous at best. And that's not all. NORAD is also tracking 8 more cubesats sitting over South America in a rough line over the border between Chile, Argentina, and Brazil."

Garcia studied Sims' map. The red dots suddenly looked like small armies strategically arranged to place the world's biggest economies and superpowers under siege.

"Look, Jaime," Deal said. "I think you can see the problem here. If those things attack the United States, our government will have no choice but to consider that an act of war by Chile. I have conveyed my theory that your government is not behind this and that I believe third-party actors are using your country as a convenient cover. Yet, my opinion will make no difference should the worst happen. So far, the U.S. has shown restraint. I can't predict how China, Russia, or any of the world's less stable governments will respond, but one thing is for certain – we are running out of time."

Garcia could tell Deal wasn't making a threat, only explaining in plain language the situation they all faced. He placed both elbows on his knees, looked at the floor, and continued to rub his temples. Now he knew precisely what was meant by "sitting on the horns of a dilemma." If he invited armed FBI agents to conduct an operation on Chilean soil, he could be tried for treason. On the other hand, if the United States or some other superpower concluded that the cubesats posed a clear and present danger, then his country could be plunged into a deadly conflict it couldn't survive. Another long moment passed as he wrestled with his thoughts. Finally, the ANI officer sat up and took a deep breath.

"What do you suggest?"

"First, has your asset communicated when the third launch will take place?" Deal asked.

"No," Garcia replied. "His last communication was just before the second launch."

"We won't need him for that information," Sims said, looking up from her phone. "NORAD has just confirmed a third launch."

Deal immediately called Bubba.

"I know," Bubba said, skipping any niceties. "I'm tracking it. That was fast. These guys don't waste time."

"I want to know immediately if it deploys more of these damn satellites," Deal said just before abruptly ending the call.

"What's our next move, boss?" Sims asked.

"We can't go in blind. We need more intelligence about these tunnels. Hopefully, Rodrigo Valdez can point us to some vulnerability we can exploit."

"Unfortunately, he has not responded to our requests for more information using the video game chat room. My people believe he turned off the device to prevent being detected. So, it is up to him to contact us."

Deal looked at Sims, who called Zach's number and handed the phone to Deal.

"Zach, are you sure the guy that helped you was Rodrigo Valdez?" Deal asked.

"Absolutely. I saw his picture several times in his parents' bed and breakfast in Talca. They still believe he is dead. Like I reported, I was with his brother Junior when they surprised us at the tunnel entrance."

"Are you still on good terms with Junior and his family?" Deal asked.

"I haven't talked to him since I got grabbed, but I would think so."

"How's the ankle?"

"Better."

"Good. You have new orders. You and Sims are going back to Talca. Michael and Sarah will investigate the Pacifico."

"When do you want us to leave?" Zach asked, his voice sounding less than enthusiastic.

"Agent Sims will pick you up in fifteen minutes."

The Cause's Underground Complex
Twenty-two minutes later

"Where is Zachary Self now"? Ruiz asked the technician monitoring Zach's location.

"Our team on the ground reported that he left the Castillo Rojo Hotel twenty minutes ago with a blonde female. The trackers in his bloodstream show that he is still in Santiago, traveling south on Highway 5. Per your orders, three members of Condor squad remained to surveil the hotel."

"Let me know if Self leaves the city. I suspect he is returning to Talca. Do we still have surveillance on the Valdez family?" Ruiz asked.

The technician pulled up a screen on his monitor displaying a live shot of the Valdez's bed and breakfast.

"Junior Valdez is at his parents' home with his daughter, Flor. At the moment, they are having dinner and discussing nothing of interest to us."

"Has Junior told his family about his little trip to the entry portal?"

"We've had him under close surveillance since he returned to Talca. He has kept his mouth shut so far."

Ruiz played with a loose strand of hair while considering her next move.

"Find out who the woman is with Self," Ruiz ordered, not revealing a growing suspicion she knew already. "And contact the squad leader in Santiago. They are to identify and then eliminate the American spies remaining in Santiago."

# CHAPTER THIRTY-NINE



Castillo Rojo Hotel
Santiago, Chile

The Castillo Rojo wasn't really a castle and didn't even look much like one. More akin to an English Tudor manor house, the four-story building's first floor was covered with rock, giving the illusion of a fortress-like foundation. Above, large arched windows sat deep in striking red-orange stucco walls. Above, a steep gabled roof with dormer windows covered the fourth floor. Outside, the busy city streets usually pulsated with cars, buses, and pedestrians, many making their way to the nearby entertainment district or Santiago's popular Metropolitan Park.

Michael and Sarah's fourth-floor room overlooked the alley that ran next to the hotel. Usually an early riser, Michael climbed out of bed around 4:30 a.m., hoping to run a couple of miles before Sarah and Deal started their day in another hour or so. The temperature in the room couldn't have been much over 55 degrees, and he shivered as he pulled on a sweatshirt and running shorts. He shook his head at the Chilean people's general disdain for indoor heating that he had first noticed at the Valdez's bed and breakfast. Grumbling about how even the cavemen figured out how to heat the inside of their caves,

Michael made his way down the narrow, steep staircase to the small lobby, where he found Daniela already working behind the front desk.

"Good morning, Daniela," Michael said, stifling a yawn. "Any advice about where I can get in a few miles this morning?"

Always prepared for guests' questions, Daniela smiled and reached under the counter and retrieved a map of the city.

"You're up early," she commented.

"We have a big day, and I wanted to get in a workout. Sarah is still asleep, so if she comes down, would you tell her I'll be right back?"

"Of course," Daniela said with a smile that Michael found impossibly bright for such an early hour. "So, most guests like running a few blocks south and then down along the river. If you want a challenge, I suggest going out through the alley, turn right, go around the hotel, and in just one block, you'll find Metropolitan Park. The path up the hill to the San Cristobal monument is only a mile, but it is steep and will give you a real workout. Once at the top, you'll also get a grand view of the city."

Michael studied the map a moment before deciding.

"I can't pass up a good view. I'll try the park. Thanks!"

Michael snaked past the tables in the hotel's small restaurant and through the hallway between the kitchen and restrooms. As he stepped out the back door, a cold breeze took his breath away.

"Geeez!" Michael exclaimed.

Instead of stretching, Michael took off at a quick trot to try and get his blood moving. As he turned the corner, he saw the steep hill rising above Metropolitan Park. High above, he could just make out the outlines of what he knew must be the monument Daniela told him about.

"You wanted a challenge, big boy," he said to himself as he ran under the park entrance.

Just as Daniela returned to the lobby with supplies to make the morning's first pot of coffee, the bell at the hotel's front entrance rang. Like most businesses in Santiago, Castillo Rojo's front door remained locked and closely controlled due to the massive city's street crime.

Glancing at the clock, Daniela checked the reservations and deliveries scheduled for the day. With nothing on the books, she went to the door to see who had rung the bell. Usually, at that time of day, she would find people looking for handouts. So, she grabbed a few coins from a little box she kept under the counter for such occasions.

Daniela opened the viewing window in the door but didn't find who she expected. Instead of a homeless person, a young woman dressed in jeans and hugging a torn green sweater around her body stood crying uncontrollably and looking over her shoulder.

"What's wrong?" Daniela asked, warily.

"I'm sorry to bother you," the dark-haired woman said quickly. "My...my boyfriend is...please...he says he is going to kill me. Please... I'm sorry...can you call the police? Oh, my god! He's coming!"

Daniela looked as far as she could up and down the street from behind the door but saw nothing.

"He thinks I cheated! I didn't! I swear! Please, can you let me in? Just until the police come? He has a gun! Please!" the girl pleaded, tears streaming down her cheeks.

Daniela was no fool. She knew this could be a trick. But the terror in the girl's eyes seemed genuine. Her tears certainly were.

"Okay. Come in quickly. I'll call the police."

Daniela hadn't opened the door more than a few inches when it slammed open, throwing her against the wall and bashing her head into the wood paneling. Dazed and gasping for air, she could only watch as two men dressed in black from head to toe and wearing ski masks forced their way into the lobby. The last thing she saw before passing out was the two men, now with rifles held in front of their eyes, scanning up the stairs as they climbed toward the guest rooms.

In his room on the second floor, Deal had just finished fifty push-ups and several rounds of abdominal exercises when he heard what sounded like a door crashing open. He almost ignored it until he heard heavy footsteps pounding up the stairs.

The FBI Special Agent had served several tours in the Middle East hunting weapons of mass destruction before joining the agency. His success had reaped him a bad reputation among the world's worst terrorists, thugs, and warlords. Ever since, his life depended on listening to his instincts, even while staying in a boutique hotel in one of the world's major cities.

Not hesitating, Deal snatched his borrowed Beretta pistol out of the nightstand next to his bed. Quietly working the slide backward to be sure a round rested in the chamber, he backed into the bathroom, turned out the light, and waited. If they were coming for him, he wouldn't have long to wait.

His room was number 101.

"Which room?" one of the men in ski masks asked the woman who had lied to Daniela at the door and now followed them up the stairs.

"How do I know? You idiots knocked out the desk clerk. We'll have to search the hotel," she replied.

"You want us to knock on every door? This place has 19 rooms."

"I don't give a shit how you do it," the woman said. "Our orders are to identify and kill the Americans. Take out everyone. I don't care."

One of the two men stepped up to Deal's room, shot the lock with a silenced pistol, and quietly pushed the door open with his boot.

After glancing around the door frame, he stepped into the room and fired several rounds into Deal's unmade bed.

"Nobody here."

Deal didn't move as his door creaked open. He took a deep breath, listening for the sound of someone entering the room. Anticipating what would happen next, he paused. Then, just as the intruder shot into his empty bed, he stepped out of the bathroom.

"Wrong," Deal said, causing the gunman to swing his gun up in his direction. But he was too late.

Deal's pistol barked twice, sending two 9mm rounds slamming into the other man's chest and throwing him backward into the hallway.

But he wasn't alone.

In the blink of an eye, a rifle barrel appeared around the door jam and unleashed a hail of bullets into the room.

The FBI Special Agent had just enough time to dive back into the small bathroom before holes appeared in the wall next to him. With nowhere to run, Deal returned fire, squeezing the trigger three times in the general direction of his room's door. He couldn't see his attackers, so all he could do was hope one of his shots found a target.

Within seconds, every guest in the hotel was awake, thrown out of bed by the unmistakable sound of gunshots.

A woman's voice shouted into the room in Spanish. "Put down your weapon and come out now. We won't hesitate to start exterminating these nice people. You have ten seconds."

Deal didn't understand every word, but he didn't have any doubt she was giving him an ultimatum. It took only seconds for him to decide how to respond. He was alone and trapped in a hotel room with only three rounds left in his weapon. Just around the corner, at least two people with automatic rifles had him massively outgunned. And he had to consider the danger to Michael, Sarah, and the other guests.

"I'm coming out," he called. "I'm tossing my weapon out now. Do you understand?"

Deal engaged the pistol's safety and tossed it a few yards into the room.

"An American?" the woman responded in English, sounding pleased. "Come out slowly."

Not knowing if he would survive the next few seconds, Deal raised his hands and stepped into the room.

"Get on your knees and place your hands on your head," the woman ordered.

In the next few seconds, zip-tie handcuffs bound his hands painfully behind his back, and a man wearing a black mask stood over him, the barrel of his gun touching the back of his neck. Deal noticed two neat holes in the man's bulletproof vest.

"Can I kill him now?"

"No," the woman replied. "You got lucky this American didn't shoot you in the head. We can use him to find the rest."

Turning to Deal, she asked, "Who are you?"

"I am a nobody. I came to buy wine," Deal responded.

The woman laughed. "You think I'm stupid? No wine merchant handles a gun like that. Now, I'll give you one more chance. Who are you."

Deal had only a split second to come up with a lie that would match his cover as a Canadian wine buyer and an expert with weapons. "A wine merchant trained by the JTF2 handles a gun like that. Major, Canadian Armed Forces, retired. Your country is beautiful but dangerous."

The woman took a minute rummaging through Deal's bag. She pulled out his passport, snapped a picture, and sent it off by email.

"I've got this one," she said to the other members of her hit squad. "You two find Michael King and Sarah Marshall. Bring them to me. Alive."

Deal didn't have to keep up his performance as an ex-military businessman for long.

A minute later, the woman's eyes widened as she looked at her phone.

"Special Agent Frank Deal, FBI," she said. "We thought you were dead."

"Obviously not," Deal replied with a shrug, no longer needing to keep up the charade.

"Sorry, but I have orders to correct that situation," the woman said, drawing her pistol and aiming it at Deal's head.

The FBI agent looked his assailant in the eye even as she cocked the weapon's hammer.

# CHAPTER FORTY

Two floors above, Sarah awoke to screams, shouted orders, and doors crashing in on their hinges. In moments, she rolled out of bed, trying to make sense of what sounded like a full-scale assault on the red castle.

"Michael?" she said, frantically looking for her boyfriend.

Hoping he had gone out for one of his early morning workouts, Sarah shoved a heavy dresser against the door and looked for another way out of the room. She chastised herself briefly for not finding the emergency exits when they first arrived but then remembered seeing a fire escape outside one of the small dormer windows. Hoping the hotel kept the ancient-looking windows in good condition, she located a handle at the window's base and turned it counterclockwise. To her relief, the window slowly but smoothly swung open.

When she heard someone running up the steps and bellowing orders in Spanish to open the door to the room next to hers, she put one foot through the window but froze when her eye landed on a fire alarm set into the wall next to the bed.

As she pulled her leg back into the room, a fist hammered loudly against her door.

"Open up!"

Sarah didn't hesitate. She dashed across the room and pulled down the white handle marked 'FUEGO.' Immediately, a blaring alarm filled the entire hotel, drowning out whoever was outside her room. Sarah didn't wait to see if her ploy would work. She slid through the open window and raced down the freezing metal fire escape in bare feet. She didn't notice the cold as she dropped the last few feet into an alley beside the hotel – and ran headlong into Michael.

"That was nice," he said. "You stuck the landing. What the hell is going on?"

"Someone is attacking the guests in the hotel. I pulled the fire alarm," Sarah explained.

"Deal? Daniela?" Michael asked.

"No idea."

"We need to be able to help them if we can. Let's get across the street. Whatever is going on must have to do with our investigation."

Michael quickly pulled off his sweatshirt and wrapped it around Sarah's shoulders just before they sprinted across the street and took refuge behind a parked delivery truck. In the distance, they heard the sound of sirens growing closer.

"What do we do?" Sarah asked.

"We wait to see if Daniela and Deal come out," Michael responded, his eyes locked on the hotel's entrance.

"What about the back door?" Sarah asked.

"Damnit," Michael replied. "I should have thought of that. I just used it twenty minutes ago."

"I've got it," Sarah said, giving Michael a peck on the cheek and racing away before he could object.

"Damnit," Michael said again under his breath as he watched his girlfriend dash back across the street and disappear around the corner of the hotel.

Inside, the blaring fire alarm bought Deal a stay of execution. While his attacker was occupied shouting orders at her men, the FBI agent sat on the floor of his room and worked the muscles in his arms, wrists, and hands against the plastic zip-tie handcuffs. The male assailant who bound his hands a few minutes before didn't notice how he had flexed his wrists, creating just a bit of wiggle room in the cuffs. Deal slowly and methodically worked the cuffs back and forth, stretching the plastic in tiny increments. Patience, perseverance, and the ability to ignore pain would be key, but freeing himself would take time. And he didn't seem to have much of that left.

"Change of plan. Get up. Now," the group's leader ordered as the faint sound of sirens grew closer. "We're leaving. You stay alive only as long as you do as I say."

Deal made a show of struggling to his feet. He glared at the woman but said nothing, walking awkwardly toward his room door, bent forward at an uncomfortable angle, and faking a slight limp.

The woman shoved him forward.

"Move it, old man."


With her head still swimming in a thick soup of confusion and pain, Daniela's eyes opened to a view of the lobby lying on its side. The sound of doors crashing in and shouted orders from the rooms upstairs helped clear her thoughts. The Chilean hotel manager struggled to her feet, and using the wall for support, staggered back behind the front desk. She picked up the phone and dialed Chile's emergency telephone number to the Santiago police, 133.

"Daniela, it's Major Garcia. Is everything alright?"

Daniela looked at the phone. She expected the Santiago Police Department to answer, not the ANI officer she had met just the night before.

Setting aside her astonishment and many questions, Daniela quickly reported how three heavily armed gunmen had invaded the hotel.

"Do you know if Agent Deal and his team are safe?" Garcia asked.

"Michael King left for a workout twenty minutes ago. Agent Deal and Sarah Marshall are still in their rooms. At least as far as I know."

"We are on the way. Are you in a safe place?"

"Yes."

"Stay there."

Daniela peeked around the corner of the desk in time to see several sets of combat boots turning the corner at the first landing. With only seconds to spare, she quietly padded across the lobby and restaurant and out the back door. As soon as she was outside, the Chilean girl had second thoughts about her escape plan. She should have known she would end up in the narrow alley.

"Daniela! Come here!"

Daniela's head snapped around toward the voice and found Sarah motioning to her from behind a massive green metal rolling dumpster.

With a gun held to his head, Deal marched down the stairs to the hotel lobby.

"Use the back door," the woman in charge ordered. "Move."

Deal continued to work his handcuffs even as he limped along behind the two male gunmen. He didn't have a plan yet on how to escape, but his captors had made a mistake by leaving him able to see and speak. Perhaps his old age act had worked. For now, he considered the situation fluid, leaving him no choice but to comply with the attackers until he could find a way to change the dynamics. Or bash their skulls in.

A few seconds later, the FBI agent followed the two gunmen into the alley. He could see a blue van waiting on the far side of the street and immediately knew that if he stepped foot inside, he was as good as dead.

Deal worked the cuffs as much as possible without being noticed, but he didn't have enough time to get free. Now, almost to the sidewalk, Deal tensed to throw himself forward, try to knock the two gunmen to the ground, and then sprint into traffic.

He lowered his shoulder and took a deep breath.

Then, from his left, what seemed like a filthy green metal wall crashed into the entire group. One of the gunmen ahead of him hit the ground hard and screamed as the "wall" rolled over his leg.

Deal didn't see what happened to the other shooter after he also slammed hard against the hotel's stone foundation.

The woman, who had been just a step behind Deal, was still on her feet. He could see her bring a 9mm handgun to her eye as she moved toward the other side of what he now knew to be a steel dumpster that had nearly squashed him like a bug.

"Run!" Sarah shouted.

Daniela didn't have to be told twice. As she sprinted out of the alley and around the corner, Sarah followed but stepped on a piece of glass that cut painfully into her foot. As she turned to escape, she found herself looking at the barrel of a pistol. She threw up her hands to surrender, but the merciless eyes behind the weapon weren't impressed. Sarah knew there wouldn't be any chitchat before the scowling woman behind the gun put a bullet in her brain.

Incredibly, the woman with the gun didn't pull the trigger. Instead, she seemed to just freeze in place. The hard sneer of a confident killer was suddenly replaced by a confused, blank look that fell across her face. Just before she crumpled to the ground, Sarah watched in astonishment as a drop of blood appeared like magic in the middle of the other woman's forehead.

Still standing with her hands in the air, she saw Michael run into the alley, holding a high-powered rifle.

"Get their guns," Deal ordered.

Michael picked up one of the gunmen's assault rifles and handed it to Sarah, who trained it on the two men still trapped between the dumpster and the wall. Deal wormed his way out and checked on Sarah.

"You okay?" he asked. "Did you push that damn dumpster across the alley all by yourself?"

"No. Daniela helped me. It rolls pretty easy, but I don't think I could have done it by myself," she admitted. "Where is she anyway?"

"I am here, Sarah," Daniela called, returning to the alley. "And I brought some friends."

Garcia walked to Deal and cut his cuffs off with a folding knife.

"Thanks," Deal said, massaging his wrists. "How did you know we were under attack."

"Daniela called for help. I decided to monitor the hotel's phones for just this reason."

"Did you shoot this piece of crap?" Deal asked, kicking the female assailant's dead body lightly with his toe.

"No. That was Michael. He saw what Sarah and Daniela were doing and grabbed a gun from one of my men. He made that shot on the run. Impressive. But I'll have to have a word with my man about losing his weapon."

Looking over the scene, Deal motioned to Garcia, "Let's get this cleaned up and these two thugs back to your headquarters. Maybe they have some information we can use."

"And I have to get my hotel put back together," Daniela added.

Michael stood with his arms wrapped protectively around his girlfriend. "It's at least a little warmer inside. Let's go before we freeze to death."

## The Cause's Underground Complex

Dr. Dave Knox, aka President Juan Cayo, paced between his massive desk – a lustrous edifice of African blackwood – and the bank of windows overlooking the rocket assembly tunnel. Below, the TS4 launch vehicle's stainless-steel skin gleamed in the bright laboratory-like lighting. The sight of his crowning achievement should have given him reason to smile. But the person on the other end of the telephone he was holding had somehow managed to bungle a simple operation and diminish the sweet anticipation of victory he should have been savoring.

"Your orders were to clean up this mess you made with the American spies..." Dave began.

"It was your incompetent people..." Ruiz interrupted.

"Goddammit! Shut your mouth," Dave shouted into the phone. "Excuses won't fix the problem you created. We are hours away from our final launch window, and you attempt to dodge responsibility? Don't even try. And you can forget blackmailing us with more threats about stealing our money or revealing our little organization to the authorities. Our people backtraced how you emptied one of our accounts. And I'm sorry to tell you that the lawyer and computer programmer that helped you have been eliminated. So that we are clear, your release of Zach Self and failure in Santiago have jeopardized an operation that cost billions of dollars. Where are you?"

Ruiz had come too far to show fear. Her mother had left her several million dollars. But Ruiz wasn't satisfied. A place at the round twelve-person table reserved for the Directors of The Cause would make her an instant billionaire, and she had no intention of giving that up.

"I'm in Talca. While the mission in Santiago failed, it also revealed that FBI agents Frank Deal and Stella Sims survived the attack at the oil tank farm. What we don't know is who helped them. Zach Self and Agent Stella Sims are here in Talca. And, if Sims is here, you can expect an attempt to stop any more launches."

"Are you anticipating an attack on the tunnels?" Dave asked.

"That bastard Deal wouldn't send her down here to screw around."

"Find out what Sims is planning and report back," Dave ordered, hanging up the phone.

Dave looked over at Alexander Monroe who had been listening to the conversation from a couch set against the far wall.

"What do you think?" Dave asked.

"I think we both know Margie Frank's daughter is too dangerous to leave alive," Monroe responded with a shrug. "Do you think this Agent Deal will try some sort of direct attack?"

"Yes. Although, our little round surprises would make that profoundly stupid."

# CHAPTER FORTY-ONE



Bubba leaned over the small trawler's railing and threw up for what seemed like the tenth time. Pulling himself upright, he wiped his mouth and looked around to see the crew quietly joking with each other about his acute seasickness in their native Spanish.

Bubba could only laugh at himself. He had flown in advanced fighter aircraft, survived a harrowing mission in NASA's high-altitude surveillance aircraft, and sat next to Michael King in his powerful convertible during a high-speed chase. But those rides were nothing compared to being tossed about in a small boat on the open ocean.

"How long have they been down there?" Bubba asked the divemaster who was monitoring communications with the three-person dive team.

"They are surfacing now."

Bubba stayed clear as three divers appeared near the back of the boat and handed several heavy instruments to the divemaster before climbing on board.

"Find anything?" Bubba asked as soon as the lead diver pulled off his full-face dive mask.

"That metal detector you brought worked perfectly. We found all kinds of metal artifacts but only a single piece of titanium," the diver replied, reaching into a mesh bag and retrieving a piece of metal no more than an inch square.

Bubba carried the sample into the ship's cabin and placed it under a powerful microscope. What he saw nearly took his breath away.

The sample had a slight curve. The outer surface bore scorch marks from its high-speed trip through the atmosphere. But it was the interior that caught his eye. Using the microscope, Bubba could see tiny etchings in the metal itself. He quickly theorized that whoever designed this weapon created all the necessary circuitry to control its flight in the metal wall of the sphere. He also guessed that the interior housed whatever allowed the sphere to maneuver in space. But he would need to study the artifact further to be sure.

"And you said this is the only titanium you found?" Bubba called out to the divers who were still on deck.

"That's all, my friend," the lead diver called back. "We could widen the search grid, but I would need at least three more divers and a couple more of your magic metal detectors."

"Thanks, but I'm out of time," Bubba said, checking his watch. He would have to pry out all the information he could from what he held in his hand.

After a rushed trip back to Cape Canaveral, Bubba enlisted the help of two NASA scientists – a materials specialist and a flight control developer – to analyze the sample of titanium that had nearly cost him his life.

First, Bubba turned to the complex circuitry etched into the surface of the sphere's interior wall. The materials specialist found that whoever had created the process for imprinting on titanium had impressively advanced the nanoimprint lithography process. But in short, the NASA specialist explained that by using the body of the sphere as its circuit board, the remainder of the interior space could be used for whatever its creator decided to install.

Next, Bubba confirmed that the sample matched the diameter of the hole made in the ER2's wing and graphed out the sphere's flight trajectory for the flight control expert. Using the interior volume of the sphere and making several educated guesses, the NASA expert agreed with Bubba's initial theory that most of the interior space would be needed for tiny maneuvering jets, liquid propellant, and a power source for the electronics. He also agreed that while technically complex, adjusting the course of a sphere four inches in diameter and with relatively little mass wouldn't take much force and could be accomplished with only six tiny retractable nozzles.

When he had completed his preliminary analysis, Bubba called Deal.

"So, what are they? And what can they do?" Deal asked as soon as he picked up the phone. "I don't have time for a nerd-heavy explanation. Just give it to us in layman's terms."

"Us?" Bubba asked.

"Yes. I have Major Garcia with me."

"Alright, my initial theory was correct. I confirmed it's a 4-inch diameter self-guided titanium alloy sphere that can hit its target on the ground at over 17,000 miles per hour. I've already described the damage it could do if it hits a target on the surface. In space, just one of these things could take out multiple satellites and then bring down the International Space Station. Now, here's the really important part. I think they are both offensive and defensive."

"What does that mean?" Deal demanded.

"Defensively, they can stop any attempt to bring down the satellites, including incoming anti-satellite missiles or any other spacecraft sent up for the same purpose. Offensively, they can vaporize whoever or whatever they wish on the surface without warning," Bubba explained soberly. "And we still don't know the real purpose or capabilities of the cubesats beyond serving as platforms for the spheres. As bad as they are, the cubesats may be even more of a threat. Someone sure went to a lot of trouble and expense to protect them with a next-generation weapon."

"Cut to the chase," Deal ordered.

Bubba paused to find words that could sufficiently describe the danger he had uncovered.

"Some men peer into the universe seeking knowledge and opportunity for all humanity. But others only want to exploit space for personal gain and to hold ultimate power over the heads of everyone back on Earth. Whoever is behind this is the latter. They placed the cubesats strategically over the world's population centers for a reason. I don't know precisely what that is yet. But I think President Lyndon Johnson put his finger on it when he said: 'Control of space means control of the Earth.'"

# CHAPTER FORTY-TWO



Dr. Dave Knox stood at the head of the massive round conference room table. To his right, the setting sun spread a warm glow over Chile's stunning coastal mountain range.

He strolled to the windows while the eleven other Directors of The Cause waited patiently for his report on the progress of his latest project. His transformation into a veritable clone of President Juan Mateo Cayo had given the Directors a bout of short-lived shock. But they had also come to expect Dave to take outlandish, even extreme measures to achieve his goals.

When he reached the windows, Dave paused and allowed the golden light to arrange itself over his face and glint off his hand-cut crystal tumbler of fine bourbon. He stood erect, looking down over the Earth like a Greek god standing in his palace on Mount Olympus.

He let the other Directors wait, confident of what their reaction would be to his most ambitious plan to date.

Returning to the head of the table, Dave set his drink down and turned to the screen slowly lowering from the ceiling behind his chair. Using a tiny remote control, Dave lit up the screen with a picture of the blue Earth covered by white clouds floating in the empty blackness of space.

Dave kept one eye on the assembled Directors. He might be the most ruthless and cunning man in the room, but every person there had an agenda of their own. After all, he himself had ordered the cold-blooded murder of The Cause's first leader as she stood in the exact spot he now occupied.

"When our forefathers first created The Cause, they believed they could carve a new country from several states in the American South. That antiquated dream began our glorious venture but never had a real chance at success. So, we evolved, pooled our resources, and have since become some of the wealthiest men and women in the history of mankind. Now, we have the resources to move forward and begin building a world that both suits and serves us. But we cannot accomplish this by forcing our will on the rest of humanity. No, the only path to taking our rightful place over the masses must come from them. They must openly and even gratefully give up any control over their lives – freedom, if you will – for a sense of security. They must live in fear. Not of us. No. We will be their saviors. They must fear whatever we tell them to fear."

One of the Directors spoke up. "That is a fine speech. And it certainly rings true. But based on your recommendation alone, we have invested billions in this space program, and I, for one, think it is high time you revealed the full extent of your plan. How does the money we spent move us toward that admittedly satisfying but lofty goal?"

Dave nodded in acknowledgment and said, "Let me show you what our planet actually looks like from a vantage point halfway to the moon."

The Cause's leader pushed another button on the remote, and suddenly, the picture depicting the beautiful blue planet became covered in a mass of red dots, apparently swarming randomly around the globe. The Earth itself almost disappeared behind the thousands of markers representing the current location of satellites, spacecraft, and discarded junk humans had been launching into space since the Russians' first simple satellite, Sputnik 1, some 70 years before.

Dave waited for the murmurs of surprise to die down.

"Now," Dave began, "I'll remove indicators for observable space junk, scientific satellites like the Hubble Space Telescope, and weather observation platforms."

While a number of red dots disappeared, the vast majority remained.

"What are all those? Communication satellites?" one of the Directors asked.

Dave responded, "Correct. Very good. Both civilian and military, regardless of nationality. Almost every form of communication now passes through the incredibly concentrated web you see on the screen. Television, telephone calls, and most importantly, the entire internet rely on the transfer of information from one point on Earth to one of these platforms, which then relays it back to the surface. It's impressive. But flawed. And that, gentlemen, is the reason for our investment."

"Can you be more specific?" a bald director wearing wire glasses asked.

In response, Dave turned back to the screen and pushed another button. Most of the red dots disappeared, leaving about two dozen that seemed to orbit in perfect unison. In addition, the cubesats The Cause launched from the Andes Mountains glowed a bright blue near each orbital track of the red dots.

"After many months of research and calculations, I determined that these 24 communications and relay platforms are the lynchpin to the global communications system. At some point, these satellites either handle direct communications duties or control the flow of information across the hundreds of other satellites in both high and low Earth orbits."

The bald-headed director removed his glasses and absently wiped them with a silk handkerchief as he stared at the screen.

"Very interesting. But…"

Dave held up one hand.

"Please watch. This one," Dave said, using a laser pointer to circle one of the red dots, "is the, well, target of today's demonstration. Pun intended."

The screen shifted to a close-up view of one of The Cause's cubesats. The camera looked down at the box-like body of the spacecraft, its stainless-steel skin shining brightly against the total blackness of space. As the entire room watched, a square door opened in the side of the craft, ejecting a small round sphere. The camera followed the sphere as it shot away and out of sight at high speed.

"You will remember the titanium sphere we used to destroy that oil platform. Which, by the way, caused a lovely spike in oil prices. As Director Monroe promised, I'm about to explain how those satellites, armed with titanium spheres, can do even more. Everyone, please take out your phones and open whatever American news app or service you use. Any one of them will do," Dave requested.

The screen's view then shifted again, this time to a close-up of the critical satellite Dave identified earlier. In the blink of an eye, the satellite seemed to disintegrate into thousands of tiny bits that flew off in all directions.

Following Dave's directions, the Directors turned their attention to the talking heads from various networks spouting opinions and conspiracy theories interspersed with tiny bits of what they considered news. Then, all at once, every screen went blank. A second later, a message appeared on their phones. It read: "Coming soon! TNI."

Dave could see the same question plastered on every director's face.

"Yes. We did that," Dave said proudly. "This was just a demonstration. The sphere we watched leave one of our cubesats destroyed ComSat42f – one of the two dozen critical communications platforms I identified earlier. As you can see, the system has already re-routed the lost signal to other platforms."

Sure enough, the talking heads returned, now trying to explain what had just happened. But without any facts, all they could offer was their usual unsupported guesses and theories that, while entertaining, provided no helpful information whatsoever.

"What is TNI?" another Director asked from the opposite side of the table.

"Truth Network International," Dave answered. "The newest and farthest-reaching news source on the planet."

"And we did all this just to compete with other news sources?" the bald director asked.

Dave laughed. "We won't have to compete with anyone. In less than a week, TNI will be the world's major source of news and information. And, oh yes, internet as well."

"Won't people question why TNI has taken over all the news networks?" the same Director asked.

Dave laughed out loud again. "That is a good question, but one that has been definitively answered over the last thirty years. And the answer is 'no.' People, as a whole, don't think for themselves anymore. It's just too much work. It's much easier to believe whatever they see or are told on their TVs, laptops, and phones. Decades ago, Russia proved that as long as there was only one news source, the vast majority of the population could be manipulated in whatever direction they chose. The Soviets called their single news source Pravda – which, not coincidentally, means 'truth.'

## Kennedy Space Center

The loss of a critical communications satellite sent alarm bells ringing all over NASA. In the history of human activity in space, no active satellite had catastrophically failed. They experienced problems and even complete shutdowns due to electronic failures, solar flares, or hacking, but none had ever just spontaneously disintegrated into a cloud of tiny fragments.

While the engineers at NASA tried to write off the satellite's destruction as a freak accident, a failure of some structural component, or even an unforeseen collision with some space junk, Bubba scoffed. He knew exactly what annihilated the satellite.

"It was one of the titanium spheres," Bubba said when Deal picked up his phone.

"How do you know?" Deal asked.

Bubba took a deep breath. He knew Deal didn't like long-winded technical explanations, so he tried to keep it short.

"It's like this, boss. Satellites are hard to attack because they are, you know, in space. And they are relatively tiny targets, making them even harder to hit. Both us and the Chinese have proved it's possible to take out a satellite in low Earth orbit with special missiles launched from high-altitude fighters. But a missile attack makes a big bang. You can't miss it. So, we can rule out something like that. And they just don't fall apart on their own."

Deal grunted. "I don't give a crap what didn't happen. What did?"

"One of the titanium spheres. I'm sure of it," Bubba said. "I think we can now make two conclusions. First, these cubesats are offensive weapons with the spheres as the ammunition, if you will."

"Yeah," Deal growled. "We got that already."

"Right," Bubba replied. "But now we also know, without a doubt, that they are also communications platforms."

"So, what was the purpose behind smashing up the communications satellite?" Deal asked. "A threat of some kind?"

"I don't think so, boss."

"Why not?"

"Whoever is behind this is supremely confident we can't stop them. What happened today proves they have the capability to demolish every communications satellite in orbit and then fill the empty airwaves, for lack of a better term, with their own programming – whatever this 'TNI' is. Today might have been a test or proof of concept of what they have in mind for the world. It could also have been a demonstration to attract investors. Whatever their motivation, it worked."

"So why haven't they pulled the trigger?" Deal asked almost to himself.

"My guess is they don't have enough cubesats in orbit yet to complete their network. It's obvious they can wreak havoc with what they already have, but they will also need a massive amount of bandwidth and computing power if they are looking to replace the existing communications grid. I believe they still need something like a master control platform up there that can synchronize the data from hundreds of millions of source devices."

"The fourth launch Rodrigo Valdez warned Zach about," Deal concluded.

# CHAPTER FORTY-THREE



Deal waited while Garcia chewed on the FBI's analysis of the communication satellite's destruction and subsequent interruption of news broadcasts that affected the United States and most of South America. Patience wasn't one of Deal's talents. But that wasn't surprising, given his job as the man most often tapped to stop some criminal, terrorist, or rogue nation from using a weapon of mass destruction. With immense effort, Deal sat quietly allowing the Chilean ANI officer to come to a decision.

Garcia didn't know it, but Deal wouldn't accept anything other than a whole-hearted effort to stop the fourth launch, even if that meant he had to order an attack on the tunnel complex without any official or unofficial permission from Garcia or anyone else in Chile.

"What assets do you propose bringing into Chile if I agree?" Garcia asked.

"I want my Red and Blue teams. I told you about them before," Deal answered. "They are the best in the world and have extensive training. I can have them on the ground outside Talca in less than 90 minutes."

"What?" Garcia exclaimed. "They were to be based in Panama. You gave me your word they would not enter my country without permission!"

"They are not in your country, Major," Deal countered quickly. "I had them board a transport as soon as we had Bubba's analysis of the satellite attack. They are currently loitering outside Chilean airspace over the ocean. Chile's navy and coast guard have been told they are searching for a lost sailor attempting a solo crossing of the Pacific."

Garcia seemed to accept Deal's explanation but remained stonily silent.

Deal stood and paced up and down the room.

"Jaime, we don't have time to butt heads. You know we can't allow another launch. We have intelligence now from at least two sources that whoever is behind this already has a weapon capable of attacking anything on the ground, in the air, or in space. We also know that they plan to take over a large portion of the information resources that the world's countries and economies, not to mention political stability, depend upon. Now, I've told you about my team's capabilities. I think we'll need more firepower if we want to get into those tunnels. What can your people add? I need an answer here."

"Or you will go in with or without Chile's permission?"

What little patience Deal still possessed evaporated.

"I'm not asking for the Chilean government's permission. I'm asking for *yours*."

Garcia ran one hand through his dark black hair while he worked on accepting what he knew to be the only viable course of action. The moment had come to make the decision he had dreaded ever since agreeing to cooperate with the Americans.

"Then the answer is yes. I have three squads of trained volunteers – all ex-military with varying specialties. There is a little-used airstrip 25 kilometers south of Talca. My people will be waiting for your teams there. Lieutenant Madres will be in command. Who will lead yours?"

Deal hid his relief. Unilateral action had not been his first choice.

"Agent Sims is already in Talca and will lead Red and Blue Teams. Zach Self has identified the entrance to the facility, and we have the coordinates for the actual launch point high in the mountains."

"Good. Let's talk tactics," Garcia said, pulling up a map of the Maule region on the room's big screen monitor.

"Then let's get started," Deal agreed. "Jaime? Where is President Cayo?"

"Why do you want to know?" Garcia asked.

"Because I think he's in this up to his neck."

"He has been campaigning around the country for the upcoming Chamber of Deputies and Senate elections. I believe he is scheduled to attend a private party at the Pacifico Hotel tonight. I'll make a call and confirm that information."

# CHAPTER FORTY-FOUR



Outside the Pacifico Hotel
Santiago, Chile
Several hours later

Michael, Sarah, and Daniela sat in Daniela's ancient Toyota Hilux pickup truck on a side street below the front entrance to the Pacifico Hotel. The evening hadn't gone as expected. Just as they arrived at the place Daniela's friend agreed to meet them for an off-the-books tour of the Pacifico's grounds – he called and canceled.

"Did he give you a reason?" Michael asked.

"No. He also said not to ask him again," Daniela responded. "Unless I'm reading too much into his tone, I think he was actually frightened to be talking to me."

"That's strange," Sarah said. "I mean, he did it before. I wonder what changed."

"Maybe that," Michael said, sticking his head out the window and looking up. "Three helicopters are approaching the roof of the hotel right now."

"Look!" Daniela said, pointing in the other direction. "And there's a motorcade coming up from the city."

Michael and Sarah looked down the steep hill leading to the hotel. Below, five SUVs followed two motorcycles toward the Pacifico. The entire convoy rolled up the tight streets at high speed, blue and white lights warning of their approach. As they flashed past Daniela's truck, all three tried to see inside the vehicles. But deep black window tinting and the fading light made that impossible.

"Who do you think was in there?" Sarah asked.

"President Cayo," Michael replied, looking up from his phone. "I just got a text from Deal that there is some kind of fundraising event tonight."

"Okay. With all that extra security and your friend backing out, getting inside seems out of the question," Sarah observed.

Daniela didn't respond immediately. She sat quietly, looking at the hotel with a blank look on her face.

"What?" Sarah asked.

"I don't know if it will help, but I remember how we got in the last time," Daniela said, with a sly smile.

"Awesome!" Michael exclaimed. "Let's go."

"Hold on," Sarah said, grabbing Michael's arm before he could get out of the vehicle. "Just what are we hoping to accomplish other than a bit of trespassing and maybe getting thrown in jail?"

"Deal said that Minister Aybar pointed out the hotel as someplace we might be interested in. I don't think someone that high in government would make a statement like that without reason. It may be a longshot, but if Cayo is in there, I think the least we can do is see what he's up to."

"Makes sense," Daniela agreed.

"Yeah. He has these little nuggets of wisdom from time to time," Sarah said, patting Michael on the shoulder.

With Daniela leading, they walked casually down the street, talking and laughing like young people headed out on the town for the night. On their left, a wall painted bright white with long ivy-like vines cascading over the top separated the Pacifico from the rest of Santiago.

"The hotel's grounds are just on the other side," Daniela said. "Keep walking to the next corner and then turn left."

Rounding the corner, Daniela stopped and held up her hand.

"My friend told me the cameras covering the grounds have one small blind spot, a narrow path on the other side of the wall right here. Michael, can you climb over the wall on your own?" Daniela asked.

Michael looked at the seven-foot-tall wall and nodded.

"Yeah. No problem."

"Good. Give me and Sarah a boost, then come over yourself. I'll go first. When you jump down, stay still and don't make any noise."

Michael had no trouble lifting the two women up to where they could scramble over the wall and drop down on the other side. Michael followed them, pulling himself up and rolling over the top.

He found Sarah and Daniela crouching in thick shrubberies, their eyes trained out across an expansive lawn that led uphill. They could see bright lights and hear music coming from behind the hotel.

"What's back there?" Sarah asked.

"The pool deck. That must be where they are having the party," Daniela responded.

"Can we get a look without being seen?" Michael asked.

"I'm not sure," Daniela replied. "I sort of remember these bushes running along the length of the wall all the way around. We can try."

With all their senses on high alert, they picked their way under and behind rows of manicured greenery. They stayed in the deep shadows, careful to move slowly and silently. Roaming security guards strolled by the line of bushes twice, delaying the trio while they froze in the deep shadows. With patience and a little luck, they found a concealed position where they could see most of the area where the party was taking place.

Strobing multi-colored lights and what seemed like hundreds of flaming torches bathed the entire pool, deck, and several levels of marble terraces leading up to the hotel in undulating radiance. Guests glided through the light, holding glasses of champagne or cocktails. Every woman wore designer fashions that cost more than an average Chilean made in two years. The men took turns regaling each other with what must have been hilarious stories or ogling the women – none of whom looked to have celebrated their thirtieth birthday.

"I think I see President Cayo," Daniela said quietly. "On the first terrace above the pool. I wish I could hear what he was saying."

"Hold on a second," Michael said, reaching into his pocket.

A moment later, he stuck one side of a set of earphones into Sarah's ear and handed the other to Daniela.

"I don't speak Spanish," he whispered as he unfolded what looked like a little umbrella perched on top of a tiny video camera.

"What is it?" Daniela asked quietly.

"A present from our friend, Bubba," he whispered. "A miniature video camera with a built-in parabolic microphone. Let's get a recording for Deal and Garcia."

Sarah just shook her head. There wasn't anything Bubba couldn't dream up and then make a reality.

Sarah and Daniela could hear Cayo's words, even after the DJ cranked up another round of European-style dance music.

"No, my friends," they heard Cayo say. "Do not worry. Your investments in TNI will be fruitful and pay dividends on schedule. You already witnessed how fragile the world's communications infrastructure is. How easily it can be broken and manipulated. We are on the brink of a major global innovation in information delivery. TNI bureaus are set to open all over the world and are hiring top talent away from, how shall we put it, old-fashioned failing networks competing for ever-thinner shares of an increasingly skeptical viewership. TNI will end all that by providing a single source of worldwide information from news to social media sites. And, of course, we will have a near monopoly on advertising dollars."

The men who were listening to Cayo seemed satisfied. They congratulated the 'president' and moved on, probably discussing the size of the mega yachts they would order with Cayo's promised profits.

"Did you hear anything interesting?" Bubba asked after Daniela and Sarah handed back Bubba's surveillance device.

"I'm not sure," Sarah said. "Daniela, have you ever heard of a news channel or television station called TNI?"

Daniela shook her head. "No. I've never heard of such a thing, and I can't imagine why the president of Chile would be promoting some kind of private news network or whatever."

Sarah mulled over what they had learned so far.

"Daniela, take another look around. Do you see anyone else you recognize?"

The hotel manager retrieved the video camera and took a minute to slowly scan the faces of the guests sipping drinks and plucking hors d'oeuvres off silver platters as they milled about around the pool.

"I think I recognize a few politicians, but I don't know their names. Almost everyone was speaking English with all kinds of accents. It seems weird for a political fundraiser in a Spanish-speaking country. I did my best to get all the party guests on the video in case Agent Deal and Major Garcia think it's important."

"Good. Let's get out of here before our luck runs out," Sarah suggested.

# CHAPTER FORTY-FIVE

Aerodromo La Aguada
Near Talca, Chile

Sims stood next to the small shack that served as the only permanent structure at the La Aguada Airport. While the single dirt landing strip carved across someone's farm could hardly qualify as an 'airport,' it served her purposes perfectly.

Isolated and rural, La Aguada sat just a few miles outside of Talca and less than twenty-five from the entrance to the tunnels. Its 943-yard length could just accommodate the Lockheed L-188 Electra cargo plane that was on its final approach.

Sims watched the unmarked white aircraft make a sharp banking turn before dropping onto the airstrip's north end. Two swirling clouds of dust appeared behind the high upright tail just before the pilot threw the four turboprop engines into reverse. For a moment, Sims worried the old white plane might not stop in time and plow a few new rows into the bean fields at the end of the runway. But the big, old-fashioned aircraft came to a halt just at the edge of the tarmac, spun 180 degrees, and taxied back to where Sims stood waving a flashlight.

One of Garcia's lieutenants, who would act as the commander of the Chilean forces, stepped up to her side. "Your pilot is quite talented to land so precisely in the dark."

"I'll tell him you said so, Lieutenant Madres," Sims answered. "And he's not really one of our men. The pilot got Deal out of several close scrapes back in the Middle East. He still does us favors from time to time."

"Like flying illegally into countries under the radar?"

"Exactly," Sims deadpanned without cracking a smile.

As soon as the plane came to a halt, a wide door at the back lowered to the ground, and four vehicles that looked like space-aged dune buggies sped down the ramp and encircled the plane. Fifty-caliber machine guns mounted over their cabs pointed outward to meet any threat. A moment later, Deal's Blue and Red teams, all dressed as civilians, emerged from the aircraft carrying duffle bags packed with equipment.

After Sims' teams unloaded the remainder of their gear, a small cockpit window opened, and the pilot stuck an arm out and waved at Sims. Sims waved a thank you in return before watching the plane lumber back down the runway, spin up its engines, and then blast back in the opposite direction before leaping into the air.

"I guess he really didn't want to stay," Madres quipped.

"Yeah, he's not overly sociable. Let's get to work," Sims said, handing Madres a tiny earpiece while placing one in her own ear. "My call sign is White One. You are on the net as Green One. My teams have been briefed and will follow your lead."

"Copy that," Madres replied, inserting Sims' earpiece. "Red and Blue teams, this is Green One. I know you have been briefed. My people are up to speed and will be approaching from the southwest."

"Red One, copy."

"Blue One, copy."

Less than two minutes later, a small convoy made up of one semi pulling an enclosed trailer and seven vans that looked like they had led strenuous lives came to a halt across from Sims and Madres.

Without waiting for orders, the trailer opened, and two ramps slid out. The four armed reconnaissance vehicles whipped around, throwing dirt and gravel into the air before charging up the ramps. Meanwhile, Red and Blue teams piled into two of the vans.

A moment later, one of Madres's people appeared and saluted.

"Report," Madres said without introducing the new arrival.

"One unit of volunteers is here and will travel with the convoy. The second unit is in place and has set up surveillance of the area around the tunnel entrance. They will stay concealed until the next phase of the operation. Our third unit will remain in Talca on reserve status."

"Thank you, Sergeant. Let's get moving."

With Sims in tow, Madres and Sims climbed into the lead van.

As they pulled back onto the two-lane highway toward Talca, Sims asked, "Volunteers? Major Garcia didn't give us much detail about your team."

"We are all volunteers loyal only to the people of Chile. Be assured, you are working with highly trained professionals with expertise in urban warfare, explosives, weapons, and the like. In fact, it was me and the two men sitting right behind you who pulled you and Agent Deal out of that warehouse and then destroyed it before the helicopter could fire its missile."

Sims turned around but didn't recognize the two men, who looked a little sheepish when she thanked them.

"I'm Stella Sims," she said, sticking out her hand.

The two men shook Sims' hand but said nothing.

"None of our people use their real names. Cayo's moles and informants have infested the military and civilian police forces and won't hesitate to accuse anyone they think may be disloyal to Cayo of treason. We don't even know each other's names," Madres explained.

"How did you manage to put together this, for lack of a better word, organization?" Sims asked. "It can't be easy to find talented people willing to stick their necks out when a dictator grabs power."

Madres nodded.

"You're right, Stella. Cayo is collecting more and more power by using his wealth and attracting the money and influence of the ultra-rich. He promises them powerful positions and, more importantly, influence in the government. Meanwhile, he is hunting down any opposition. Our 'organization,' as you call it, has no name. A handful of officers in Chile's law enforcement and military services assembled several small units of dedicated men and women who have proven their loyalty to the country, its people, and the constitution. I entrust my life to these people, and they entrust theirs to me."

"Have things become that bad here?" Sims asked.

"Yes. But Chile is not alone. Dictators and authoritarians are rising to power all over the globe using the most effective weapon possible – information. Dictators use social media and news networks to ignite fear and suspicion, then claim to be the only person that can save them from threats that don't exist. History teaches this is how brutal authoritarians have always risen to power. But we just don't seem to learn."

For the next few minutes, Sims sat silently in the passenger seat, staring out at the dark, unfamiliar landscape of rural Chile. Long, thin clouds slashed across the face of an ominous full moon hanging low over the Andes, lending a creepy, foreboding backdrop to her thoughts.

A shiver ran up her spine as she thought of home.

Sims' reverie disappeared when Madres announced they were only a mile from the tunnel entrance.

Then, without warning, the Earth itself exploded.

As if swatted off the road by the hand of a giant, Sims' van spiraled like a football in mid-air before hitting the ground and rolling over and over, finally coming to a rest against the trunk of a massive tree.

# CHAPTER FORTY-SIX

The Cause's Underground Complex

"Was the attack successful?" Dave Knox asked a technician monitoring the landscape surrounding the tunnel entrance.

The tech used his mouse to zoom in on several smoke plumes just west of the highway that passed closest to the entry point.

"This is from one of our remote security cameras. We'll have drone coverage capable of providing a detailed damage assessment over the site in fifteen seconds," the tech reported without emotion.

Dave waited patiently for the drone to begin sending real-time video footage. When the picture changed a few seconds later, even he was surprised at how much damage one of his relatively tiny titanium spheres could produce.

A thirty-foot wide crater centered just off the two-lane blacktop marked the impact point. The shock wave had scattered the vehicles about like so many dry leaves after a sharp gust of wind.

Off to one side of the road, a dirty white trailer looked like it had been crushed flat. The truck that used to be attached had rolled over several times, coming to rest completely upside-down. Thick black smoke from burning diesel fuel poured out from around the destroyed engine cover.

"Zoom in closer," Dave ordered. "I want a body count."

Sims' skull felt like someone had tried to crack it open with a hammer – which explained the fact her face rested in a pool of blood and broken glass. Time seemed to pass in slow motion as she tried to understand why she was lying on her side, still strapped into the van's seat.

But when smoke began filling the cabin, Sims' mind snapped into sharp focus.

With the passenger side of the van now resting against the ground, Sims had no hope of opening her door. Above her, Madres hung awkwardly from her seat belts, one arm draped across Sims' torso.

Sims summoned all her concentration to find the seatbelt release. Thankfully, she didn't think she had any broken bones and could maneuver her body around enough to stand. A random thought crossed her mind that this was one of the few times she was thankful to be short.

Turning to Madres, she checked her pulse and was relieved to find it strong and even.

"Lieutenant! Wake up!" Sims shouted, holding Madres' head up to relieve the strain on her neck.

When the Chilean officer didn't respond, Sims scrambled around her body and, using the steering wheel as a foothold, pulled herself up through the broken driver's side window. Sims quickly surveyed the situation from her perch on the toppled van's door. Fire engulfed the tractor-trailer rig. Beneath the smoke, five of the seven transport vans burned brightly, adding to the apocalyptic scene. Sadly, she could see several bodies lying in the tall grass.

Turning her attention back to her own vehicle, Sims pulled open the passenger door and helped extract several members of Madres's team.

"Two of you help the lieutenant. The rest gather any survivors and move them into that stand of trees. It's the only cover around here."

Sims grabbed her phone and looked at the screen. No service. "Shit!"

Without working communications with Deal, they were on their own in the middle of the open Chilean countryside.

The Cause's Underground Complex

Dave and his technician studied the drone footage to see if anyone survived the sphere's surprise attack.

"I'm sorry, Mr. President," the tech said. "The smoke is too thick to get a good visual."

"Go to infrared," Dave ordered.

The tech entered a few commands, and the screen changed. But the raging fires and hot smoke obscured everything on the ground.

"Keep the drone on station and let me know when you have an accurate assessment of damage and casualties," Dave ordered. "If anyone attempts to move toward the entrance, you will contact me immediately. And this time, I won't program the weapon to miss."

"And if an attempt is made to extract the survivors?"

"They are no longer a threat. Let them go," Dave said. "Our fourth rocket will soon be leaving the launch pad and taking our final satellite into orbit. After that, there won't be anything left for them to find."

The technician's eyes flew open, and his eyebrows nearly raised to his hairline.

*What did that mean?*

Sims was trying to determine the status of the combined team of Americans and Chileans. And the news wasn't good.

Whatever hit the convoy had targeted the tractor-trailer and destroyed the four combat vehicles it carried. To make matters worse, every van that had transported the assault personnel was now useless.

Sims spent the next twenty minutes marshaling the teams and any remaining supplies and weapons.

"How's the lieutenant?" Sims asked one of the Chileans who, fortunately, had training as a combat medic.

"Conscious and giving orders. She probably has a concussion and could use a CT scan."

"Okay. Thanks. How many wounded do you have?"

"We have four in critical condition. Almost everyone has suffered minor injuries. I've seen at least ten with broken bones and more lacerations and contusions than I can count. I'll patch up the others when I get the four in critical condition stabilized."

"Do we know how many people we lost?"

Madres appeared and answered Sims' question.

"Eight. Five Chileans and three Americans. At least that is what we know so far."

Sims had to put those deaths aside. She would mourn later.

"Are you in contact with your advance team?" Sims asked. "We have no cell service out here."

Madres pulled out a yellow walkie-talkie.

"It is old technology, but we always carry these as a backup. We have four men concealed 500 meters from the tunnel entrance doors in a creek bed. They hiked in from five miles away last night and believe they were not spotted."

Sims thought for a minute. "Okay. Contact them again, but keep it short. We don't want anyone tracking the radio signals. They need to remain in place and stand by for further orders. And have them get in touch with Agent Deal. He can arrange an extract for us. I think I know what hit us. And if I'm right, we're sitting ducks. This operation is over."

# CHAPTER FORTY-SEVEN

Garcia's Apartment
Santiago, Chile

Deal had to restrain himself from throwing his phone against the wall. The assault he had fought for and planned came to a deadly end before it even began.

Now, three of his people from Blue Team were dead, along with five brave Chileans.

With Sims and her forces out of commission, he didn't have anyone in position to stop the critical fourth launch. And he desperately needed to recover Sims and the survivors.

Deal turned to Garcia, who had just gotten off a call.

"Can you arrange to get them out of there?" Deal asked.

"I have two private cargo helicopters on the way. Madres reports that there has been no further attack on our teams. This weapon they have is devastating. Hopefully, the helicopters can get in and out without getting hit as well," Garcia responded.

Deal nodded somberly. "We can't predict with any certainty what they will do. But they can't have an unlimited number of these things in space. It's not like they can just reload when they run out of ammunition. So, unless they perceive another direct threat, my bet is they stand back and observe."

"I hope you're right," Garcia said. "We don't have an unlimited number of people either. We suffered losses today that will be hard to replace."

"Yes, and we are not a millimeter closer to stopping the fourth launch."

"We will find another approach," Garcia said confidently a moment before his phone notified him of an incoming message. "But we don't have much time."

Garcia held the phone's screen up so Deal could read the message. *Number 4. 14 hours 30 minutes.*

"Rodrigo?" Deal asked, already knowing the answer.

Garcia nodded as the tension in the room spiked.

"Luckily, my team is excellent at improvising," Deal replied almost to himself as he stood and ran one hand over his head.

Deal's thoughts turned to Bubba and his research. The eccentric genius might be their last hope, but he didn't want to show Garcia all his cards. At least not yet. He might have to use whatever Bubba thought up without Garcia's permission.

Deal and Garcia paused their discussion when a guard opened the door for Michael, Sarah, and Daniela. Deal took a moment to bring them up to speed.

The news of three deaths on Blue Team shocked the young Americans. Michael, in particular, took the news hard. He trained from time to time with Deal's Red and Blue teams, hoping to one day earn his way onto one of the FBI's vaunted elite operations units.

"They knew the risks," Deal said, his voice low but determined. "And they won't be forgotten. But right now, we need to figure out how to stop this next launch. We have less than fifteen hours. Sims and the rest of the original assault force are being extracted. Most of them are banged up, and a few are seriously injured. I have no doubt Red and Blue teams would be more than eager to pay back whoever is in those tunnels. But with those weapons orbiting overhead, getting inside may be impossible."

"There will be access to the tunnels at the launch site," Michael observed. "And we know of one more – the escape hatch Zach used. And I bet he could find it again."

"Maybe..." Deal began.

"Michael's right," Sarah agreed. "Get us to Talca, and we'll find it."

"Assuming he can locate one small hidden door high in the mountains, how will you get in?" Garcia asked.

Deal shook his head. "You guys don't have the training or equipment to mount an assault of any kind."

"At least let Zach try," Michael pleaded. "He could probably find the escape door or hatch or whatever in a couple of hours. And I know the guys on Red Team will want to hit back. How about dropping them off in Talca and having Sims and them follow Zach?"

Deal didn't want to put Zach in harm's way again, but he didn't have a choice.

"Get him on the phone."

# CHAPTER FORTY-EIGHT



Despite the toasty warmth from the wood-burning heater, Zach sat uncomfortably in the Valdez's living room while Fernando, Rosa, and Junior sat around the kitchen table, working through the stunning revelation their son was still alive.

After several minutes fidgeting in an armchair, Zach stood and paced around the room. On a table next to the front door, he stopped to look at several pictures of Rodrigo Valdez arranged around a statue of the Virgin Mary. He studied the photos carefully, reassuring himself that the person who helped him escape from the tunnels had the same face as the one who smiled brightly out from the little shrine.

A ringer mounted over the door, announcing someone was at the gate, broke his concentration. Not wanting to overstep, Zach waited for one of the Valdez family to respond.

When a second ring went unanswered, Zach opened the door to the kitchen.

"I'm sorry to intrude," he said, seeing Fernando sitting at the small table with Rosa, their hands intertwined and tears flowing from their eyes. "I think someone is at the gate."

Without saying a word, Junior motioned for Zach to come into the room and patted his shoulder as he strode toward the front door. The American stood shifting his weight from foot to foot and trying not to look as uncomfortable as he felt.

Finally, Fernando motioned for Zach to come and sit at the table.

Rosa looked up from the floor and into Zach's eyes. She slowly reached two trembling hands across the table and gently folded them around Zach's forearm.

"Gracias, Zachary. Gracias. Gracias."

Zach's eyes filled with tears. He had not brought Rodrigo back from the grave. But the look in Rosa's eyes told him she believed he had.

"De nada, you're welcome," Zach responded with the few words of Spanish he remembered from high school. "But I'm no hero, and we still have to find a way to get him out of those tunnels."

Fernando seemed to understand what Zach said even without Junior there to translate. He reached over, grabbed Zach's shoulder, and nodded soberly, his eyes burning with determination.

Junior pulled on his coat as he opened the front door. No guests were scheduled to stay with Valdez family that night, and it was too late for a visit from neighbors.

When he got to the gate, he found a lone woman dressed in casual hiking clothes and holding a backpack upright by her side.

"Buenas noches," Violet Ruiz said through the gate. "I'm sorry I'm so late."

"Good evening," Junior responded warily, looking up and down the street.

"Yes, uh, I made a reservation some time ago. I was supposed to be here this morning, but I got held up in Santiago and had to catch a later bus," Ruiz explained acting like an exhausted traveler. "The reservation was under the name of Ruiz. Violette Ruiz."

"I didn't know my parents were expecting a guest tonight," Junior said. "Let me go in and check with them."

Ruiz couldn't let that happen.

"Let's see. I have the confirmation here somewhere," Ruiz responded quickly, reaching into the backpack and pulling out a silenced 9mm automatic pistol.

Junior took a step backward. "What...?"

"Open the gate, Junior," Ruiz ordered.

"What...? How...?" Junior stammered at the stranger who knew his name and now pointed a gun at his chest.

"Now. Take me to Zach and your parents."

Without any other option, Junior unlocked the gate and pushed it open far enough for Ruiz to enter before leading her into the house and through the kitchen door.

Zach glanced over his shoulder to see the strange sight of Junior walking into the kitchen with his hands raised. Then he noticed Ruiz.

"You!" Zach exclaimed, jumping up from the table. "What the hell are you doing here?"

"Hello, Zach. Your leg looks better," Ruiz purred.

Zach took one step toward the Argentinian officer but stopped short when she leveled her weapon at Rosa's head.

"Sit," Ruiz ordered, waving vaguely at the kitchen table with the weapon's barrel. "Hand me your phones."

"What is this about?" Fernando demanded.

"Shut up," Ruiz barked, dropping four cell phones into the pocket of her hiking vest. "I've got unfinished business with someone. And I will require your assistance."

Before Ruiz could explain further, her coat pocket buzzed. Reaching inside, she withdrew one of the four phones she had just confiscated.

"Answer it," Ruiz said, tossing the phone to Zach. "Put it on speaker and be very careful about what you say."

Zach could see the call was from Sarah and Michael.

"Hey," Zach said, swiping the phone open.

"Hey yourself," Michael responded. "Are you okay?"

"Yeah. What's up?"

Zach could tell Michael knew something was wrong.

"Uh, Deal wants to know if you can find that door you used to escape from the tunnels. Are you positive you're okay? You don't sound like yourself."

Ruiz pointed her gun at Rosa again.

"Yeah. Yeah. Sorry. Just tired, I guess. Why does he want to know?"

"We have to find another way into the tunnels. The fourth launch is happening in a few hours. Can you find it or not?"

"Geez, cool your jets. Yeah. I think so. What does he want me to do? Climb up there and pull a surprise attack all by myself? I know I have a big head sometimes, but ..."

"No, dumbass. Backup is on the way. We just don't have time for them to meet you in Talca. Get into the mountains, and we'll track your phone," Michael explained.

"But there's no cell signal up there," Zach protested. "I found that out the hard way."

"Bubba built a long-range tracker into your replacement phone. We can see where you are right now. Tell everyone we said hello."

"I'll see if Junior can give me a ride. One way or another, I'll be out of here in five minutes," Zach said before ending the call.

Ruiz took his phone back and dropped it in her pocket.

"They want you to go back to the escape hatch? Good idea. That's almost exactly what I had in mind – except you won't be going. Some of us will. And I have the code," Ruiz said, holstering her gun.

"What?" Zach asked, confused. "I don't get it. First, you kidnap me. Then you show me the rockets inside the tunnels. And after I escape, you track me down again. What gives?"

Ruiz crossed her arms over her chest and cocked her head. "My reasons don't concern you. All you need to know is our interests happen to align for the moment. You want to stop the fourth launch. These nice folks want Rodrigo back. And I want something from the people running that operation. And, Zach, you didn't escape from the tunnels. I let you go."

"No," Zach objected. "Rodrigo Valdez, the son of Fernando and Rosa Valdez, helped me."

"Well, that's partially true. Rodrigo is alive and has been feeding Major Garcia of the ANI information when he can. But you wouldn't have made it out of your cell if I hadn't set it up."

"It is true?" Junior blurted. "I had no reason to doubt Zach, but now you say it is true as well. How do you know?"

"Once they accepted me as one of their own, I ran a security sweep of every employee. I wanted to find a mole to use for my own purposes and found one in Rodrigo. Of course, he doesn't know I'm using him. When Zach 'escaped,' I protected Rodrigo's identity by saying he was actually a man named Manuel Mancha. Rodrigo is alive. But he is far from safe."

"Then we must go get him. I am going with you," Junior announced.

"As am I," Fernando added, standing from his chair.

"Everyone sit down. Now," Ruiz demanded, putting her hand back on her holstered weapon. "Like I told Zach, my reasons don't concern you. I will need Junior and Fernando to convince Rodrigo to help me once we access the facility using the escape door."

"And what about me?" Zach asked.

"You will be hiking back to the launch site. I'll have your phone."

"What good will that do?" Zach asked, confused.

"Before you left the tunnels, you drank water that contained millions of nano-sized tracking devices. The rather unpleasant people inside are tracking you even now. And so am I. You will be a decoy."

"Why don't I just stay here?" Zach said, pressing the issue.

"God, you are irritating," Ruiz responded. "Have you never seen someone in the movies throw meat over a fence to distract vicious guard dogs? You will get back to the launch site. I will know if you don't do as I say."

"And if I don't?"

As if by some sleight of hand, Ruiz's pistol appeared in her hand.

"The Valdez family ceases to exist."

# CHAPTER FORTY-NINE

35,000 feet over Southern California

"Where are they now?" Deal asked Bubba.

From a deeply padded leather seat inside the FBI's long-range passenger jet, Bubba typed a series of commands into his laptop.

"The tracker on Zach's new phone is working perfectly and shows him climbing into the mountains. From his description, he should be only a half hour or so from reaching the escape hatch he described," Bubba reported a moment later. "Is Agent Sims safe?"

"Blue Team is on their way back to Santiago. Sims and Red Team will be dropped off in the mountains in an hour," Deal said. "Michael and Sarah are with Garcia at his headquarters working on intel they gathered about President Cayo and the Pacifico Hotel."

"What kind of intel?" Bubba asked.

"I'm waiting to hear as well. Tell me where you stand. How can we take down this next launch with those titanium spheres hanging over our heads – without starting a war with Chile?" Deal asked.

For once, Bubba's boundless optimism seemed to have disappeared.

"After sitting down with the best aerospace guys at NASA, I'm afraid the news isn't good. Whoever designed this orbital weapons system had to be a certified genius. Maybe even as smart as me. They can obviously tap into every surveillance platform, both military and private, and will have advance warning of any attempt to take out their satellites. They will be able to track any aircraft or rocket. Nothing in our current inventory is stealthy enough to avoid detection and capable of operating anywhere near the upper atmosphere, much less space. GBI or Ground-Based Interceptor missile systems are out of range, and we don't have time to get a ship with the Navy's Aegis system into the area. Heck, even if we had a ship close enough, the bad guys would just sink it. And, the powers that be don't want to start a war by ordering an overt military attack on a civilian space program."

"No weapons system is invulnerable," Deal said.

Bubba nodded. "Our only chance is to catch the launch vehicle while it is outside being fueled or shortly after it launches."

"Tell me you have an idea." Deal responded, the frustration in his voice evident.

"I'm on my way to Edwards Air Force Base in California now to look at a classified prototype. It's old and a long shot, but it may be our only hope of bringing down the fourth rocket before it reaches space."

"Make it quick. We're running out of time."


Edwards Air Force Base
California, USA

Four nervous scientists and three stern Air Force officers greeted Bubba as he stepped out of the FBI jet. Over the past few years, Bubba had built an enviable reputation in the aerospace industry that had also spilled over into all branches of the military. Every major player had offered him research and development positions at gaudy salaries but the young genius from rural Alabama couldn't be tempted by money. He loved the challenge of working with the FBI and the excitement of teaming up with his three closest friends.

But even Bubba's high standing in his field wouldn't open the impenetrable doors concealing the country's black projects. Thankfully, FBI Director Glover had the ear of the president and the Joint Chiefs of Staff. So, despite massive pushback from the Air Force and several defense contractors jealously guarding their secret innovations, Deal's genius engineer had been granted access to several highly classified projects. Bubba had no time to waste. He moved quickly to try and find something capable of stopping the fourth launch while also offering some defense against the mysterious and deadly weapons orbiting high above.

Only one held any promise.

After a quick round of introductions on the tarmac, an Air Force security detachment hustled Bubba and the others into a shiny black van. A few silent minutes later, they sped through a set of partially open hangar doors. The van's darkly tinted glass and dim interior lighting prevented Bubba from seeing whatever the Air Force, or whatever clandestine agency was actually in charge, had secreted away inside.

Nobody said a word as the van's passengers gathered at the front of the vehicle. One of the Air Force officers pulled a small radio from his belt.

"Lights."

Bubba watched as the hangar's dark interior slowly brightened like some kind of dramatic stage lighting change. He wasn't sure if this was done to impress him, but what slowly materialized in the gloom did that all by itself.

"She's a real beauty," Bubba exclaimed, leaving the group of scientists and military men. "I wrote a paper as an undergraduate about the X-30, but I didn't expect it would ever become operational."

A gray-haired man wearing a slightly wrinkled lab coat appeared at Bubba's side.

"You can call me Dr. Jason," the kindly, grandfatherly scientist said, holding out his hand. "I've read some of your papers, Mr. Adcock. Impressive."

Bubba didn't recognize the man calling himself 'Dr. Jason.'

"Yours?" Bubba asked, waving vaguely at the aircraft still partially concealed by the dim lighting.

"For the last thirty years. Yes. They never recognized the major leap forward this would have provided," Dr. Jason explained, not able to keep deep disappointment out of his voice. "Come on then, take a look. Believe me when I say I don't get many visitors in here, so I'll be glad to answer whatever questions you have."

Bubba took a long moment to take in the sleek 50-foot-long vehicle that looked like the child of an unholy union between a cruise missile, a jet fighter, and a duck. Unlike modern fighters and missiles, the X-30's nose was thin, wide, and flat. Bubba reached up and ran one hand across the oddly shaped assembly he knew was necessary for ultra-high-speed flight. The fuselage rose gently from the nose toward the rear of the craft, where two dorsal fins were mounted at the top of the plane. Below, two small triangular stabilizers sprouted from the craft's almost comically pregnant belly.

"Have you tested this for stealthiness?" Bubba asked.

"Yes. But we didn't design the X-30 for stealth. Speed, Mr. Adcock. It didn't need to be stealthy because nothing in the world could have caught the X-30."

"Unmanned?"

"Of course. As you know, even if a human pilot could withstand the g-loads this creates, the weight of a cockpit and life support would significantly reduce its performance envelope."

Bubba ducked under the X-30's short, thin wings and walked to the back of the vehicle, where he found an odd configuration of three engines.

"Scramjet with rocket assist to orbit. Nice," Bubba observed.

"Indeed. After being released by a modified B-52 at 45,000 feet, its internal engines provide plenty of thrust for orbital insertion. Maneuvering thrusters for space navigation are in the usual positions around the fuselage but protected by doors until the vehicle reaches orbit. At the end of each mission, the X-30 reenters and recovers unpowered like the old space shuttle or uses its scramjets if necessary to reach a designated landing site."

Bubba took another few minutes to examine the vehicle and asked, "Can she carry a weapons load?"

The scientist shook his head.

"No. And that's one reason they put us on the back burner. If it can't kill people, the government isn't interested. This is now a testbed for flight faster than Mach 5, or hypersonic speed. But I'm afraid this is rather dated technology at this point. Other programs, ones I can't tell you about, will probably make this sweetheart a dinosaur in just a few years," Dr. Jason explained, wistfully running his hand over the X-30's smooth white belly.

Bubba stood in front of the experimental aircraft, admiring its design and the engineers and scientists who had worked for decades to perfect its advanced aerodynamics. After a moment, he turned to Dr. Jason, who was justifiably proud of his creation.

"Is this the only working prototype?"

The scientist turned to Bubba, cocked his head slightly to one side, and looked at him with squinted eyes.

"Yes. Why do you ask?"

# CHAPTER FIFTY

The Cause's Underground Complex

Dave stood with both hands stuck deep into the pockets of his white lab coat while a small army of engineers, technicians, and scientists swarmed over the fourth rocket. The brilliant aerospace engineer, physicist, and leader of The Cause walked along the entire length of the massive vehicle, his practiced eye critically assessing every coupling, fitting, and valve until he reached its nose, where a clear plastic wall had been erected to protect delicate electronics from dust or other contamination.

Standing outside the barrier, Dave motioned for one of the engineers to come and give him a report.

A moment later, a man dressed in white clean room apparel approached. Dave had worn identical outfits many times but still thought it made the wearer look like an overly cautious surgeon. The one-piece jumpsuit with built-in shoe coverings closed in the front with a long zipper. A separate hood covered the head and face and flowed down over the shoulders. The only part of the body Dave could see was the man's blue eyes from behind the visor built into the outfit's hood.

"We are preparing the mount for the master satellite now, sir," the engineer said in a muffled voice through the wall of thin, clear plastic.

"Any issues?" Dave asked.

"No, sir. We should have the payload in place and the nose cone installed in eight to ten hours."

"Seven," Dave ordered. "Keep me informed. I'll be in ops."

A few minutes later, the maglev tram delivered Dave to the flight center a half mile away. Inside, Dave found the darkened room buzzing with preparations for the master control satellite's launch and initiation. His incredible ego wouldn't allow him to worry about whether the launch would succeed or whether his constellation of cubesats would function as he intended. His mind was preoccupied with security.

The accomplishment of Dave's entire scheme, not to mention the promised return on the billions invested by The Cause, now depended on maintaining operational security for the next few hours. His ingenious orbiting weapons system had already halted one attempt to breach the tunnels. With just one shot, he had taken out a heavily armed assault force. But, like a tiny stone in one of his shoes, one irritating problem kept Dave from enjoying the sweet anticipation of success.

Dave stopped and stood behind one of the officers who was monitoring several video feeds and various security systems.

"Show me the location of Zach Self."

A moment later, one of the screens displayed a map of the Maule Region and a bright red dot about 30 miles east of Talca.

"Zoom in."

With a tap on his mouse, the security officer enlarged the map. According to the information on the screen, Zach was only five miles from the launch site.

"Is there anyone with him?" Dave asked.

"No, sir. I ordered drone surveillance of the target when he breached the five-mile perimeter. He is limping and leaning on a hiking stick of some kind."

Dave rubbed his chin and scowled at the screen for a moment.

"Keep an eye on him. I have to go to Santiago for the Independence Day parades. If he becomes a problem, you are authorized to eliminate him."

"Yes, sir."

"Where is Lieutenant Ruiz?" Dave shouted at his head of security, who stood behind several officers monitoring security camera feeds showing the tunnel entrance and the launch site high in the mountains.

"She hasn't reported in from Talca, sir."

"Well, find her, damn it."

Ruiz was supposed to be dealing with Zach Self and the other American agents. Dave couldn't make sense of her failing to report or allowing Self near the launch site just as the most critical part of his plan was about to unfold.

A cold knot in his gut made him reach for his phone.

"Where are you?"

"You're in luck, sweetie. I'm in Buenos Aires."

"I'm sending a jet. I may need you for another job. Meet me at The Pacifico."

"Deposit the usual fee into my account, and I'll see you in two hours," Amina Kent replied while refreshing her bright red lipstick.

## The Pacifico Hotel
## 12th Floor Conference Room
## Two hours later

"It's one of the president's constitutional duties as Commander-in-Chief of the armed forces," Alexander Monroe said almost jokingly. "The whole country will expect you to be at the Independence Day celebration."

Dave sat across from Monroe dressed in a bespoke tailored suit, Turnbull and Asser tie, and Italian leather brogues. He blew a stream of pungent cigar smoke into the air.

"Where?"

"O'Higgins Park here in Santiago."

Dave laughed. "What do I have to do? Dress up in that ridiculous uniform with all the medals and sashes and crap and salute as a few old, useless tanks roll by?"

Monroe chuckled. "Exactly."

Dave scratched at the mustache that seemed to continuously tickle his nose.

"And the whole country will be watching?"

"Yes. If all goes as planned, the master satellite will have reached orbit by the time you take the stage, but I understand it won't be in position yet to take control of the entire network. We still have time to take out the com satellites covering Chile and Argentina with our titanium spheres, leaving TNI to carry the ceremony exclusively and live in both countries."

Dave nodded, already knowing the timetable. "In less than 24 hours, we will control most of the global information delivery systems and be able to manipulate public opinion in whatever direction we wish. I don't want any more complications. Perhaps I should have ordered the American agent, Zach Self, eliminated after all."

Monroe took a sip from his drink. "Relax. Your nano-trackers are working perfectly. He can be dealt with any time we choose. Security just updated me. He is alone and not a threat to the next launch. Probably freezing to death by now. Let's not get sidetracked by minor irritants."

"Fine," Dave reluctantly agreed.

"Good. Everything is on schedule," Monroe said, the alcohol in his bloodstream making him chatty. "It's a brave new world. People swallow whatever preposterous bullshit pops up on their phones. All we will have to do is decide who and what they see. We are the puppet masters now."

Dave stood and walked to the floor-to-ceiling windows that ran along the entire west wall and looked at the face reflected in the glass. He had taken on Cayo's identity weeks before, but even his immense intellect couldn't easily reconcile the face looking back at him in the glass with how he saw himself.

"Good. You're right, of course. But I want my old face back," Dave said wistfully.

"You don't want to become Chile's dictator? Could be a lot of fun," Monroe said sarcastically. "Or is Chile not big enough?"

Dave laughed. "No. It's not. I'm going to change our plans just a bit."

"How so?" Monroe asked, intrigued, just as an unexpected voice broke into their conversation.

"You two look a little too self-satisfied. Smug even."

Dave and Monroe spun around to find Amina Kent sitting in Dave's chair at the conference room table, her black Christian

Louboutin pumps resting on the polished surface. Amina wiggled out of a bright red coat and threw it casually onto the table, revealing a form-fitting black jumpsuit that did little to hide her fit twenty-five-year-old physique.

"I thought you might call when you got into town," Dave replied, his mouth drawn into a tight line.

"You called me. Remember? Anyway, I didn't want to pass up the chance to test my skills against your security setup. And, so you know, it's a joke."

Dave looked at Monroe. They both knew about Amina's unique talents. But her sudden, unannounced, appearance sent a chill up both men's spines.

"How much of that did you hear? And get the hell out of my chair," Dave demanded.

"Not enough to give a shit," Amina replied, ignoring Dave's orders. "I only care about your money. So, let's not waste time arguing over who has the bigger set of balls, and you just tell me who you want dead. I have dinner reservations in less than an hour."

Monroe had to stifle a laugh.

"Fine," Dave said, throwing both hands into the air. "Do you remember the last time you were in this room?"

"To be precise, I've been here twice. The last time I murdered the real president. Before that, some foul-mouthed old lady died about where you are standing now," Amina said, pointing her index finger at Dave like a pistol.

"Bang."

"Do you know who she was?"

"I couldn't care less. Now, can we dispense with the guessing games?" Amina asked, tapping the face of her Rolex watch.

"I want that woman's daughter dead. Lieutenant Violet Ruiz. Oh, and one more as well."

Monroe's eyebrows raised, but he said nothing.

Amina didn't bat an eyelash. "Just deposit another fee. And, by the way, there's no quantity discount. Who is the second target?"

"President Juan Mateo Cayo."

Amina just shrugged. "It's your funeral."

# CHAPTER FIFTY-ONE



"Just what the hell do you think you are doing?" a red-faced Air Force colonel shouted up at Bubba, who sat precariously on the rounded upper fuselage of the X-30, his legs grasping the cold titanium alloy skin like a bull rider.

Bubba looked down and waved.

"Hey there, colonel. Just installing a couple of upgrades to this baby's radar tracking program."

The Air Force officer's face turned an even deeper shade of red.

"Get your ass down here. You are not authorized..."

Bubba cut off the officer's rant by drawing a single sheet of paper from his pocket and letting it float down toward the concrete floor like the last leaf in late fall.

"Let me know if you have any more questions," Bubba said as the colonel snatched the paper off the floor.

After scanning its contents, the officer looked back at the almost comical appearance of an overweight, shaggy-headed twenty-something perched on top of one of the country's most closely guarded black projects. But he couldn't argue with orders signed by the president of the United States, the director of the CIA, and the chairman of the Joint Chiefs of Staff.

"You don't have to salute or nothin'," Bubba joked in his thick country accent. "I'm almost done here. Can you tell them to get that B-52 warmed up? This thing needs to get into the air."

The officer looked at the paper again.

"Well, I'll be damned. *You're* that genius FBI scientist?"

"That's what they tell me," Bubba responded affably.

"Alright then. I'm Colonel Thornton. Most people call me Bronco. I fly the B-52 mothership," Bronco said in a thick accent.

"Other than the obvious connection to Texas, why Bronco?" Bubba asked, not looking up from the laptop between his legs.

"Seems one of my flight instructors found my style a little aggressive. Said he almost got thrown out of his seat. What the heck are you going to do with the X-30?"

"Wish I could tell you, Bronco."

"Alright, I get it. Fly the plane and shut up. Story of my life. I've got my ground crew gassing up the BUFF now. We can have the X-30 mounted and ready to take off forty minutes after you're done up there," Thornton said, looking at his watch.

"Big Ugly Fat...uh...Fellow. Always loved that name," Bubba laughed.

"They ain't pretty, but they get the job done."

Bubba closed his laptop, unplugged its connection to the experimental plane, and closed the access hatch he had been using. A moment later, he climbed back down to the concrete floor.

"Let's go."

Less than an hour later, Bronco Thornton pushed the B-52's throttles to full military power. The gigantic black aircraft slowly rolled down the runway with the X-30 tucked under its right wing. Long black smoke trails from all eight jet engines traced the plane's path into the sky.

For the next fifty minutes, Bubba monitored the condition of the X-30's complex software from the electronic warfare officer's station behind Bronco.

"What's our position, Bronco?" Bubba asked over the ship's intercom system.

"One hundred twenty miles west of Cabo San Lucas on the southern tip of the Baja Peninsula. Eight hours thirty-two minutes to the drop point off the coast of Chile," Bronco answered.

"Any chance we can improve on that ETA?" Bubba asked. The X-30 had to be in position before the fourth launch – and over eight hours wasn't going to cut it.

"Not even if you got out and pushed."

Bubba used the BUFF's communication array to contact Deal in Santiago.

"Where are you?" Deal demanded.

"Cruising past Mexico, but we're still over eight hours from even a maximum-range initiation point. Any update on when the fourth launch is happening?" Bubba asked.

"Major Garcia is still hoping his man on the inside, Rodrigo Valdez, can get a message out to us with an exact time. But so far, nothing."

# CHAPTER FIFTY-TWO



Ruiz held up a fist, signaling Fernando and Junior to stop. Throughout the late afternoon, she and the two Valdez men had climbed into the Andes, retracing Zach's steps after his escape. But unlike Zach, they were trying to get into the tunnels and not out.

"We have to be silent, and you must stay directly behind me from this point on," Ruiz ordered. "Sensors are scattered all along this ridge and up to the escape hatch. We will be fine as long as we don't set off the vibration or sound detectors. Do you understand? All our lives, including Rodrigo's, depend on it."

Fernando and Junior nodded their understanding.

"Lieutenant," Junior said quietly. "We don't care what you are about to do or why. All we want is Rodrigo."

Ruiz shot Junior a threatening look.

"Just do as I say, and your family might survive this."

Ten minutes later, Ruiz settled the group outside the camouflaged escape hatch. It took a full minute for her to locate and open a hidden control panel and enter a seven-digit code. A satisfying click accompanied the door popping open.

"Let's go."

As they stepped through the door, a figure emerged from the shadows.

"Pappa? Junior?" Rodrigo Valdez said, his eyes the size of dinner plates. "What are you doing here?"

Fernando and Junior didn't say a word. Tears fell in rivers of liquid happiness as they wrapped their arms around the son and brother they fully believed to be dead just twenty-four hours earlier.

Ruiz let the reunion play out for another ten seconds before stepping in and physically separating the men.

"We don't have time for this right now. Rodrigo, when is the next launch?" Ruiz demanded.

"Less than four hours. They are almost finished inserting the master control satellite into the nose of the vehicle. Once that is done, the rocket will be taken out to the launch site, where it will be lifted into position and fueled. Final checks will be run during the last few minutes of the countdown. The entire process outside the tunnel will take less than twenty minutes so that it is exposed for the shortest time possible. So, now what?" Rodrigo asked. "What do you need us for?"

Ruiz waved her pistol at the stairs.

"Don't act like you forgot what we talked about. Lead the way down to the assembly station. I don't have to remind you that if we get caught, we all die."

Rodrigo led the group down eight floors to the assembly area door. He stopped and retrieved four matching sets of light blue coveralls, masks, and headgear which Ruiz had ordered him to keep on hand.

"Get us close to the rocket," Ruiz demanded.

"Fine. We can use my credentials. Leave any talking to me."

Fernando put a hand on his son's shoulder and looked at Ruiz.

"What are we to do once we get inside? You have the only weapon. Could we not just leave the way we came in?" he pleaded.

The gun in Ruiz's hand that now pointed at his stomach answered Fernando's question.

"Rodrigo here is going to make sure this rocket never makes it to orbit. I don't care if it blasts off, but I want it to end up in the ocean or smashing into the mountains. You two are here to make sure he does his job."

"I told you, I'm a mechanical engineer. I work on the transport systems and infrastructure," Rodrigo objected.

"And I told you to figure something out. Just open it up and start cutting wires or pipes or something," Ruiz ordered.

"And when I cut the wrong wire, and it blows us to pieces, or I sever the wrong line, and it releases a gas that kills us all instantly?"

"You have sixty seconds to figure that out. When we get out there, you better have a plan. I didn't bring your family here so they could give you a big hug and take you home," Ruiz growled, placing her hand on the door to the assembly area.

"Okay. Just a second. This is important," Rodrigo said. "Final preparations of the rocket itself are complete, and operations are now concentrated at the nose where the satellite is being mounted. We should have a few minutes alone back by the engines. Anyone interested will see a work crew looking at the assembly/launch platform."

Ruiz glared at Rodrigo and then snatched Junior by the collar and held her pistol to his head.

"Quit stalling," she hissed through clenched teeth while waving the barrel of her pistol at the closed door.

"Let him go. I can disable the transport system. They won't be able to get the vehicle outside."

"That only delays the launch. You don't seem to understand. I want this to fail. Fail! Do you hear?" Ruiz almost shouted, now pointing her gun at Rodrigo.

"Yes. Yes, of course. Please. Give me a second to think," Rodrigo pleaded.

All but forgotten by Ruiz, Fernando worked his way around to the Argentinian officer's side. He caught Junior's eye and motioned for him to take a step back from the woman brandishing her pistol at Rodrigo.

Junior got the hint.

"Hey!" Junior suddenly said excitedly, pointing up the open stairwell. "Who's that?"

Ruiz took her eyes off Rodrigo and looked up at where Junior was pointing.

At that moment, Fernando's right arm shot out like a snake and wrapped around Ruiz's neck. The next instant, his left arm bent around his right, putting Ruiz in a tight chokehold.

Without hesitation, Ruiz fired her right elbow backward into Fernando's side. A second blow broke one of his ribs. But Fernando had lost a son once, and now he fought to keep both of his children alive. As a youth, his wiry frame had been hardened by unending farm work and later honed into a deadly weapon by the Chilean army. The struggle lasted only a few seconds before Ruiz tried to raise her gun. In an instant, Junior grabbed her wrist with both hands and twisted the pistol away before she could pull the trigger.

But Ruiz wasn't finished. With her free hand, she pulled a short but razor-sharp knife out of her boot and plunged it into Fernando's thigh. The older man grunted with pain but held on.

Ruiz snarled and twisted, trying to find another target for her blade while desperately fighting to pull away from Fernando's determined chokehold. Neither seemed to have the advantage until Rodrigo smashed Ruiz's own pistol into the side of her head.

The Argentinian officer crumpled to the floor, and Rodrigo wasted no time dragging her limp body under the staircase.

"What now?" Junior asked.

"I wasn't lying to this woman. I can't disable the rocket. I wish I could. But I can delay the launch for a few hours. I'll be right back," Rodrigo said just before casually walking out the door, giving Junior and Fernando a glimpse of the stainless-steel rocket.

In less than two minutes, Rodrigo reappeared.

"What did you do?" Junior asked.

"I disabled the electric motors that power the rocket's moving platform. They will have to be completely replaced. It will take hours to repair. Now, let's get out of here," Rodrigo said. "Right, Pappa?"

Fernando was already tying a strip of cloth torn from his overalls around the wound in his leg.

"Yes, son. Yes."

"I don't think we can get back out the way we came in," Junior observed, looking up at the imposing escape stairwell. "Pappa won't make it back up. Even if he could, hiking out of the mountains would be impossible."

Rodrigo smiled. "Luckily, I work on the transportation systems. We'll take the maglev tram down to the tunnel entrance. From there, I know a way out. Then I need to make an important call."

Fifteen minutes later, Ruiz pried her eyes open and winced as she touched the side of her head. It took a moment for her to recognize she was looking up at the underside of the metal escape stairs. After a few deep breaths to get her bearings, she suddenly realized the Valdez family was nowhere to be seen.

Ruiz couldn't very well sound the alarm and have the entire complex looking for intruders she herself had brought into the tunnels to sabotage Dave's master plan.

Her scheme to discredit the man who killed her mother had failed.

She needed a 'Plan B.'

Ruiz found her radio and called the operations center.

"This is Ruiz. Where is President Cayo now?"

"The president was looking for you, Lieutenant. He left for Santiago to attend the Independence Day celebrations tomorrow, ma'am."

"Have operations get a helicopter warmed up and fueled for a flight to Santiago," Ruiz ordered.

Before walking to the helicopter pad, Ruiz covered the nasty knot on the side of her head with a black cap and took a deep breath to gather herself.

In the control room, The Cause's head of security called The Pacifico's conference room.

"Please tell President Cayo that Lieutenant Ruiz is on her way to Santiago."

# CHAPTER FIFTY-THREE

Garcia's apartment
Santiago, Chile

Deal sat on Garcia's couch, closely monitoring Bubba's flight. Once the B-52 arrived off the coast, it could only loiter for an hour before low fuel would force it to turn around, severely limiting the timeframe Bubba could launch the X-30 in an attempt to intercept the fourth launch.

"Where are they now?" Garcia asked for the fifth time in the last two hours.

"Off the coast of Ecuador," Deal said. "They need more time."

Garcia stood and paced around the room, one hand rubbing his forehead. Deal had waited to fill in the ANI officer until after Bubba's flight was on the way to Chile. At first, Garcia had been alarmed and incensed that the United States had decided on a unilateral attack inside his country. But when Deal explained Bubba's idea and that the X-30 was an unarmed test plane, Garcia relented.

But now, it looked like the launch would take place long before Bubba had the chance to try his hair-brained scheme.

"If they aren't in position by the time your launch detection satellites pick up the rocket lifting off, the fourth satellite will make it into orbit," Garcia said, running one hand over his thick black hair.

Deal looked at his watch. Time was running out.

"We'll cross that bridge…"

Garcia's phone rang, cutting off the discussion. He didn't recognize the number.

"Yes?"

"This is Rodrigo Valdez. I need to report."

Garcia got Deal's attention and put his phone on speaker.

"Excellent. State your status."

"I am outside the tunnels. I had help escaping. Right now, you need to know the fourth launch has been delayed. My guess is an hour. Maybe two. I'll explain why later."

"Understood. What else?" Garcia prompted.

"An Argentinian, a Lieutenant Ruiz, brought my father and brother into the tunnels using the escape hatch high in the mountains. She wanted to use them as leverage to force me to sabotage the fourth launch. Her motives were not clear to me. I think she was seeking revenge of some sort against the owners of the project."

"Did your investigation determine who is behind this?"

"No. But President Cayo has been in the tunnels many times. Usually in the company of gringos. Mostly Americans," Rodrigo responded.

"What about Zach Self?" Deal asked. "He was supposed to be trying to locate the escape hatch. Is he with you?"

At that moment, Michael, Sarah, and Daniela walked in the door. Deal waved them inside and pointed to chairs.

Rodrigo spoke quickly. "No. My father and brother reported that Ruiz sent him toward the launch site as a diversion while they accessed the tunnels through an escape hatch. His current status is unknown. But you need to know the real purpose of the satellites.

"First and foremost, they are creating a web of communications platforms that can reach almost every person on the planet. The fourth satellite is the master control unit. As soon as it's in orbit, they plan to destroy the existing global orbital communications array and hijack most, if not all, access to the internet. They also plan to replace most major news services with their own broadcast. They call it TNI or Truth Network International. TNI will spout propaganda to prop up whatever regime, dictator, or oligarchy is willing to pay their price."

The global scope of the plot Rodrigo described sent shockwaves across the room.

Garcia asked, "What else can they do?"

"They carry titanium spheres that can be used to hit and destroy satellites or spacecraft in orbit. They can also drop through the atmosphere and strike targets on the ground or in the air with unbelievable force."

"Yes. We've seen that happen already. But you have no information on the exact time the fourth launch will take place?" Garcia asked.

"No. I'm sorry."

"Excellent job. Your service will not be forgotten," Garcia said.

"I'd rather it was," Rodrigo answered quickly. "My family has been through enough. But if you need me, call."

After Garcia hung up, Deal asked, "Do you trust this guy?"

Garcia nodded. "I do. I happen to know his family. His father, Fernando Valdez, was the highest-ranking enlisted man on base when I attended Officer Candidate School. Back in the eighties, Master Sergeant Valdez worked tirelessly to maintain the military's independence when our last dictator tried to use them against his political rivals and his own people. Some failed their oaths. Not Valdez. If not for men like him, we might still be living under the iron hand of some authoritarian tyrant. It appears he instilled the same sense of duty in his sons."

Deal turned to Michael, Sarah, and Daniela.

"What did you learn at The Pacifico?"

Daniela handed Deal the memory card from the camera they used while hiding under the bushes.

"President Cayo attended what was billed to be a fundraising event. But everyone there seemed to be a foreigner," Daniela said. "After hearing that report from Rodrigo Valdez, I think you'll find the conversation he had about TNI interesting. We also made sure to get a shot of every guest, just in case. But what about Zach? Where is he?"

# CHAPTER FIFTY-FOUR

Near The Cause's Launch Site
Andes Mountains
Two hours later

When Zach recognized the place where he, Michael, and Sarah had been attacked, he knew he was going in the right direction. Thankful for the familiar landmark, he stepped through the entrance to the narrow canyon they had found during their first trip into the mountains.

At the other end, Zach took a quick break in the fading light and took a long pull from his water bottle. Looking around, he noted the rather obvious lack of anyone concerned about his approach.

*I'm not sure I make much of a diversion.*

Zach considered his next move, but with Ruiz and probably the entire underground complex able to track his position, he couldn't risk Junior and Fernando's lives by giving up at this point. Sticking his water bottle back in his small backpack, Zach looked up to see the ridge they had found just days before. Bubba's launch site was supposed to be on the other side. Though nearing exhaustion and once again feeling drained by the altitude, Zach pushed on.

Ten minutes later, he scrambled over the rock-covered ridge and found himself peering down into a flat valley. To get a better view, Zach scrambled across the rocky hillside until he reached the same boulders Ruiz and her late partner, Bruno Miranda, had sheltered behind days before. Despite studying the entire valley end to end, the young American saw nothing indicating this place had ever been used to launch rockets into space.

In the tunnel's operations center, a quiet but insistent alarm alerted the Chilean special forces operators that Zach had breached the final security perimeter.

"Can we pick up this guy now, sir?" one of the operators asked the sergeant Dave had left in charge. "We've been watching him for over an hour."

"He's completely alone and unarmed. Anyway, we are too close to rolling the TS4 out to the pad. Just keep an eye on him. Let him watch the show. If he stays, the exhaust blast from the spacecraft will either incinerate him instantly or blow him off the mountain. The trackers in his blood are working perfectly. If he's bright enough to run, he won't be able to get away."

Outside, Zach's eyes grew wide as he suddenly noticed a black slit opening in the side of the mountain. As it slowly grew wider, the afternoon sun revealed the nosecone of a massive rocket. Zach watched, somewhat spellbound, as a gleaming stainless-steel launch vehicle rolled smoothly through the door on what must have been partially buried tracks of some kind. When it reached the center of the valley floor, its nose rose into the air until it pointed straight up. In a well-rehearsed and efficient operation, about twenty men wearing white overalls and hard hats appeared and attached multiple fueling lines to round ports on the rocket's side. A minute later, thin clouds of evaporating liquid oxygen, vented from internal fuel tanks, floated off to the side of the vehicle. Zach tried to mentally record everything he saw so he could describe it to Bubba in detail.

Five minutes later, three short blaring alarms sounded, sending the workers below running back into the tunnel opening.

"Looks like it's time to go," Zach said to himself, suddenly realizing he was way too close. Not wasting another second, he turned and took off at a dead sprint down the hill and away from the valley.

Zach's rush to get away from the launch site took him higher into the mountains. While he would have loved to make his way back toward the old truck Fernando Valdez let him borrow and drive it back to Talca and civilization, he had ruled out that option, at least for the night. After running for what seemed like miles on a bum ankle, he dropped to the ground out of sheer exhaustion. The good news seemed to be he wasn't being followed. At least not yet.

Zach grabbed his water bottle and poured the last ounce of liquid into his burning throat.

"Well, crap," he said, dropping the aluminum bottle onto the rocky ground.

Just as the harsh reality of being alone in the mountains without food and water sunk in, the American student heard a familiar voice.

"You look awful."

Zach jumped to his feet. "Stella?"

"Hey, Zach," Agent Stella Sims said, stepping out from behind a boulder.

"How did you find me?" Zach responded with a wide grin.

"Deal diverted us to this area after he received new information from Rodrigo Valdez. I'll fill you in on that later."

"So, how did you get all the way out here?" Sims asked.

Zach recounted how he had been coerced to drive into the mountains and then climb back to the launch site as a diversion. He also quickly described how his blood carried nano-sized trackers that let whoever was in the tunnels monitor his position.

"You're kidding," Sims exclaimed. "I've never heard of technology like that. Why do you think they haven't come after you?"

"I can't be sure. I suppose they were too busy with the giant rocket they are about to send into space."

# CHAPTER FIFTY-FIVE

The Cause's Underground Complex

The operations center suddenly burst into life as several alarms turned everyone's eyes to the immense map spanning the front wall where a single red diamond-shaped icon advanced toward Chile's border.

"Identify," the officer in charge of the op center ordered the tech sitting behind a console.

With a few quick movements of a mouse and lightning-fast keystrokes, identification symbols appeared next to the dot.

"American. B-52. Training flight scheduled to overfly Easter Island and recover at Diego Garcia," the tech reported.

"Cleared by the Chilean Air Force?" the officer asked with his head cocked to one side and his eyes narrowed.

"No, sir. The president ordered the Air Force and Navy to copy us with any such notices. I have nothing on this."

"Damn," the officer spat under his breath. "How long to launch?"

"TS4 is fueled and on the pad. We are T-Minus 12, sir."

With only 12 minutes until the crucial final launch, and with the president and Mr. Monroe in Santiago for Independence Day, the decision to act or not was his.

"Take it out. Two spheres."

"Two, sir?"

"That's a big plane."

"Are you in position?" Deal asked Bubba over the secure link with the B-52 mothership.

Without looking up from his screen at the Electronic Weapons Officer's position behind the B-52's two pilots, Bubba responded, "Barely. The delay Rodrigo Valdez reported gave us just enough time."

"Give me a status report."

"I'm a little busy here, boss."

"Bubba, I've got the president, the Joint Chiefs of Staff, and a pack of angry prime ministers from Europe to Japan breathing down my neck. Half of them want to start lobbing ballistic missiles into the Andes."

Bubba glanced at the screen. He could see Deal needed some news – good or bad – so he spoke quickly.

"Okay. Using Rodrigo's time estimate and what we can see from our surveillance satellites, we expect the final rocket to lift off any minute. We don't know exactly when, but we'll know from our dedicated launch detection systems. When that happens, we'll have only two and a half minutes before it reaches MECO or Main Engine Cut Off. After that, it will stage and be going too fast for even the X-30 to catch. And, to make this harder, I have to release the X-30 so it has enough time to cross Chile and intercept the rocket without running out of fuel."

"Okay...," Deal said just before realizing that Bubba had already ended the call.

High in the Andes, Zach and Agent Sims felt the earth shake as they knelt behind a ridgeline almost a mile away from the launch site. Huge clouds of white smoke billowed over the canyon walls just before they watched the rocket rise slowly into the air. A moment later, deep, rumbling sound waves crashed into the pair, nearly taking their breaths away with the sheer power necessary to thrust the massive rocket out of the earth's atmosphere.

Over the Pacific Ocean, two words appeared in red on Bubba's main screen:

LAUNCH WARNING

Bubba checked their exact position, looked at his watch, ran several complex calculations in his head, and pressed the intercom button.

"Bubba to Bronco. Release the X-30 on my mark. Five, four, three, two, one – mark!"

From his position facing the rear of the massive aircraft, Bubba felt the plane shudder hard, not once, but twice. Bronco had described the plane's reaction to the release as a single mild jolt as the weight of the much smaller aircraft dropped away. But the two sharp shocks that passed through the massive aircraft felt scarily familiar.

"Oh, crap," Bubba said to himself, even as he tightened down his harness straps. "Come on! Not again!"

"I do not have visual on the X-30," Bronco said over the intercom.

Then all hell broke loose. Warning lights flashed across Bronco's instrument panel like some demented Christmas tree.

"X-30 still attached!" Bubba heard the navigator shout over the intercom. "Pilot! Engines four, five, and six on fire."

"Bronco, Comms, engines one and two are just – gone."

The giant plane suddenly pitched down and began a shallow dive. As Bronco tried to pull the nose up, four feet of the right wingtip tore off and tumbled away.

For the first time in his nearly 30-year career, Bronco Thornton realized he was going to lose his aircraft.

And Bubba was about to get the ride of his life.

"Emergency manual release the X-30," Bronco said as calmly as possible to his co-pilot, who reached down and yanked up a metal handle installed between the seats.

"X-30 away!"

"Alright, everyone, let's go swimming. EJECT! EJECT! EJECT!"

Bubba slammed down his helmet's visor just before he rotated two arming levers, blowing the hatch above his head into the atmosphere. Less than a second later, he pulled the eject triggers on the two yellow and black handles on either side of his seat. In a series of chaotic events he would have a hard time recalling later, the rockets in his seat fired, sending him hurtling out of the aircraft and into a crazy kaleidoscope of blue sky, white clouds, and green ocean tumbling over and over each other. The aerospace genius could do nothing but try not to lose his lunch. Finally, the drogue parachute automatically deployed and stabilized his fall. Bubba barely regained his bearings before the ejection seat dropped away, and air filled his main parachute, jerking him to what felt like a dead stop in midair.

While Bubba, Bronco, and three other crew members watched their B-52 slam into the Pacific Ocean from under their parachutes, high above their heads, the X-30's rocket engines burst into life. The ungainly bird leaped ahead, gaining speed at an incredible rate. Only seconds after it began powered flight, a sonic boom rolled across the beaches along Chile's west coast, signaling the X-30's transition through the sound barrier. But it was far from hitting its top speed.

Preprogrammed by Bubba back in the United States, the X-30 swung south toward its first waypoint, its flat, thin nose beginning to glow red and then white from the friction produced as it cut through the atmosphere.

The nearly thirty-year-old experimental aircraft screamed over the coastal mountains and across the central plains. When it passed directly over Talca, just a minute later, the radar in its nose began looking for a target. And a moment later, it found one. The X-30 charged into the Andes and then lifted its nose toward the sky to chase down its prey. The hypersonic aircraft's internal computers and Bubba's upgraded navigation system used the onboard radar to get a hard lock on the stainless-steel rocket. The X-30 adjusted its trajectory thousands of times every second as it chased the TS4. However, Dr. Jason's creation was never designed to be a weapon. Only Bubba's ingenious upgrades gave the old testbed a chance to make its last mission a success.

But they only had one shot – and it would have to be a bullseye.

Both vehicles were moving so fast that even with the X-30's computer crunching millions of calculations every second, not even the most reckless gambler in Las Vegas would bet on the X-30 destroying a ballistic missile climbing toward space at over 4000 mph.

Yet, without any other way to avoid its attacker, speed was the TS4's only defense.

A high-speed video of the event taken from an E-2 Hawkeye orbiting off the coast of Argentina would later reveal what a human could not have seen with the naked eye. The X-30's flat nose missed the much larger vehicle by almost two feet just before the rest of its wide fuselage passed by with inches to spare.

At the last possible instant, one of the control fins mounted under the belly of the experimental hypersonic aircraft sliced a tiny wound through the TS4's skin. While only a couple of inches long, the jagged laceration caused an explosive depressurization of the rocket's interior. In milliseconds, the change in pressure tore the TS4 apart just before a cloud of highly volatile rocket fuel ignited, totally enveloping what was left of The Cause's critical rocket, the master control satellite it carried, and the X-30, in one spectacular orange fireball.

Several minutes later, bits of blackened debris rained down across an empty 20-mile-long swath of the Atlantic Ocean.

# CHAPTER FIFTY-SIX

Garcia's apartment
Santiago, Chile

Deal snatched his phone off Garcia's coffee table as soon as the call from the E-2 Hawkeye pilot came in. After listening for a few seconds, Deal's shoulders relaxed, and he breathed for the first time in what felt like an hour. Garcia overheard the report and slapped the FBI agent on the back before standing and pouring them both a stiff drink. Just as he hung up the phone, Deal shot a thumbs up toward the rest of the room.

"He did it."

Michael let out a *WHOOP* of celebration before embracing Sarah and Daniela in a mighty bear hug.

After touching Deal's glass with his own, Garcia took a sip and fell back against the cushions of his armchair.

"Well, my friend, your man cut that close but pulled it off. Congratulations."

Deal allowed himself a rare smile.

"Thank you for trusting me and my team. But the news isn't all good, I'm afraid. The B-52 got hit. Probably by the damn spheres."

Michael and Sarah's heads snapped in Deal's direction.

"He's okay," Deal said quickly. "Everyone, including Bubba, eject-ed safely and are unhurt."

"Where are they now?" Sarah asked with a sigh of relief.

"Floating in the Pacific about fifty miles offshore," Deal replied.

"He's going to have a real story to tell," Michael said, shaking his head.

"Yep," Deal agreed. "And I'm never going to hear the end of it."

"I've already spoken with the Coast Guard," Garcia said, looking up from his phone. "They have a rescue helicopter inbound to their location and will have them on board shortly. Let's keep in mind though, while our adversaries have lost considerable capability, they still have a constellation of satellites that can devastate anything in space or on the ground."

"And have the ability to control a broad swath of communications in discreet areas," Deal added.

"Geez. Take the win," Michael chimed in.

"The major is right," Deal warned. "This isn't over."

As the short-lived celebrations died down, Garcia inserted the mem-ory card Daniela, Michael, and Sarah gave him earlier into his com-puter, hit a few buttons, and then picked up his phone.

"This is Garcia. I just sent a large video and audio file. I want every face that appears on it run through the facial recognition sys-tem. Everyone. No exceptions. Confirm each identity. I don't care how many people you need to get this done. I want your report in an hour. No more."

"Can they do it that fast?" Deal asked.

"Well, this is one time President Cayo's paranoia comes in handy. You remember how quickly we identified you and Agent Sims when you crossed the border? Cayo acquired the system but never said where it came from," Garcia explained.

The ANI officer paced around his apartment's living room for almost an hour, waiting for his phone to ring. When it finally did, he listened to the caller for less than ten seconds and hung up.

"We have the facial recognition results from the party," he said, opening his laptop and casting the screen to his 65-inch television. "My technician seemed upset but said I should review the results for myself."

Intrigued, Michael, Sarah, and Daniela gathered behind Deal.

Garcia opened the file. Thumbnail images of every guest attending the party appeared on the screen above each person's name and a brief dossier.

The ANI officer moved slowly through the list, identifying several major players in President Cayo's political party and most of his cabinet. But when Cayo's picture appeared on the screen, Garcia nearly jumped out of his chair.

"My god!"

"How can that be?" Daniela asked. "This program, or device, or whatever it is, must be tragically inept if it cannot identify the president of our country. Why does his name appear as Dr. David Knox?"

Deal nearly exploded out of his chair. "Did you say, Dr. David Knox?"

"This can't be correct," Garcia responded, puzzled.

"Precisely how accurate is this facial identification system?" Deal asked, trying to tamp down the excitement and tension in his voice.

"We have been using it for almost a year. It has never failed. Not even once," Garcia responded. "But that is Cayo. There can be no doubt about it. Who is this Knox?"

Deal didn't answer. Instead, he approached the screen and studied the image carefully before asking Garcia to add an image of President Cayo taken at the Independence Day celebrations a year before. When Garcia queried the facial recognition program, the year-old image was immediately identified as President Juan Mateo Cayo of Chile.

Everyone in the room agreed that the side-by-side comparison showed the same person. They had the same build, the same eyes, and even stood with the same pompous upward tilt of their chins and condescending smirk plastered across their faces.

Michael asked, "Hey, boss. Isn't Knox one of the Area 51 scientists that the FBI was looking for during the failed secession a couple of years ago?"

Sarah answered for Deal. "Yes. And if I remember correctly, he was a certified genius in aerospace technology and physics."

Deal rubbed at a knot forming in his neck muscles while he explained to Garcia how the FBI suspected Knox, along with his partner Dr. Rick Donnelly, of the theft of highly classified technology and the murder of two other brilliant scientists. Deal and his team had managed to foil a plan to use the stolen technology and had captured Donnelly. But Knox had seemingly disappeared off the face of the earth.

Until today.

"So, what does all that mean?" Daniela asked.

"And where is the real Cayo?" Sarah added.

For a moment, everyone in the room sat in stunned silence at the incredible ramifications of one of the FBI's Most Wanted criminals posing as the president of Chile.

"If this program is correct and that is not President Cayo, then Cayo is dead," Garcia answered. "But let's not get ahead of ourselves."

Deal's mind raced with possibilities. He had been sent to Chile to investigate a rogue space program, and he had gained invaluable intelligence about the satellites launched from the Andes – not to mention neutralizing a threat to the world's communications system. But now, with Knox's sudden appearance on the scene, he desperately needed to turn his mission into a manhunt.

"We know from Minister Aybar that Cayo is tangled up with whoever is behind these satellites. Now we know that it wasn't Cayo after all. Jaime, I've been chasing Dr. David Knox for years. I'm sure he is the mastermind behind this insane plot and that he has used your country to carry it out. He is more dangerous than you can imagine. Just look at how he fooled an entire country into believing he is the president," Deal began. "I want him."

Garcia could see the determination burning behind Deal's light blue eyes.

"I'm sorry, Frank. There's nothing I can do. Not right now."

"Why not?" Deal demanded. "It's your system, not mine, that discovered your president is an imposter. You can't just ignore that. It's your duty to arrest him!"

Garcia stood and pointed a finger into Deal's face.

"You will not tell me my duty. I know my duty."

"Yes? Then tell me this. What duty do you owe to someone posing as president?"

"Do not preach to me in my own house. In my own country. My duty is to the law. The ANI will investigate this properly. But I cannot and will not arrest the president when one computer program says he is not who he appears to be. If you were in America, you could not march into the White House and arrest your president on such little evidence. Even if I could do such a thing, Cayo's security will not let anyone spouting wild accusations like this within a mile of the president."

Deal held up a hand. He had gone too far.

"Jaime, you are correct, of course," Deal said, moderating his tone. "My team and I stand ready to assist. And please let me add that Dr. Dave Knox is not just a danger to the people of your country and mine. He just tried to throw the entire world into chaos and came damned close to succeeding. I'd like permission to remain in Chile while you launch your investigation. We make a good team."

Garcia understood Deal's intensity and eagerness. An outstanding law enforcement officer should have such passion.

"I agree, for now. But you will take no action against who you believe to be this David Knox. Do not test me on this point. I will personally arrest and prosecute anyone who breaks Chile's laws. Including you. The Independence Day parades are tomorrow. Cayo, or Knox, will be closely guarded, and his entire staff and cabinet will be present. I will start approaching a few of his ministers and military officers with our evidence after the event. But let us be realistic. Cayo's influence reaches deep into the bank accounts and careers of many in the government. However, a few, like Minister Aybar, will put the people of Chile and the law above their own personal gain."

# CHAPTER FIFTY-SEVEN



Dave paced back and forth in the lavish tent erected behind the massive viewing stand he would use to watch Chile's Independence Day parades. In a few hours, troops, tanks, armored vehicles, police, firefighters, and civilian groups of all kinds would parade through the park while he saluted and waved while dressed in a ridiculous faux-military uniform.

"What happened?" Dave asked Alexander Monroe, who sat stretched out on a chaise lounge sipping on a fragrant cup of coffee.

Monroe shrugged and answered, "They got lucky. The American Air Force disguised the attack as a routine training flight. Our security guys destroyed the bomber with two spheres, but it was too late. They think it released a hypersonic weapon. Apparently, they never got a lock on the thing. It just moved too damn fast. The real question now is – how does this affect our plans? The other Directors will want to know, and some of them may not share the same unshakable confidence that I have in you."

"Don't start kissing my ass now, Alexander. Whoever came up with using a hypersonic aircraft was clever as hell. They used the only type of vehicle that we couldn't effectively defend against. Anyway, I have already prepared for just this situation," Dave replied with an arrogant grin before picking up his phone and contacting the operations center back in the tunnel complex. "Initiate contingency plan A. And target all communications satellites covering South America with remaining spheres."

"What is contingency plan A?" Monroe asked, confused.

"Just a surprise nobody will see coming," Dave responded evasively.

"Great. Okay, so don't tell me. But, aren't you taking a big gamble with the spheres?" Monroe asked. "If we don't have the master control satellite in place, shouldn't we save the spheres for when we do? We just suffered a rather significant, uh, setback. And with our attacks on the aircraft and ground forces that threatened our facilities, not to mention the demonstrations where we took out that satellite and oil platform, our supply of spheres is already severely depleted. And now you are going to expend most of what we have left. Do you think that's really worth the risk you're taking?"

Dave chuckled confidently.

"I'm about to make a very dramatic exit, and TNI's exclusive coverage will make for great TV. And as for the risk I'm taking, I'm about to show you and the Directors how to properly deal with an unexpected setback, as you called it."

## Andes Mountains
## Approximately 1 mile from the launch site

Zach rolled over on his back and let out a deep breath.

"That was too close," the young American commented after witnessing the fourth launch. "Any closer and that thing would have barbequed us."

"Agreed," Sims said, her binoculars once again trained on the shallow valley. "They have an impressive operation. The sled or whatever that carried the rocket outside and raised it into position has already disappeared back into the tunnels. Just like that, the whole valley is just empty. Unbelievable."

"So, can we get the hell out of here now?" Zach asked. "Deal said Bubba's plan worked, whatever that means, and I still feel like I'm being tracked like a chipped dog."

Sims laughed, still scanning the launch site. "Yeah. I don't blame you. We should probably start moving...wait! Look!"

Zach quickly put his own spotting scope up to his eye. The cold and lack of sleep had sapped his energy, making it difficult for him to hold the telescope-like device steady. But he had to admit most of his trembling came from knowing Ruiz and the security forces in the nearby tunnels knew his exact position.

Zach focused on where Sims now pointed – the same place where the mountainside had opened to let the fourth rocket roll out to the launch pad. Even from almost a mile away, the military-grade optical equipment he held in his hand provided an impressively sharp image. At first, he saw nothing. But a moment later, he rubbed his eyes, thinking they must be playing a trick on him.

The camouflaged doors were slowly opening once again. Zach held his breath, hoping he was mistaken. But he wasn't.

From out of the dark tunnel, the glossy nosecone of a fifth rocket appeared.

"Come on! You have got to be flipping kidding me!" Zach exclaimed.

Sims snatched the satellite phone from her backpack and called Deal. She spoke quickly, relaying the appearance of the fifth rocket. She had just finished reporting when her tactical radio crackled to life in her earpiece.

"White One. Red Two. I have movement to the northeast."

"White One. Red Five. Movement to my southeast. I can see four, repeat four, tangos moving directly toward your position."

Sims swung her binoculars around, searching for the threats.

"Someone must have finally gotten irritated with you spying on them," Sims said to Zach. "But don't worry. We have one big advantage. They don't know Red Team is here."

Sims got back on the comms net.

"White One to Red Team. Stay out of sight and prepare to engage. Priority one is to keep them away from our position on the ridge. Buy us some time. We have another imminent launch. Repeat, a fifth launch vehicle is rolling out to the launch area."

"What the hell is going on? That was supposed to be the final launch, right?" Zach asked, turning toward Sims, who was busy checking her weapon and swinging her backpack onto her shoulders. "Hey! Where are you going?"

"I'm going to get a closer look. You coming?"

As Sims took off toward the launch site, Zach slammed the dirt with his fist before grabbing his backpack and following the FBI agent.

Sims hustled down a steep, rock-covered slope using an awkward, long-legged stride that at least let her stay upright.

Zach plugged along behind, slipping and sliding and muttering to himself while doing his best not to lose sight of Sims.

"This is a bad idea. A really, really, bad idea."

Almost a mile away, Red One had taken cover behind a pile of rocks that slid off the side of the mountain during some forgotten avalanche. He couldn't tell if they had been there two days or two millennia. But it didn't matter. They provided a natural barrier across one of the only paths up toward Sims' and Zach's last position.

"What have we got?" Red Two asked Red Team's leader.

"Four tangos moving in roughly line abreast formation. They have skills. I suspect ex-special ops. Red Two and Three are in high cover positions to our right. Our left flank is protected by the mountainside. Red Four and Five have a similar situation to our rear. They are covering this same pass a half click behind us. I had them set some booby traps. Anyone coming much closer is going to get a nasty surprise."

Satisfied with the preparations, Red One issued his final orders before the enemy made contact. "Red One to Red Team. I don't want to start a war here unless we have to. Hold your fire. Red Four, give them one warning shot before they reach your trip wires. If they insist on making trouble, give it to them. They're after Zach. He is with White One investigating the appearance of another rocket. So, let's have their backs."

Red One's headset crackled with four individual clicks acknowledging his orders.

"You think they'll turn around before they get here?" Red Two asked.

"Nope. This is going to get hot real soon."

"Good. We have a score to settle with these guys."

## Garcia's apartment
## Santiago, Chile

"We have another problem, Jaime," Deal said after ending the brief call with Sims from her satellite phone.

"What is it, my friend?" Garcia asked, seeing the worried look on Deal's face.

"There's a fifth rocket. And it's about to launch."

Deal's news silenced the entire room. They had received no intelligence from Rodrigo about another launch. If, as Deal fully believed, Knox was behind the rogue space program, he had masterfully concealed the existence of a fifth launch vehicle.

"What about Zach?" Michael wanted to know immediately.

"No idea. Red Team is fully engaged with security forces deployed from the tunnels," Deal replied. "Get Bubba on the phone."

Fifteen seconds later, Bubba's face appeared on the big screen. He looked like a giant half-drowned rat. He wore a towel over his head and a rough wool blanket draped around his shoulders. After Deal explained the situation, Bubba just shook his head.

"The X-30 was a one-and-done, boss," Bubba said over the racket from the Coast Guard helicopter. "Even if we had another one, we couldn't get it there in time. If they have that thing outside already, we know it will launch in no more than thirty minutes. Probably less. We're out of options. Without a miracle, that rocket's payload is going into space."

"Shake the seawater out of your brain, Bubba. Use it to find that miracle. Sims and Zach are in position overlooking the launch site. How do they stop this thing from taking off?" Deal asked.

For the next several seconds, Deal couldn't hear anything but the thumping of helicopter blades.

"Bubba?"

"Okay. Okay. Do they have a shoulder-mounted missile? Something that has some range and will make a big loud bang?" Bubba wanted to know.

"Will a grenade launcher do?" Deal asked. "Red Team uses a rifle-mounted system and carry four rounds each."

"What kind of range does it have?"

"About 350 yards," Deal replied.

"If Sims can get in range of the target and manage to place several grenades close to the engines or damage the launch tower... maybe. But if she misses..."

Bubba's voice trailed off.

"What?" Deal demanded.

"She'll be burned alive in the rocket exhaust."

### Andes Mountains

Still fifty yards behind Sims, Zach tried to pick up his pace. Fighting the pain in his leg and crippling fatigue from lack of sleep and thin air, he pushed himself as hard as possible to catch up.

Zach's stomach seemed to turn to ice when sharp cracks and pops of small arms fire began echoing across the mountains. Now he knew what it truly meant to be 'trapped between a rock and a hard place.' Just ahead, he knew that a fueling crew was making the last preparations needed to ignite seven massive rocket engines that would incinerate everything in the area – including him. Less than a mile behind, Red Team was engaged in a firefight with trained security forces bent on taking him out.

For the next few minutes, Zach tried to ignore the growing panic clawing at his gut as he climbed the rock-covered slope up to the ridge overlooking the launch site. Ahead, he could see that Sims had almost reached the exact position where he had first watched the fourth rocket roll out of the mountainside.

A moment later, things took a decided turn for the worse when he felt as much as heard the thumping of helicopter blades approaching. Exposed on the barren slope, he could only watch as Sims turned toward the sound and calmly raised her Heckler & Koch assault rifle toward the threat.

Suddenly, the noise from the helicopter blades grew deafening as the black and green camouflaged aircraft swung around a low peak only a quarter mile away.

With nowhere to hide, Zach threw himself on the ground, buried his face in his arms, and froze. Seconds later, he heard Sims' rifle firing at the helicopter on fully automatic. Zach could feel the rotor wash whipping dirt and debris over his body just before a loud WOOOSH announced a rocket ejecting from a pod mounted under one of the helicopter's small winglets.

Zach rolled over in time to see the missile impact the ground just below Sims, throwing the FBI agent bodily into the air.

"Noooo!" Zach shouted, getting to his feet.

Ignoring the helicopter now pirouetting in the air and turning back toward the ongoing firefight, Zach clambered up to where Sims lay unconscious.

"Stella! Stella!" Zach said, gently laying Sims' head on his backpack.

She was still breathing, and he didn't see any blood. But he could tell her right arm and leg took the brunt of the explosion. Both were definitely broken.

Not knowing what else to do, Zach poured water on a spare shirt from his pack and wiped it across Sims' forehead. The FBI agent groaned, and her face contorted into a mask of pain. But she was alive.

"Zach?" Sims said. "What...?"

"Stay still. You're injured."

"No shit. What about the rocket?" Sims said, trying to pull herself up to a sitting position – and failing.

"Still on the pad. Otherwise, we'd be toast," Zach responded.

"Take these. Go shoot that goddamned thing," Sims said, pushing her rifle and ammo belt to Zach. "Use the grenade launcher. Here."

"I don't know how..." Zach objected, looking at the short, wide barrel mounted underneath the assault rifle.

"Shut up and listen," Sims said through clenched teeth. "Unlatch the barrel here and swing it out to one side. Insert a grenade. Slam it shut. Aim at the base of the rocket and pull the big trigger. You've got four grenades. The top of the ridge is just within range of the launch platform. It will be a tough shot. Make them count."

"But..."

"No buts. I can't do it. Red Team is down there risking their lives to give us this chance. Now put on your big-boy panties and move your skinny ass!"

"This is a very bad idea," Zach responded, reluctantly grabbing the weapon.

"Yeah. I know. Now go!"

Zach scrambled sideways across the slope and then up to the top of the ridge, crouching behind the same boulder where he had hidden earlier in the day. Below, the launch alarm blared, sending the fueling crew running back into the tunnel. He had only a few brief minutes before the doors in the mountain closed completely, and the engines on the fifth rocket came to life.

Sweat soaked through his clothes, and his hands shook, trying not to think about what would happen to Sims and him if he failed.

Behind him, he could hear the near-continuous rattle of automatic weapons fire and the helicopter pounding through the peaks and valleys.

Zach hadn't been lying. He had never even seen a grenade launcher. It looked like a big pistol of sorts mounted below the rifle. It took him valuable seconds just to find the latch that released the contraption's barrel so it could swing off to one side. The squat, fat rounds looked like little bombs, several inches in diameter, with no fins. Zach pulled a round out of the ammunition belt and nearly fumbled it onto the ground before managing to shove it into the barrel. He had no idea if he had loaded the weapon correctly, but he was about to find out.

Rolling over on his stomach, the American student looked through the rifle sights and found the rocket. He took a breath and squeezed the trigger.

Nothing.

"Well, crap!"

Zach turned the weapon over and found the safety was still engaged. A second later, he re-aimed and fired.

The grenade flew from the barrel with a quiet POP and sailed straight toward the rocket. Halfway to the target, it hit the ground, bounced twice, and exploded.

"Holy crap!" Zach exclaimed, surprised by the magnitude of the blast from something small enough to hold in one hand.

But as the smoke cleared, he saw that his shot had landed short and that the rocket and launch platform remained completely untouched.

Inside the operations center, the detonation of Zach's first grenade flashed across the big screen that monitored the launch pad. Alarms blared as the technicians in charge of the missile tried to determine what had caused the fireball that still rose from the valley floor. To their relief, every system needed to send the rocket into space still showed green, ruling out any failure with the spacecraft or its fueling system.

"Damnit! That's no accident," the sergeant in charge of security shouted. "Someone is attacking the launch site! Where is Condor Squad?"

"You sent them to eliminate the intruder. But they now report being in a firefight with unknown forces almost a mile southwest of the pad," one of the security officers in the control room reported. "Now the nano trackers show Zach Self only 283 meters or 310 yards from the tunnel entrance."

"Pan the cameras around to the perimeter of the launch site. Find him. Now!"

While security personnel scanned the perimeter, the sergeant checked the countdown clock.

*T-1:35.*

"Okaaaay," Zach said to himself, inserting another grenade. "Let's try it this way."

This time, Zach raised the barrel above his target, hoping to get more distance. When he pulled the trigger, the grenade flew well past the rocket, exploding violently but harmlessly on the open ground outside the tunnel doors.

Before the security personnel in the operations center could fully survey the ridgeline, another explosion ripped across the launch site – this time closer to The Cause's last hope of placing the master control satellite into orbit. Just a moment later, the monitor caught a glimpse of Zach behind a large boulder, loading what could only be a rifle-mounted grenade launcher.

"Get the helicopter over there. Take out that son-of-a-bitch!" the sergeant shouted.

"Sir, the vehicle is fully fueled, and final checks are complete," the launch director reported. "We are at T-50 seconds."

"Launch, goddamnit it! Launch!" the sergeant screamed.

"No, sir. We are still forty seconds outside the window."

Well aware that he had allowed Zach Self to remain in the area despite repeated requests from his team to eliminate the intruder, the security officer pulled his sidearm out of its holster and pointed it at the launch director's head.

"Do it! Now!"


Zach could tell his attack hadn't gone unnoticed. He could hear the helicopter somewhere behind him charging toward his position.

Ignoring the approaching threat, Zach pushed his next-to-last grenade into the launch tube and estimated an aiming point halfway between his first and second attempts. Knowing he was running out of time and ammunition, the student who studied the peaceful art of diplomacy put his finger on the trigger and drew a deep breath to calm his nerves and steady his aim.


Inside the operations center, the launch director's hand shook as he flipped the protective cover off a red button marked "Launch." But he hesitated, knowing an early launch would ruin the chance to place the master control satellite into the proper orbit.

The now panicked security sergeant viciously shoved the launch director aside and slammed his hand down on the button. Immediately, high-pressure pumps inside the rocket forced thousands of kilograms of liquid oxygen and rocket-grade kerosene surging toward the engines.

Zach's eyes narrowed as he lined up the rifle sites just above where he wanted the grenade to land and pulled the trigger. The grenade bounced once, and for a split second, Zach thought he had missed again. But then, the fat little explosive rolled directly underneath the heavy steel launch platform. A millisecond later, the platform and scaffolding-like structure holding the rocket upright quaked violently as two great tongues of flame burst out from both sides. Zach couldn't see the shards of steel and shrapnel that sliced through the engines and fuel lines just as the highly volatile mixture of liquid oxygen and rocket-grade kerosene erupted from the mangled engines. In an instant, the rocket and launch platform disappeared in a spectacular blast that shook the ground and sent a churning fireball into the sky.

Zach had the good sense to quickly tuck himself behind his boulder and cover his face. Nearly unbearable heat washed past him, but then it passed. When he felt like he wouldn't be cooked alive, Zach took a quick glance into the valley. Nothing remained of the tall, stainless-steel rocket – and the launch platform had been reduced to a pile of twisted black metal.

"Well, I'll be damned."

## Garcia's apartment
## Santiago, Chile

"He did what?" Deal asked incredulously.

"I swear, boss," Sims reported. "He shot a grenade that landed under the platform. A perfect shot. The kid had never even seen a grenade launcher but figured it out with just three tries. Three! I couldn't have done it better myself. After the rocket blew up, the tangos just disappeared."

"Casualties?" Deal asked.

"Red Two has a flesh wound, and my arm and leg have been better. Otherwise, we got lucky. We're on our way back to Talca. Can Major Garcia arrange transport back to Santiago from outside of town?"

Garcia nodded.

"And Zach?"

"He's fine. Exhausted. Dehydrated. And his back is sore from my guys slapping it so many times."

"That's my boy!" Michael shouted.

"Amazing!" Sarah agreed.

Daniela beamed with pride. "Ask Agent Sims to let Zach know I'd like to see him as soon as he gets back to the hotel. Room 106."

# CHAPTER FIFTY-EIGHT

O'Higgins Park
Santiago, Chile

"The Directors won't be happy," Alexander Monroe warned. "They spent billions on those rockets and satellites just to have not one, but two, literally blow up in their faces."

Dave Knox ignored Monroe while he stood before a full-length mirror.

"How do I look? I'm going for bombastic dictator. You know, a Mussolini vibe. I think the gold epaulets really work with the dark blue tunic and fake medals."

"I'm serious. These guys don't play. Maybe you better go ahead and tell me how you're going to spin all this," Monroe said, standing and placing both hands on his hips.

Dave sighed loudly. "I have to say I'm a little disappointed. You are generally smarter than this, Alexander. We made a long shot play at silencing and then taking control of much of the internet and almost every source of news on the planet. Our real chance of accomplishing such a thing was always near zero."

"If you knew all along such a colossal plan wouldn't work as advertised, why did you choose to waste so much of The Cause's resources?" Monroe demanded, his hands outstretched as if pleading for a lifeline that would save him from the consequences of losing enough money to buy a small country.

"Because," Dave replied, holding up one finger, "the Directors, like all greedy ultra-rich assholes, have colossal egos. I needed an entire space program to accomplish my real goal. They wouldn't have responded to spending billions on an idea that didn't match their unreasonable expectations."

Monroe didn't back off. "You're *real* goal? You can't just manipulate the Directors like that. They might not have your intellect or talent, but they'll want answers."

"Or what?" Dave laughed. "They'll have me killed? First, that would be stupid. Who else has the brains to make The Cause the kind of money I have in just a few years? And you can pass this tidbit on. Amina Kent is not the only professional with special skills I have on call. Anyone with ambitions about taking my chair better think twice."

Monroe sat back down. "Then maybe you'll at least indulge *me*. I've had your back ever since you grabbed control. My butt is on the line here, just like yours."

Dave checked his watch. "That's a good point. Okay. You heard me order our spheres to take out every communications satellite serving the southern half of the South American continent."

Monroe interrupted Dave's explanation. "Yeah, but why South America? Why not choose somewhere in Europe, North America, or Asia?"

"Now you've asked an intelligent question. Excellent. Most of the internet relies heavily on undersea fiber optic cables. However, only a few such cables serve this continent, where much of the internet is provided by satellites. We can control a higher percentage of data with our cubesats here than in any other developed part of the world. Very shortly, we will be the sole internet provider, and TNI will be the only source available for news, commentary, opinions, and political analysis over a broad swath South America. The Cause will have unchallenged command of almost all information available to the good people of Chile, Argentina, Peru, Uruguay, Bolivia, Paraguay, and half of Brazil, including its capital and largest cities, Sao Paulo and Rio De Janeiro."

"Sweeping power, indeed," Monroe commented, starting to grasp the reasoning behind Dave's concept.

"Exactly correct," Dave agreed. "Information is the world's most potent weapon and its most valuable asset. With the vast majority of the population exposed exclusively to our content, we can feed them whatever content suits our purposes. For instance, nature's strongest emotion is fear. With a creative array of stories and half-baked facts, they will become frightened of anything we choose. From there, it's child's play to place our people into powerful government positions just by promising to protect the citizens from the very boogeymen we brought to life. People will accept any law or policy, no matter how outlandish or absurd, as long as it makes them feel safe. We can start wars to sell arms or manipulate markets to our advantage. And that's just a start. If I do say so myself, I am about to give The Cause power that will rival or exceed the greatest empires the world has ever seen."

When Monroe grasped the scope and brilliance of Dave's vision, his smile lit up the entire tent.

"When does the show start?"

Dave looked at his watch.

"Now."

Far above their heads, communications satellites that provided interlocking relay channels serving much of South America began to fail. As the titanium spheres fired from The Cause's cubesats smashed through fragile aluminum frames and complex hardware, a deathly electronic silence fell across half of South America.

Television screens turned black, cell phone calls abruptly dropped, and computers accessing the internet suddenly froze. However, the destruction of the crucial satellites did much more than interrupt people's soccer games and internet searches. Critical infrastructure and transportation services reliant on internet access and satellite communications stopped working, causing massive chaos. Traffic lights failed, clogging the streets with accidents and traffic jams. Air traffic controllers stared at blank radar screens while desperately trying to raise pilots on radios that didn't work.

In the glass and granite towers of Santiago, Sao Paulo, Rio de Janeiro, La Paz, and Lima, bank tellers couldn't access customers' accounts, and financiers trading stocks, commodities, and currency fell into shocked silence when the screens that usually flashed prices and trades went black. Markets around the world took note, sending the value of South American currencies plummeting.

"It must have worked," Monroe commented, holding up his phone. "This thing is dead."

Dave reveled in the knowledge that, with the push of a button, he could inflict such wide-ranging chaos. When he had first conceived his latest plan, he realized that even a few minutes without the internet would send a tsunami of panic surging across any affected country. He even built in time for people's fear and confusion to grow. So, for the next ten minutes, he sipped his drink and listened to the crowd outside become more and more agitated as their phone screens remained stubbornly blank.

As the ten-minute countdown ended, Dave looked at his watch. "Check again in three, two, one. Now."

Monroe's phone beeped twice, and a message appeared on its screen that read:

WELCOME TO FREE HIGH-SPEED INTERNET AND CELL PHONE SERVICE

COMPLIMENTS OF TRUTH NETWORK INTERNATIONAL

TNI - THE WORLD'S NEW LEADER IN NEWS, ENTERTAINMENT, AND SPORTS

Monroe laughed out loud.

"Brilliant! Free? Nobody is going to turn that down," Monroe crowed. "I can even hear the crowd outside. They sound confused but also happy."

"Just as I planned it," Dave said confidently. "We own their screens, so we own them. And nobody will be able to take a shot at challenging what we have built for years to come. And by that time, The Cause will be solidly in control of every country in South America below the equator."

"Will you try again? Launch more rockets?" Monroe asked.

"Oh, no, my friend. In fact, I ordered the tunnels evacuated after the last launch failed. And now comes the fun part," Dave said, lifting his phone and showing Monroe a comically large glowing red button that covered the entire screen.

"Isn't that a little dramatic?" Monroe asked with a chuckle.

Dave raised his index finger in the air and, with unnecessary flourish, brought it down onto the button.

Several hundred miles to the south, the ranch once owned by the late President Juan Cayo trembled as a long series of explosions rolled through the tunnels. Over the next two minutes, seismic sensors throughout the continent registered what appeared to be a low-level earthquake that shook the ground from Chile's central plains high into the Andes.

Five minutes later, The Cause's vast underground network of tunnels had utterly disappeared.

Monroe raised his eyebrows. "I guess the question is clear – why?"

"The Cause is, and has always been, invisible. This assures we remain so."

<br>

Garcia's apartment
Minutes later

"What?" Deal asked, seeing the strange look on his Chilean counterpart's face.

"I ordered the helicopter that picked up your team to overfly the launch site and take pictures. The pilot just reported a series of explosions that brought the side of a mountain down and covered the entire area. It looks like someone spent billions on that project and then just blew it up," Garcia said, his voice betraying near-complete confusion.

"Covering his tracks," Deal said confidently. "Now I know it's Knox. He's ruthless to a fault. But he's good. Too good. No wonder he has stayed under cover this long."

"Hey, let's look at the bright side," Michael chimed in, trying to lift the mood. "We came out on the plus side of this thing. We sure didn't lose."

"Yeah," Sarah agreed. "But we didn't win either."

# EPILOGUE

O'Higgins Park
Santiago, Chile

The Independence Day celebrations kicked off in earnest at noon when the first of several parades wound its way from downtown into the park. Smiling school children dressed in traditional costumes marched by waving little Chilean flags and singing the national anthem.  Dr. Dave Knox, posing as President Juan Cayo, surrounded on both sides by his cabinet and high-ranking generals and admirals, waved from a raised platform set high above the throngs of people packed into the roughly five-acre park.

The sun shone brightly overhead, but thankfully, a cool breeze kept Dave from sweating through his dark blue wool tunic while he waited for the next parade to pass below the viewing stand. With one hand, he double-checked the bullet squibs taped to the left side of his chest. They would ignite one by one when sound detectors in each recorded the sharp crack of blanks fired by Amina Kent from the eighth story of an apartment building on the far side of the park. He had adapted the design and placement of the squibs from the movies, ensuring they would fool the hundreds of cameras that would record his "assassination." But he didn't have to worry. With

TNI reporting on the incident, any question about the authenticity of the president's death would be quickly snuffed out.

Dave wanted to look at his watch but had been told by his staff it would be bad form. They didn't want videos of him posted on social media looking impatient or bored with the festivities. But that didn't keep him from wondering when Amina Kent would strike.

Inside the presidential tent, Lieutenant Violette Ruiz found the party in full swing. Waiters circulated with Chilean sparkling white wine in crystal flutes that disappeared almost as fast as the trays of local delicacies. People danced in front of a band at the far end of the tent. In contrast, a contingent of scowling security guards in black suits and sunglasses stood nearly motionless at the opening onto the viewing stand. She would have to wait until Dave Knox appeared inside to complete her plan. In a couple of hours, she would be sitting at the head of the table in The Pacifico's twelfth-floor conference room and take her mother's rightful place as the leader of The Cause.

After grabbing a glass from a passing waiter, Ruiz made her way to one of the tables away from the action and lowered herself into a chair. As smoothly as possible, she reached down and removed one black pump and slipped her short combat knife out from where it was installed in the steel arch.

"Nice shoes," a voice said from behind her. "I have a pair just like them."

Ruiz turned slowly to find a striking young woman dressed in a form-fitting red dress, red shoes, and matching red lipstick smiling at her.

"Just a little protection," Ruiz answered smoothly. "Chilean men can get insistent. I'm sure you understand."

Amina Kent brushed a strand of glossy black hair behind her ear and lowered herself into a chair next to Ruiz before displaying the double-sided 4-inch dagger she had concealed in her hand.

"I do, indeed."

Ruiz looked the other woman up and down.

"You didn't hide that in your shoes. How did you get it past security?" Ruiz asked, her eyes searching behind Amina for any backup.

"Oh, I'm alone," Amina said, recognizing what Ruiz was doing. "Anyway, Dave Knox said I could use anything I wanted to kill you. I thought this would be fun. I like to kill women face to face. It's more, well, satisfying."

Ruiz didn't react to Amina's taunts other than to instantly slash her knife toward the other woman's gut. But the professional assassin was ready. She expertly blocked the move with her left hand, snatching Ruiz's forearm in a death grip while striking like a cobra with her right.

Ruiz partially knocked the blade aside and grabbed Amina's wrist but gritted her teeth as a deep laceration opened just under her left arm.

Locked in a silent struggle for survival in the middle of hundreds of partiers, the two women glared into each other's eyes. To a casual observer, they looked like two friends sitting face to face having an intimate, if intense, conversation.

"What now?" Ruiz asked. "Do we finish this here at our table or take it outside?"

One side of Amina's mouth lifted slightly.

"Here, Lieutenant Violet Ruiz of the Argentina Air Force."

"You have me at a disadvantage," Ruiz responded. "I don't think we've been introduced."

Muscles on both women's arms and shoulders hardened and shook with effort as each tried to move their knife toward the other's chest.

"You're right, Violet. But I know a lot about you," Amina growled. "While you played with other privileged children at your private school, I sold bread for pennies on the streets of Cairo. While you chased cute boys in high school, I was a sex slave trying to fight off men twice my size – and losing. And while you practiced killing in the military, I choked the life from people I no longer remember with shoestrings, lamp cords, and piano wire."

Ruiz kept her eyes locked on the killer's but could feel blood soaking her black top and puddling on the wood floor beneath her feet. The standoff couldn't last much longer.

And it didn't.

Without warning, Amina slammed her forehead into Ruiz's right eye. Stunned, the Argentinian's grip relaxed for only an instant, giving the assassin the opening she needed. In less than a second, Amina's short combat knife pierced Ruiz's chest three times. The final thrust, aimed expertly between the third and fourth ribs, tore into her heart.

"Tell your mother Dave Knox says hello," Amina whispered into Ruiz's ear as she eased the dead woman's head onto her lap.

Checking that nobody was paying any attention, Amina lowered Ruiz to the floor and used her legs to shove the body under the table, making sure not to get any blood on her shoes. The long tablecloth would hide the body long enough for her to make her way out of the tent and set up for her next "kill."

Ten minutes later, Dave didn't have to fake his reaction when the first gunshot painfully triggered the explosive squib taped over his heart. Less than a second later, another shot rang out, firing the second squib. With just the right amount of blood soaking the front of his shirt, the leader of The Cause did a masterful acting job, falling slowly backward with one hand over the bullet "wound" and the other reaching out in a desperate attempt to stay upright. Dave slowly closed his eyes as screams of panic rose from the crowded park.

But the phony president didn't have to keep up the act for long. Within seconds, three burly men from his security detail scooped him off the ground and ran with him into the tent. In another few seconds, he was strapped onto a gurney and rolled into a waiting ambulance.

"How did that look?" Dave asked Monroe, who was already loosening the restraining straps so Dave could sit up.

"We can catch it on TNI in a minute. But by all the screaming, I'd say you pulled that off quite well. Where to now?"

"Back to Switzerland. I have a date with a plastic surgeon. I want to use my own face for what I have in mind next."

www.ingramcontent.com/pod-product-compliance
Lightning Source LLC
Chambersburg PA
CBHW071351300726
48976CB00006B/1844